The house was quiet and dark.

Mike sat in the living room, on the couch. Waiting.

It would be like a holiday from real life for them both, Christine decided. For just a little while there would be no tangled, complicated pasts for either of them. Nor need they consider their uncertain futures.

She went to the couch, knelt beside him, put her arms around his neck, kissed his lips. She meant for it to be light, preliminary, but he had little patience. He was a man, as he had said, who didn't think for a long time about things but simply did them when they were right.

"Oh, God, oh, Chrissie."

The arms that pulled her close were so caring. His mouth, hard in wanting, covered hers with such heat that she felt wild inside.

"Mike," she whispered against his open mouth. "Mike."

They couldn't simply kiss for a while first, as if they were on a date, Chris realized. She lived in his house; she had come to him and put her arms around his neck. It was not a seduction and could not be construed as one. It was surrender.

Dear Reader,

Magic. It dazzles our senses, sometimes touches our souls. And what could be more magical than romance?

Silhouette **Special Edition** novels feature believable, compelling women and men in lifelike situations, but our authors never forget the wondrous magic of falling in love. How do these writers blend believability with enchantment? Author Sherryl Woods puts it this way:

"More. That's what Silhouette **Special Edition** is about. For a writer, this Silhouette line offers a chance to create romances with more depth and complexity, more intriguing characters, more heightened sensuality. In the pages of these wonderful love stories, more sensitive issues can be interwoven with more tenderness, more humor and more excitement. And when it all works, you have what these books are really all about—more magic!"

Joining Sherryl Woods this month to conjure up half a dozen versions of this "special" magic are Robyn Carr, Debbie Macomber, Barbara Catlin, Maggi Charles and Jennifer Mikels.

Month after month, we hope Silhouette **Special Edition** casts its spell on you, dazzling your senses *and* touching your soul. Are there any particular ingredients you like best in your "love potion"? The authors and editors of Silhouette **Special Edition** always welcome your comments.

Sincerely,

Leslie Kazanjian, Senior Editor
Silhouette Books
300 East 42nd Street
New York, N.Y. 10017

ROBYN CARR

Informed Risk

Silhouette Special Edition

Published by Silhouette Books New York

America's Publisher of Contemporary Romance

For Pat Warren
and Vicki Lewis Thompson,
thanks.

The author would like to thank
John and Georgia Bockoven
for their interest in this project.

SILHOUETTE BOOKS
300 East 42nd St., New York, N.Y. 10017

ISBN: 0-373-09517-1

First Silhouette Books printing April 1989

Printed in the U.S.A.

ROBYN CARR

has been writing for thirteen years, publishing primarily hardcover historical novels and, more recently, branching out into contemporary fiction. A frequent contributor to writers' magazines, she also won the Romance Writers of America's coveted Golden Medallion Award for best historical novel in 1986.

Before she became a full-time writer, her "previous occupations" included "domestic engineering and pregnancy." Her many hobbies have now given way to "keeping a household of one busy husband, two teenagers in braces (and every activity available), three dogs, a bird and five houseplants all in health, clean clothes, tight braces and laughter, according to individual needs."

Robyn and her family live in Arizona.

MIKE'S FIRE TRUCK AND US
MIKE
ME
MOM
KYLE
CHEEKS
by Carrie

Chapter One

Chris heard a loud thump. The furnace had turned on; soon warmth would begin to flow through the rickety little house. She wrinkled her nose, then remembered that heaters always smelled of burning dust and soot the first day they operated. She returned her fingers to the typewriter keys, and her concentration to the last chapter of her story about a twelve-year-old boy named Jake. After seven rewrites, Jake was finally about to enjoy some resolution to the previous 122 pages of pubescent tribulation he'd suffered in his first year of junior high school.

This was her fourth attempt at a young adult novel, and Chris knew she was getting closer. Of earlier attempts editors had used such words as *brisk*, *lively*, *smooth*. Also words such as *awkward*, *unresolved*, *clumsy in places*.

She stopped typing and wrinkled her nose again. Should it smell *that* bad? She had asked the landlord if the furnace should be serviced or cleaned before she set the thermostat, but he'd assured her it was fine. Of course, he said everything was fine, and this old rattrap was anything but. To be fair, she had never actually seen a rat, but she *had* swept up plenty of suspicious little pebbles, which she assumed were mouse turds. The traps she set, however, remained—thank you, God—abandoned.

She and the children had made do with oven heat until now, waiting as long as possible before turning on central heat. Utility bills were hard on a Christmas budget, and, when you got right down to it, hers was hardly a budget. But the temperature might drop to freezing tonight, and sleeping bags alone wouldn't keep the kids warm.

She looked at the kitchen clock. Nearly midnight. Her eyes were scratchy, but tonight she was determined to finish the last chapter. To be published . . . finally? Much of this great push, she had to admit, was for Jake himself, a great kid who deserved a resolution that was not awkward or clumsy in places. As did she.

As for publishing, the responses she collected had been consistently more encouraging, asking her to send future work. "Write what you know," a writing instructor had advised. Chris certainly knew what it was like to be twelve, to be struggling for self-reliance while simultaneously fighting feelings of incompetence. She knew this dilemma even better at twenty-seven.

The shrill siren of the smoke detector interrupted her musings. The sound wrapped strangling fingers around her heart and squeezed. Stunned, she looked up from the gridlock of library books, photocopied magazine articles, paper, typewriter and loose manuscript pages all around her on the kitchen table. Through the kitchen door, her wide eyes quickly scanned the little living room with its two beanbag chairs, old television, clutter of secondhand toys and card table littered with the remnants of the macaroni-and-cheese dinner she had given the kids hours earlier.

And there, from the floor vents in the living room, poured smoke.

She bolted from the chair, fairly leapt to turn off the thermostat and raced into her kids' room. She grabbed one in each arm—five-year-old Carrie and three-year-old Kyle.

"There's a fire in the house," she said, hustling them through the thick smoke and toward the door. "We have to get outside, quick." As she rushed past the smoking vents, she prayed the situation wasn't as grim as it looked. Maybe it was only dirt? Soot? Dead bugs? But she didn't pause in her flight out the front door.

Only when they were safely outside did she stop to take stock of her predicament. The neighborhood was dark. Even in broad daylight it left something to be desired; at night it seemed almost threatening. There was not so much as a yard light shining. Her seven-year-old Honda sat on the street, and she opened the car door, nearly threw the kids inside and reached into the back seat for a blanket. "Wrap up in this, Carrie. Wrap Kyle up, too. Come on, that's a girl. I have to get someone to call the fire department. Don't get out of the car. Don't. Do you hear?"

Kyle started to whimper, rubbing his eyes. Carrie pulled the blanket around her little brother and nodded to her mother. Then she began to comfort Kyle with little crooning, motherly sounds of "'s'okay...'s'okay...."

Chris slammed the car door shut and ran to the house next door. Like her own house, it was small, ramshackle and in need of a paint job. She rang the bell and pounded on the front door. After a minute or two she gave up, ran to the house across the street and began ringing and pounding and yelling. She was panicked. How long do you wait for someone to get up? She jumped from one foot to the other. No light came on there, either. "Come on, c'mon! Anybody home?" The porch light across the street went on, where she had begun. "Damn," she muttered, turning away from the door to run. The porch light behind her came on. "Jeez," she hissed, doubling back.

A sleepy, unshaven and angry-looking man opened the door. He was holding his robe closed over boxer shorts. That was when Chris remembered she was wearing only an extralarge T-shirt, moccasins and her undies. Purple silk undies, to be precise. That was it.

"Call the fire department," she begged her unsavory-looking neighbor. "The furnace is on fire. My kids are in my car. Hurry. Hurry!"

She turned and ran back to her car. She opened the door. "Are you okay?" They looked like two little birds peeking out from under the blanket.

"Mommy, what about Cheeks?" Carrie asked.

"Cheeks is in the backyard, sweetie. He's okay." She lifted her head to listen. "He's barking. Hear him?"

Carrie nodded, and her yellow curls bounced. "Can Cheeks come in the car with us?"

"I'll get him in a minute. You stay right here. Promise?" Again Carrie nodded. "I'll be right back. The fire truck is on its way. Pretty soon you'll hear the siren."

"Will our house burn down?"

"Burn down?" Kyle echoed.

"It'll be okay. Stay here now. I'll be right back."

Chris knew it was stupid to go back into a burning building; people died that way. But under these circumstances, she rationalized, it wasn't entirely stupid. First of all, she had seen only smoke, no other evidence of a bona fide fire. Second, the house was so tiny that the kitchen table, where her manuscript and all her research lay, couldn't be more than ten steps inside the front door, which she intended to leave open in the event she had to make a fast getaway. Third, she wasn't going inside unless it looked relatively safe.

She heard the distant trill of the siren. The station was only about a mile away. She would be quick. And the smoke was not terrible, not blinding or choking. She had a plan.

She filled her lungs with clean air and bolted toward the kitchen. Even if the whole house burned to a cinder, the refrigerator would remain intact, like the bathtub in a tornado, right? Since she couldn't possibly gather up all her materials and her typewriter and get them out of the house in one trip, she opened the refrigerator door and started heaving papers into it. It wasn't even supposed to be a long book. How had she ended up with so many pages? And the books—the sourcebooks and expensive reference volumes—went in next. One marked *Sacramento Public Library* landed in the butter dish, but she didn't have time for neatness. She yanked out a half gallon of two-percent milk to make room for a pile of photocopied pages—the sirens were getting closer—and replaced a jug of apple juice with the large, old dictionary she had gotten at a garage sale. The sirens seemed to be winding down.

Suddenly Chris started feeling woozy. The typewriter, she thought dimly. Could she carry it out? But things started to blur. She looked toward the vents. That sucker, she thought remotely, was really smokin'....

The first fire engine stopped behind an old green Honda, and the men sprang off. The truck with ladders and hydraulics was right behind. As his men pulled a hose to a hydrant, Captain Mike Cavanaugh glanced at the burning house and approached the man in boxer shorts and a ratty bathrobe who stood on the curb. The furnace, he'd been told. He saw heat waves come off the roof. A furnace fire could have started in the basement, but in these old houses without fire-stops there could be an attic fire already. The ladder company would go up. Over his shoulder he called, "Take the peanut line in to fog it, and we'll open up the top." Then he turned to the bathrobed man. "Anyone in the house?"

"It ain't my house. Some woman's house. She's only lived there a couple of months. Them's her kids, there."

"Did you call it in?"

"Yeah, she was pounding on my door, said her furnace was on fire and her kids was in the car."

Mike felt someone tugging on his coat, and looked down. The face that stared up at him jarred him, almost cut through him. A little blond girl with the face of an angel, a face something inside him seemed to remember. She wore pajamas with feet, and beside her was a similarly attired little boy, one hand dragging a blanket and one hand holding on to his sister's pajamas. "Our mother's in the house," she said. "She told us to stay in the car."

"Then you'd better get back in the car," he said. "I'll get your mother." He spoke gently, but he broke into a run, pulling at the mouthpiece of his air pack so he could cover his face. "There's a woman in there," he informed a fire fighter nearby. "Number 56 will initiate rescue. Take over incident command." The man, Jim Eble, turned to pass the word.

"Women," Mike muttered. Women invariably thought there was something worth saving in a fire. Usually a purse or some jewelry, but sometimes they were goofy enough to go back after a pair of shoes, or a robe.

Even these thoughts left him totally unprepared for what he found just steps inside the front door: a small woman, her thick, wavy hair in a fat ponytail, wearing only slippers, an oversize T-shirt and purple—yes, purple—silk underwear. He knew about the underwear because she was actually bending over, digging in the refrigerator, in a house cloudy with smoke.

He tapped her on the shoulder. "What are you, hungry?" Through his mask it came out something like "Bflust uurrr doooo, flungee?"

When she turned toward him he instantly recognized the ashen pallor and the glassy eyes. She coughed, her knees buckled, and he put his hands on her waist. She folded over his shoulder like a duffel bag. He supposed she might toss her cookies down his back; it wouldn't be the first time.

He pointed that purple silk rump toward the front door. It was right beside his ear, creating an indelible impression even in the midst of chaos.

Once he got her outside, he put her down by the rear of the engine and pulled down his mask. "Anyone else in the house?" he barked.

"Cheeks . . . is in . . ." she wheezed and choked ". . . the backyard."

"Cheeks?" he asked.

"Dog . . . wirehaired terrier," she managed. She gagged and fell against Jim, who held her shoulders and backed her up to the tailboard of the engine so she could sit down.

"I'll get the dog," Mike said to his friend. "Furnace is in the basement. We'll have to go down. Right smack in the middle of the house. That's not a new roof." He headed toward the backyard.

"Here," said Jim, pushing a mask toward Chris. "You'll feel a little better after some oxygen."

Chris decided this fireman was much gentler than the one who'd deposited her on the sidewalk. But his voice seemed to become smaller and more distant as her head whirled and her stomach flipped. She abruptly leaned away from him and lost dinner and several cups of coffee in the street. Bracing a hand on the tailboard, she heaved and shuddered. The man handed her a bunch of gauze four-by-fours to wipe her mouth. "Sometimes you feel a lot better after that." He touched her back. "It'll be okay now. Take it easy."

Chris, mortified, accepted the wipes and mopped her nose and mouth, meanwhile dying of all kinds of embarrassment. A large green trash bag miraculously appeared and covered the mess. All of this, she assumed, must be standard business at a fire.

"Is our mother sick?" Carrie asked in a small voice.

"Mama?" came Kyle's echo.

The fireman hunkered down and smiled into their little faces. "Naw, not really. She smelled too much smoke, and it made her sick to her stomach. She feels better now. Dontcha, Mom?"

She straightened up, eyes closed, and nodded. She couldn't speak yet, but she felt her pea-green face turning red. The irony was not lost on her that her house was burning down, and all she felt was shame because she was wearing practically nothing and had thrown up in the street.

"Our mother is going to be upset if her book burns up," Carrie told the fireman.

"Well, now, we can always get another book, can't we? But it sure would be hard to find another mommy as special as this one. That's why we *never* go back into a house where there's a fire."

"Our mother is *typing* her book, and it takes a very long time and is very hard to do," Carrie informed him rather indignantly.

As the fireman glanced at Chris, she stretched her T-shirt down over her thighs. She was recovering now. "Never mind that, Carrie. The fireman is right—I should not have gone back into the house. It was very dangerous and very stupid." She looked up at the fireman. "I don't suppose you have a drink of water?"

"Well," he said, standing and looking around, "water is pretty hard to come by."

She noticed three different hoses reaching across the lawn toward her smoking house and shook her head.

"I'll ask a neighbor," he said, moving away.

A minute or two later he returned with a paper cup filled with water. After she had taken a few swallows she noticed that he was holding a blanket toward her. "Thanks," she said, trading the cup for the cover. "If I'd known you were coming, I would have dressed."

"No problem," he said. "Besides, you don't have to be embarrassed by those legs," he added as he turned away. The blanket, thankfully, reached her ankles.

"Whoa!" came a baritone shout, followed by a crashing sound.

Part of the roof where men had been poking opened up, and flames leapt out. Two fire fighters came shooting out the front door of the house, then two others dragged a larger hose in. They were everywhere—inside, outside, on the roof.

It was amazing, Chris thought. Just a few minutes ago she'd only seen a little smoke. Now there was a great deal more than smoke; red-orange flames were eating up the little house.

Out of the darkness the tall fireman who had saved her life approached them with a silver ball of fur that went *grrrr* in his arms. He handed Cheeks to Chris. Cheeks, very particular about who carried him around, snarled and yapped in transit. He was cranky.

Carrie and Kyle pressed closer to Chris, and her arms wrapped around them reassuringly, enfolding them in a circle of safety she herself didn't quite feel. As she drew Kyle up onto the tailboard and hugged Carrie closer with her other arm, she saw that all the neighbors she had never met were up, watching her house burn down.

"Maybe we should have a block party," she muttered, kissing one child's head, then the other, then getting a dog's tongue right across her lips and nose. *"Phlettt."* She grimaced.

"Do we have a second alarm?" one fireman asked another.

"Yep." Just that fast another huge rig rounded the corner, bringing the total to four. They had not heard the sirens, Chris assumed, because of the general pandemonium immediately around them: shouting, engines, radios, gushing water and the hissing, creaking, crackling sound of everything she owned in the world turning to ash.

This new fire truck blinked its headlights like a great behemoth, and soon its ladder and basket rose like a stiff arm over the tops of the eucalyptus trees. A hose that was threaded upward began to pour water down on the little house.

Fire fighting had turned to demolition, from Chris's point of view. She flinched at the sound of crashing glass and splintering wood as windows and doors were smashed in. She looked back to the mounting traffic. Police cars blocked the street, and an ambulance had arrived. Chris and her kids and dog sat quietly on the bumper of engine 56.

Tears ran down her cheeks. There it all went. And there hadn't been very much. Five weeks until Christmas. She was twenty-seven years old, and this was the third time in seven years that she stood by, helpless, hopeless, while everything she had, everything she thought she *was*, disappeared—this time, before her very eyes. First, when her parents both died in a small plane crash. She had been twenty, and an only child. Then, when Steve walked out on her without so much as a goodbye after having used up her every emotion and every penny of what her parents had left her. Now this.

"Mommy, where are we going to sleep?"

"I . . . uh . . . we'll work that out, baby. Don't worry."

"Mommy? Did our sleeping bags burn up? How can we sleep without our sleeping bags?"

"Now, Carrie," Chris said, her voice breaking despite her effort to fake strength, "don't we always m-manage?"

The house was thirty-two years old and, because of the landlord's minimal maintenance, badly run-down. It didn't take much time for it to look like one big black clump. Chris sat watching, stunned, for less than two hours. She wasn't even aware of being cold.

The last fire truck to arrive left first. The neighbors went to bed without asking if there was anything she needed. Hell, they went back into their houses without *introducing* themselves. A policeman took a brief statement from her: the furnace came on after she set the thermostat, then it made smoke. Not much to tell. He gave her a card that had phone numbers for Victims Aid and the Red Cross and headed back toward his car. The disappointed ambulance was long gone. Kyle snored softly, his blond head against her chest, the fireman's blanket that she wore wrapped around him and Cheeks. Carrie leaned against her, wrapped in her own blanket, watching in fascination and fear. She was silent but wide-eyed. It was after 2:00 a.m., Chris estimated, when she found herself sitting on the bumper of engine 56 with no earthly idea of what she was going to do next.

The fireman who had saved her life stood in front of her. He seemed even taller now that her house was a mere cinder. His hair, thick and brown and curly, was now sweaty and matted to his scalp. Dirt and perspiration streaked his face. His eyes were deeply set and brooding under thick brows, but there was a sympathetic turn to his mouth.

"If you take this fire engine out from under me, I have absolutely no idea where I'll sit."

"You don't know any of the neighbors?"

She shook her head. If she attempted to say a word about how all the neighbors had just gone off, she might cry.

"Is there someone you can call?"

She shrugged. Was there? She wasn't sure about that.

"You can go to the police station and make some calls. Or we can wake up a neighbor so you can use their phone. Or you could come to the firehouse and—"

"The firehouse," she requested abruptly. "Please." She couldn't face a police station tonight. Or her ex-neighbors. At that moment, looking up at the man who had carried her out of a burning house and even managed to rescue Cheeks, she had the uncanny feeling that he was all she could depend on.

"Got any family around here? A husband? Ex-husband?"

"Oh, there's an ex-husband . . . somewhere," she said.

"Don't I know you?" he asked.

She frowned.

"Iverson's," he said. "The grocery store."

Of course, she thought. Before tonight, that was the only thing she had known about the local firemen. They shopped for their groceries together, finicky and cohesive, in much the way women went to restaurant rest rooms together. Chris was a checkout clerk at Iverson's grocery store, and it had always amused her to see the truck pull into the parking lot and five or six big, strapping men wander in to do their shopping for dinner. "Yes. Sure."

"Well, you must have some friends around here, then."

How that followed, she was unsure. Did being a clerk in a grocery store ensure friendship? She had only moved to Sacramento from Los Angeles in late August, just in time for Carrie to start school. She had a few friends at work, but their phone numbers, which she'd rarely had time to use anyway, were in that big ash heap. And she couldn't call anyone in L.A. She'd live in a tent in the park before she'd go back there.

"I'll think of someone on the way to the firehouse," she emphasized. "There are probably fewer criminals there than at the police station." She looked down at her slippered feet. "I'm not dressed to fend off criminals tonight. How long can I use the blanket?"

For the first time Mike remembered the purple panties and was glad it was dark. His cheeks felt warm. *He* felt warm. It was a vaguely familiar feeling, and he liked it. "Until you're done with it, I guess. You can get some things from the Red Cross. I'll get the officer to drive you to the firehouse. We can't take you on the engine."

"What about my house?" she asked.

"Well," he said, looking over his shoulder, "what house?"

"Won't it be looted or something?"

"Lady, there isn't a whole lot left to loot. You have any valuables that might have survived the fire?"

"Yeah," she said, squeezing her kids. "Right here."

He grinned at her approvingly; it was a great, spontaneous smile of crowded, ever-so-slightly protruding, superwhite teeth. A smile that did not hold pity but humanity. And one deep dimple—left side. "You got the best of it, then." He started to turn away.

"The refrigerator," she said, making him turn back. "Did the refrigerator go?"

"Well, it'll never run again."

"I don't care about the refrigerator itself," she said, her voice gaining strength. "I put my manuscript in there. And research papers. It's a book manuscript. It's the very last thing of any value I—" She stopped before her voice broke and she began to blubber. She hugged her children tighter. Inside she felt like a little girl herself, a defenseless, abandoned, pitiful orphan. *Won't someone do something, please. Why, oh, God, why does my luck get worse and worse, and just when I think I might make it, it goes wrong and I don't even know what I did to deserve this and, oh, my God, my kids, my poor kids.*

"Is that what you were doing?" he asked her.

She looked up at him. Brown eyes? No, green. And crinkled at the corners.

"What . . . what did you think I was doing?" she asked.

He reached into the engine cab for an industrial-sized flashlight. "I had absolutely no idea. I'll go see if the fridge made it."

She stood suddenly, struggling to hold on to Kyle and Cheeks. "Well, be careful."

The hoses were being put away, and the shortwave radios were having distant and eerie conversations with one another.

He came back. He had it. A thick stack of white pages. He showed it to her, smiling. It wasn't even singed. "It's got butter on it. And something red. Ketchup, I think."

"I don't believe it," she breathed.

"Well, I hope it's good. It almost cost you way more than it could possibly be worth. Don't you know better than to go into a burning—"

"The typewriter?"

He shook his head, exasperated. "Really, there wasn't time to save anything in there. We tried, but... Come on, let's get you into the squad car. These old houses, jeez."

Chris walked ahead of him in the direction of the police car. She carried Kyle and Cheeks while Carrie held on to Chris's blanket, trailing behind. The fireman followed with the manuscript. "I've known women to go back for their purses, but I couldn't imagine what you were doing in the refrigerator! They'll never believe this one. You're lucky, all right."

"I'm not feeling all *that* lucky."

"Well, you ought to. That old house went up like kindling."

Taking her precious manuscript, Chris managed to get into the police car without saying anything more, and they followed the fire engine to the station. The policeman carried Kyle inside, but Chris was stuck with Cheeks because of his obnoxious attitude. She struggled to hold the terrier and her manuscript.

Inside the station she was taken into a little living room that boasted two couches, several chairs, a desk, a telephone and television and even a Ping-Pong table. This must be where they lounged between fires.

The big fireman, out of his coat now, suspenders holding up his huge canvas pants, a tight T-shirt stretched over his enormous chest and shoulders, was standing in the living room as if he were the welcoming committee.

Carrie tugged on his pants. "Our mother types on her book every night because she is trying to be a book writer and not work at the grocery store anymore."

"Oh?" the fireman said.

"And it's worth a very lot," Carrie informed him proudly.

Chapter Two

After the other firemen were finished, Mike Cavanaugh took his turn in the upstairs shower to wash away the acrid odor of smoke that clung to his hair and skin. While he lathered his hair he thought of his mother, who lived nearby. She would have heard the sirens and might be lying awake, wondering if her firstborn was all right. Mike knew this because his father had told him; his mother had never admitted it. He could give her a call, his father had suggested, making Mike suspect it wasn't only his mother who worried. But, hell, he was thirty-six years old. He was not going to call his mother after every middle-of-the-night alarm so she could fall back to sleep without worrying. Besides, it would start a bad pattern. If he obliged, sometimes his phone call would come fifteen minutes after the sirens, occasionally it would be hours. Calling would become worse than never calling. Sooner or later she would have to get used to this. He had been a fire fighter for more than twelve years.

He did, however, check in with his parents during the daytime. And he had bought them a multiband radio scanner so they could listen to the radio calls. He wasn't as stubborn as he pretended.

It had been 3:00 a.m. when he left the woman—Christine Palmer, he'd learned when they finally had a moment to exchange names—and her kids in the rec room. He'd given her a couple of pillows and blankets to tuck her little ones in on the couches, and some extra clothing for herself—the smallest sweatpants and sweatshirt that could be found. He'd told her which line to use to make her calls. He'd told her to go ahead and close her eyes for a while if she could; the men would be getting up for breakfast and a shift change in a couple of hours—around 6:00 a.m. She could have someone pick her up in the morning so as not to upset the kids' sleep any further.

Upstairs in the sleeping quarters there had been some grumbling. It was not customary to bring homeless fire victims to the firehouse. It was very rare, in fact. Jim had said it might set a bad precedent. Hal had said the kids might be noisy and rob them of what little sleep they had left. Stu had said he suspected it was that little purple tushie Mike had carried out of the house that had prompted this innovative move. Mike had said, "Go to sleep, darlings, and try not to get on my nerves." Mike was in charge tonight.

He couldn't stop thinking about her, however. It wasn't the purple silk butt, even though that did cross his mind from time to time. It was the way she seemed unusually alone with those two little kids. He thought he'd picked up a defiant loneliness in her eyes. Blue eyes, he remembered. When she thrust out her chin it gave her otherwise soft face a sort of challenge. It was peculiar, especially during a catastrophe as exciting to the average man or woman as a house fire, not to have people rally around the victims. Even in neighborhoods where folks were not well acquainted or friendly, it was odd not to have someone break out of the crowd and ask all the right questions, take the family in, call a church or a victims' aid organization. The Salvation Army. But Christine Palmer seemed to hold them all at bay with her look of utter isolation.

Mike could have called the Salvation Army himself. Or the Red Cross. He'd taken a shower instead. His first reaction had been to distance himself from this little family; their aloneness made *him* feel vulnerable. But he felt them pulling him like a magnet. Now he decided to go downstairs and see if she was awake. He wouldn't bother her if the lights were out. Or if her eyes were closed. He was just too curious to go to sleep.

Christine Palmer was a curiosity—an attractive enough one, to be sure—but it was that precocious little blond bombshell who'd gotten right under his skin. He had had a daughter once. And a wife. They had been dead for ten years. Joanie had been only twenty-three and Shelly three when a car accident stole them away and left holes in Mike's soul. He had felt a charge, like a shot of electricity, when that Shirley Temple reincarnate tugged on his coat. What a kid. He felt a giddy lightness; then a familiar, unwelcome ache.

When his foot touched the bottom step he heard a predictable *grrrr*. Then he heard "Shut up, Cheeks." So he knew she was awake. Mike stood in the doorway of the rec room and saw that Cheeks was sleeping on the end of the little boy's couch, right on the kid's feet. He liked that, that the dog guarded the kids. He felt as though these kids needed that. They slept soundly; the boy snored softly.

Christine Palmer sat at the desk nearby, her feet drawn up and her arms wrapped around her knees. The phone book was open in front of her, and her back was to him.

The terrier stiffened his front legs, showed his teeth and growled seriously. She turned to see Mike standing there, surprise briefly widening her red-rimmed eyes. Then she turned away quickly and blew her nose as though it was humiliating to be caught crying after your whole world had burned up. "Shut up, Cheeks," she commanded sternly. "Down." The terrier obliged, but he watched.

"Has he ever actually bitten anyone?" Mike asked, working hard at sounding friendly and nonthreatening.

"No," she said, wiping her eyes before swiveling the chair around to face him.

She had pulled sweat socks up to her knees over the sweatpants, probably to take up some slack; she was drowning in the smallest sweats they could find. Small boned, but with a wiry toughness that showed. She was a very pretty woman. Her blue eyes were fierce, her thick, light brown hair willfully wavy, springing loose around her face. If they hadn't just been through a fire and if he hadn't caught her crying he would wonder if contacts gave her eyes that intense, penetrating color.

"Cheeks is only crabby," she said. "He's not dangerous. But I don't mind if strangers are wary around my kids."

"Why'd you name him Cheeks?"

"His mustache. When we first got him, Carrie grabbed him by that hair around his mouth and said, 'Mommy, look at his cheeks,' and it stuck." She shrugged and tried to smile. The rims of her lips were pink, and her nose was watery. "This is very embarrassing," she said, becoming still more fluid.

"Look, it was a bad fire. Of course you're upset."

"No...no, not that. I...I have no one to call. See, I'm new in Sacramento. I only moved here the end of August, just before Carrie started school. I got a job at Iverson's about a month, no, six weeks ago. I only know a few people. I don't know anyone's phone number except Mr. Iverson's at the store. I have a baby-sitter for Kyle and for Carrie after school, but she doesn't have—" She stopped. *Anything* was the next word. The baby-sitter, Juanita Jimeniz, was the mother of another grocery-store clerk; the Jimenizes were practically destitute themselves. There were more family members living under one roof than there appeared to be beds. No help there.

"I could give you a lift to the bank after my shift change if you—"

"My checking account has $12.92 in it."

"Where'd you come from, then?" he asked, moving to sit on one of the chairs near the desk. Cheeks growled, watching. Mike wasn't convinced he wouldn't bite.

"Los Angeles."

"Well, that's not so far away. Maybe someone there could send you a few bucks? Or invite you back down till you get, you know, reestablished?" He felt his heavy brows draw together, and he tried unsuccessfully to smooth out the frown. His mother had warned him that he looked mean, threatening, whenever he got that brooding look, his heavy brows nearly connecting over the bridge of his nose. But his forehead took on contemplative lines now because he was confused.

Something about Christine Palmer did not sit well. She appeared indigent, yet he'd shuffled a goodly number of indigent families off to Victims Aid, and she didn't fit. People totally without resources, without family, friends, money, without memberships in churches, clubs or unions, did not usually rush into burning buildings to save the books they were writing. Strange. What's missing from this picture? he asked himself.

"L.A. was also . . . pretty temporary," she said.

Her hesitation and her downcast eyes made Mike think she was lying.

"Mrs. Palmer, are you in some kind of trouble?"

Her head snapped back. "Yeah. My house just burned down, my car keys are in there somewhere, I have no money—oh, I *had* forty-two dollars and some cents in my purse for groceries for the rest of the week till payday, but I imagine that's gone, too. And I lied about L.A. I was there for more than three years. I had already borrowed as much as my former friends were willing to—" She stopped abruptly, took a deep breath and quieted herself. "There was no farewell party, all right? I didn't actually do anything wrong, I just . . . had a run of bad luck. An unpleasant divorce. My ex is a . . . scoundrel. It gets rough sometimes."

"Oh," Mike said, pretending to understand. "Make any calls to the Red Cross? Victims Aid?"

She nodded. "And two crisis counseling centers, four shelters and a church group that's helping illegal aliens. Do you know what? My house burned down on the first freezing night in Sacramento. Everyone, it seems, has come in off the streets."

"No luck?"

She shrugged. "I have two more numbers here. The Opportunity Hotel and a place called Totem Park. Do you suppose you have to sleep outside in Totem Park?"

"I know so," he said, frowning. "Here, let me try the hotel," he offered, pulling the phone across the desk. She turned the pad on which she had written the number toward him. He glanced at the sleeping kids as he waited for an answer on the line. Their shiny yellow heads were clean, their pajamas the warm and tidy kind. They were obviously well cared for, with healthy skin and teeth. Bright, alert eyes, when they were awake.

This particular shelter, called a hotel because they took a few dollars from people who either overstayed or could afford it, was possibly the sleaziest place in the city, Mike knew. Some people actually preferred the street to places like this; protection from the other homeless was difficult to provide. Even though she didn't have anything to steal, Christine Palmer didn't look tough enough to fend off an assault. He glanced at the kids again; the ringing continued on the line. The shelter was filthy, nasty. He wondered if there were rats.

Finally there was an answer. "Hi, this is Captain Mike Cavanaugh, Sacramento Fire Department. We're trying to place a homeless family—woman and two small kids. Any room down there?"

The man on the line said yes.

"Oh, too bad. Thanks anyway," Mike said, making his decision and hanging up quickly.

"I'll call Mr. Iverson in the morning, when the store opens. He's a pretty decent guy. Maybe he'll advance me some pay or something."

"Are you *completely* orphaned?" He didn't mean to sound incredulous, but he came from a large family himself and had trouble picturing a life without relatives. Cavanaugh. Irish Catholic. Six kids.

"My parents are dead; I'm an only child. There's this unmarried aunt back in Chicago, where I grew up, but she probably hates my guts. We parted on very unfriendly terms a long while back." She gave a short, bitter laugh. "Actually, it was all my fault. But I'm sure if I grovel and beg and apologize enough, Aunt Florence will invite me and the kids back home. Chicago. Ugh. I hate the idea of crawling back to Chicago, all ashamed and sorry." She slapped the manuscript on the desk. "I was going to go back, you know. Patch things up with Aunt Flo, who is the only family I have in the world besides the kids. But later, hopefully with my tail straight up and not tucked between my legs." Her voice quieted. "I'm not a bad writer. Some people have liked my work."

"'It's worth a very lot,'" he said, quoting the little girl.

"Oh, to her," Chris said, her voice becoming sentimental, almost sweet. "Carrie's my biggest fan. Also the greatest kid in the whole world. Never lost faith in me—not once." A large tear spilled over.

"No one, huh?" he asked her.

"I'm sure I'll think of something in the morning. I've been called resourceful. Gutsy, even. Probably nice ways of saying I'm contrary and not easy to get along with."

He laughed. She wasn't nearly as hysterical as she could be, under the circumstances. Nor as scared. And he could relate; he wasn't always easy to get along with, either. "Just so you get along," he said.

"One way or the other."

"Well, this doesn't look good," he supplied.

"No, but them's the breaks, huh? I'll think of something. I hope."

According to six o'clock news stories, Mike considered, this was how it happened: some perfectly nice, smart, clean, decent individual hit a cultural snag—illness, divorce, unemployment. Fire. Then, with no money for rent deposits, utilities turn-on, child care or retraining, he or she was suddenly living out of a car. After about three weeks of living out of a car, no one would hire them. Then, if they did land a job by some miracle, they couldn't work it because there was nowhere to shower, leave the kids or do the laundry. A mean social cycle. No money, no job.

No job, no money. The forgotten people who were once accountants or engineers.

The press indicated the homeless situation was getting worse every year. The reported living conditions were terrifying. Hopeless and vile. The one common link among these people seemed to be aloneness, lack of family. Mike had family. Boy, did he.

"You know what?" he began. "Maybe we could help you get a news spot. A little—"

"What?"

"You know, get channel five to do a spot on the fire and your circumstances."

"What? What are you talking about?"

"Donations to a post-office box or bank or—"

"*Be* on the news?"

"Yeah, because your house—"

"Oh, *please*. Please don't do that. I'd die!"

"Well, it's nothing to be ashamed of. It's not like it was your fault, you know."

"No. No. That would be awful!"

Okay, he thought, she's hiding. From the ex? She didn't look like a bank robber or kid— Kidnapper? He wondered if the ex had gotten custody. Yeah, he decided. That was probably it. Well, maybe. Whatever, she was hiding something. He wondered how much.

"Tell you what. I live alone. You could use my place for a couple of days. It's a roof."

"What?" she said, almost laughing. "Come on, that's not your usual policy. In fact, judging from some of the looks we've gotten, I'd say you don't have a whole lot of fire victims in your rec room, either."

"It's not usual," he admitted. He shook his head. He had surprised himself as much as her with the offer. But Christmas was coming, and the kids were clean, cute, precocious. She had some secrets, but he was sure they weren't the dangerous kind. Bad luck, she had said. Most of all, they had no one. No one. Well, what the heck, he was someone.

"Fact is, none of this has been policy. The only other time we brought a fire victim here in the middle of the night, it was a relative of a fire fighter. Upstairs they think I've gone soft in the head."

"We'd better get out of here."

"Naw, no problem. Here's the deal, Christine. Can I call you Christine? Chrissie?"

"How about Chris."

He nodded. "Well, here it is, Chris: I'm a little soft in the head. You seem to be having some rotten luck, and I don't have to know what happened to you, but that little girl of yours reminds me of my little girl. She was a lot like that one," he said, jerking his head toward the sofa. "Blond, opinionated, had an IQ of about four thousand. She died in a car accident with her mother about ten years ago. She was only three. And hell, it's almost Christmas."

Chris stared at him. She had only lost a house and everything she owned. Suddenly it didn't seem like much.

"So," he said, watching her watch him. "I don't spend all that much time at my house. I sleep here when I'm on duty, I have a cabin I like to use when I have a few days off in a row, and I have family all over Sacramento. It's a pretty good-sized place, I guess. Three bedrooms. You could make a few calls, get some things like insurance paperwork started. You might say a few things to that landlord about the furnace, and he might settle with you real quick, but there could be a lawsuit in it. You didn't hear that from me, okay? And then, before you grovel to your old-maid aunt, you'd have a little edge. There don't seem to be many alternatives." He shrugged. "It would be too bad to have to take those kids to one of those crappy shelters. Most of them are pretty awful."

"Your house," she said, her voice barely a whisper. She looked at him a little differently. She judged his size and musculature.

"My parents live just around the corner, and I could stay with them when I'm not here. I might be soft in the head, but I'm pretty safe. Anyway—" he smiled "—you have *him*," he said, glancing at Cheeks.

"Gee, that's...really generous of you," she said, but she said it cautiously, suspiciously. Mike wondered if she had been abused by the ex. He wondered *how* abused.

"It's a pretty well-known fact that fire fighters have a weakness for little kids. It's up to you. I live alone, but I have this house. I didn't even want it, to tell you the truth, but my family started hounding me about doing something with my money—real estate, you know. Sometimes you have to do something just so that everyone in your very nosy family will get off your back. So they talk you into buying something, investing. Then they stop worrying and start calling you moneybags." He chuckled to himself. "In my family, everyone minds everyone's business but their own. It's an Irish tradition."

"What will your very nosy family say if you take in this completely unknown, whacked-out, poverty-stricken divorcée with two kids and a dog?"

"Oh, I don't know. They'll probably shake their heads and say, 'It figures.' They gave up on me a long time ago; I'm the one they always shake their heads over. They call me ornery. Probably just a nice way of saying I'm not easy to get along with," he said, and grinned that big grin again.

"You?"

"Yeah. Don't I seem ornery?"

She tilted her head and looked at him. He smiled confidently through her appraisal. "No," she said after a moment. Gentle. Generous. Never ornery. "But they know you better than I do."

"They have their reasons, I suppose." Reason number one, they couldn't get him remarried after Joanie and Shelly were gone. Not a one of them—not three brothers and their wives, not two sisters and all the friends they had in Sacramento. Tough, he told them. He had never liked dating, and he kept his few liaisons to himself; they had never come to much, anyway. Though he missed Joanie and Shelly, he no longer minded being alone. He had gone through school with Joanie, married her when he was twenty and she was eighteen. And he had known he was going to do that the first time he kissed her.

He had liked being a husband and father. And he wasn't anymore.

What he also liked was to hunt, a reclusive sport. He liked the department's baseball team, the gym, the little one-room house in the mountains, and sitting in front of a television set with his dad and brothers when they couldn't get tickets to a game. He liked to read, and he liked to putter under his car. He was solitary but not antisocial. Sometimes he needed sex, someone to make love with, but he didn't like doing it with strangers and there hadn't been very many women over the years who'd become friends. It had been quite a while, in fact. He was a little disappointed in himself for that, but he had become a man who put his energy into a lot of physical things and thereby coped with a primary physical need left unmet. The longer he waited, the less urgent he felt.

He was a quiet, private, sometimes lonely man who had no one to spend his money on except his mom and dad, his brothers and sisters and their spouses and kids. Uncle Mike. He knew what he was becoming—the odd uncle, gentle with some, crotchety with others. Difficult and sometimes short-tempered. Like Cheeks.

"What do you think? Got any better ideas?"

"I... uh... it's hard for me to take... you know, charity. I don't know if..."

He tilted his head toward the sleeping kids. "They won't know the difference. You oughta see some of those shelters. You've got a job, so pay me a little rent if you want, later, when you get it together. Or maybe you could do a few things around the house? Like cleaning or laundry?" He tried not to draw his eyebrows meanly over his nose, which happened whenever he lied. His house was immaculate, and his mother did his laundry. She insisted.

"What if I'm a crook or something? What if I hot-wire my old Honda, clean out your house and haul your TV and stereo off to Mexico?" She was weakening.

Mike laughed. "They'd never let you across the border with that dog." Cheeks growled on cue. "God, he's a piece of work. If he bites me, he's out. Does he, um, make any mistakes?"

"No," she said, smiling. "He's really a very good dog, just crabby. And the kids are pretty good, too." And there it was. Without her saying anything more, he knew it was decided. She and the kids would move in tomorrow.

In the morning, while Jim scrambled eggs for the whole crew, Carrie tugged on Mike's sweatpants. He looked down into her pretty blue eyes. "Our mother says we're going to stay at your house for a little while, because our house is burned."

"Do you think you'll mind?" he asked her.

"No," she said. She smiled at him. "Do you want us to?"

"I invited you, didn't I?"

"We always pick up our toys and our dirty clothes," she informed him. "Kyle is just learning, but he's learning very good."

"I'm sure you're very neat," Mike said. "But I'm a little bit sloppy."

Carrie's expression changed suddenly. She looked over her shoulder toward her little brother, who was sitting on the couch with his thumb in his mouth. Then she looked back up at Mike's face. "Our toys burned up," she said, her expression stoic.

"Oh, didn't I tell you? I must've forgotten. I have toys. They're at my mother's house, but she'll let you borrow them. If you promise to pick them up, of course."

She smiled suddenly, and her eyes became very like her mother's. "We'll pick them up. We're learning very good."

Cheeks growled.

"Can you make him stop doing that?" Mike asked her.

"If he gets used to you, he stops it. You must not hit him. It will make him mean."

"He already sounds mean."

"Yes," she said, smiling a wild young smile that was tangy with innocence and made Mike feel warm all over. "But he only *sounds* it," she added with a giggle.

He wanted to crush her in his big arms. He became afraid of himself, his hard and trembling shell, his gushy innards. He was an uncle who had cuddled many nieces and nephews since he'd lost his own child, but he suddenly, desperately, wished to hold a child who *needed* to be held.

He picked her up, gently. His loneliness, his aching desire for a family of his own, pressed against the backs of his eyes. What was he doing with this child in his arms? A long time ago he'd stopped trying to replace what he'd lost. After ten years, he'd built a strong enough wall that he didn't have to face what he had lost. But holding this little girl shook loose the bricks he had used to build his wall.

Everything they had was gone, and it hadn't been much to start with. Yet these people were not the destitute ones.

Chapter Three

Mike opened the front door for them but did not go in to show them around. He and Chris had talked on the way over. He said he had a lot to get done on his days off, and she had important decisions to make, phone calls to place. Calls that Mike suggested might be easier if he wasn't there to listen.

"You go ahead and look around," he told her. "You won't have any trouble recognizing the two extra bedrooms. The one with the desk and the couch, well, the couch folds out into a bed. And keep the kids out of the garage, okay? There are power tools out there. I'll be back around lunchtime."

"Look, I feel kind of funny, going in alone and everything. There's no reason you should trust me, you know. I mean, it's not too late to—"

"Is there anything you're looking for besides a way to take care of your kids?" he countered.

"No," she answered.

"That's what I figured. Just make your calls. I'm going to stop by the house you rented. If I found an ash that might have been a purse, would your car keys be in it?"

"Yes." She smiled. "Hey, that would be great. Really, I don't know how to thank you for all this."

"Don't worry about that. I don't usually do things I don't want to do. It just isn't that big a deal."

"It is," she said, peeking into the house. "It's a very, very big deal."

"Naw." He shrugged. "The place just about stands vacant. I'll see you in a few hours, then. And listen, I'm going to be pretty tied up for a couple of days, so I hope you can handle all your reorganizing without my help." As if it had just occurred to him, he added, "Since I'm going to stay with my folks, take...uh...the master bedroom, if you want."

Then he vanished. Chris cautiously placed Cheeks on the floor inside the front door. As she and the children stood watching, he ran down the stairs from the foyer into the carpeted living room. "Please, God," she said, "don't let him pee." He scooted around the floor like a windup toy, his whiskers flush against the rug, zooming a pattern of certainty that no other dog had marked the place. He paused for a long while at the coffee table leg. "I'll kill you," Chris warned. The terrier looked over his shoulder at her, then zoomed on.

As Cheeks sniffed and scooted around downstairs, Chris and the kids peeked up the short flight of steps leading to the bedrooms. The three of them were all a little frightened of the fireman's house. It was quiet, new, immaculate, not theirs. Chris finally stepped across the parquet entry onto the thick gray carpet that flowed down the steps.

The living room was decorated in masculine colors of blue, gray, dark purple and dark rose, mostly velour. Walnut accent tables held a few decorator items—an unused ashtray, a scented candle, coffee-table books. A fireplace with a great granite hearth took up most of one wall. Even the logs in the tray beside it looked impossibly clean.

The kids stared at the entertainment center as if it were a rocket ship. Stereo, video recorder, large television, tapes, records, speakers, knobs by the dozen, dials, all enclosed in smoky glass. Spotless, smearless, dark glass. And paintings—prints, actually. Could he have chosen the prints? Also behind glass. Two McKnights. McKnight was known for his happy, homey, bright settings of rooms devoid of people. No hazy pastels, but sharp-featured living-room scenes crowded with things, not people, paintings of rooms that seemed to celebrate themselves with vibrant aloneness. Like Mike?

"My God," she muttered, "I might have to feed you kids in the bathtub."

"He said he was a little sloppy," Carrie told her, "but I think he's learning very good."

"Yeah," Chris replied absently. "Don't touch anything. See that coaster there, on the coffee table?" She pointed. "That brown thing that you put your glass on so you don't leave a mark on the table?" They nodded. "That's the only thing in this room that I can afford to replace."

"Are we going to put our glass on it to not leave a spot?" Carrie asked.

"No," she said. "You're not going to eat or drink anything in the living room." She looked around fretfully. "I'm going to keep a bottle of Windex strapped to my belt."

"I never eated in the bathtub," Carrie said.

"Ate. And I'm kidding. Maybe."

She felt a lump in her throat and turned them around before they could look with envy at the living room any longer. "Come on, let's see if we can find where we're going to sleep."

Upstairs was not the showplace the downstairs was, but it, too, was immaculate. The bedrooms were large and airy and practically unfurnished. The only furniture in one was a set of twin beds, with not so much as a lamp or cardboard box in addition. The other room had a love seat, which, upon inspection, Chris found was the hide-a-bed. And there was a desk where Mike paid his bills. The desk had a glass top. Underneath the glass were a few pictures. One was a picture of a woman and child, and by the woman's hairstyle, Chris guessed it was them. She stared at it a long time, the ones he had lost. Her heart began to split into a bleeding wound. Poor guy. How could you lose that much? It was incomprehensible. She had buried her parents before becoming a mother. She had since decided that the overwhelming pain of that still could not approach what a parent must feel when burying a child. Her throat began to close.

"Is that me with the lady?" Carrie asked.

"No," she said, her voice soft and reverent. "No, honey. That's Mr. Cavanaugh's little girl and his wife. They died a long, long time ago. Way before you were even born."

"Does he miss them, then?"

"Yes, of course. This is his private stuff, all right?" Private feelings. "I don't think we should ask him questions about it. Okay?" Chris crouched so she could look into Carrie's eyes. Her own wanted to water, but she tried not to cry over borrowed heartache. "In fact, I don't think we should even mention we saw the picture, okay? Please?"

"Okay. Can we watch TV?"

"Sure," she said, straightening. "If I can figure it out. Come on. Back downstairs, where you may sit on the floor and touch nothing."

"I thought you said we could touch that brown thing?"

Chris was not in awe of Mike's moderate, tasteful wealth, even if her children might be. She was in awe of *him*. There was stuff to steal here. How was he so sure she wouldn't? How did he know she'd be careful? How could he do this, trust her like this? He knew nothing about her, nothing at all. Except that she was alone and had nothing. She felt a trifle insecure about using his discriminately chosen, carefully placed things, but her chief insecurity was that she didn't deserve this charitable act.

Chris had grown up in a house that would make Mike's place look like the maid's quarters. The fireman's house, in fact, was much like the place she and Steve shared the first year they were married. The kids wouldn't remember anything so comfortable, however. The comparison to what they *did* know made her shudder, and the tightness in her throat grew into a lump of self-pity as she took the children downstairs to deposit them in front of the television while she made some calls.

Mr. Iverson excused her from her job for a few days and agreed to give her a hundred-dollar advance on her salary, which he would deduct from her pay over an extended period of time. She gave him the phone number where she could be reached and called the baby-sitter. Juanita asked her if there was anything she needed. In spite of the fact that they needed everything, she said nothing. Juanita, good-hearted and hardworking, had too little to share. At Carrie's school, the secretary offered the names of places that might offer help. Chris didn't mention she had already tried most of them, but simply informed her that Carrie would not be back for a while. Actually, she didn't know where Carrie would go to school next, and she was grateful it was only kindergarten.

The call to the landlord was another story. Not a story of compassion, either.

"Well, Mrs. Blakely, when do you think Mr. Blakely will be able to return my call?"

"I'm sure I don't know, Mrs. Palmer. He's a little upset about the house, you know. We don't know how that happened."

Chris laughed hollowly. "It happened because the furnace was old, in poor repair and hadn't been serviced in a good many years."

"Ah, I see. You, of course, have the arson report?"

"Arson report?"

"Could you possibly have been . . . smoking?"

"I don't smoke! Hey, listen, I've got two little kids, and we could've all been killed! We didn't even get the car keys out of that old house, it went up so fast! Would you like to take down this number, please?"

"I'm sure we don't need your number, dear, as long as the police know where you can be found."

"What!"

"Well, we don't want to make any accusations, naturally, before the investigation is complete, but I'll take your word that you won't leave the area."

Chris was stunned for a moment. Then, thanks to the finesse she had learned too late from her missing ex-husband—who she hoped was at that very moment being subjected to some incredible Chinese torture that would leave vicious scars—she let out a knowing sigh.

"Mrs. Blakely," she said smoothly, "my lawyer suggested that I find out when your husband will be available for a settlement meeting. We should probably talk before any further medical tests are run on my children so that you'll be fully and fairly apprised of all possible expenses and punitive suits that could be forthcoming."

"Tests? What kind of tests?"

"Smoke inhalation. Possible internal injuries. Possible brain damage. And, of course, stress, trauma, emotional—"

"What is that number?"

She recited Mike's phone number.

Click.

Chris's husband had been a con man. A wheeler-dealer. A schemer. A crook, a louse, a liar. But she couldn't prove it. The sad truth was that she knew where every freckle on his body was located, she would be able to pinpoint his very individual male musk in a stadium holding twenty thousand people, but she had not known what he did for a living. Or what he did with her money. The word *incomprehensible* popped into her mind again, associated with catastrophic loss and the fact that she knew nothing at all about a man she had been married to for four years. Because she had been inside-out-in-love and feeble with idealism and ignorance.

While her children watched a nature program on a cable network, Chris brooded about her past. It was checkered indeed. Poor Aunt Florence.

Chris's grandfather had started a furniture business as a young man; he had started his family as a much older man. By the time Chris's father was twenty-two and married, Grandfather was nearly ready to retire. His company, Palmer House, was respected and very successful.

Chris was born into a family that included her young parents, her elderly grandparents, her father's younger sister and piles of money.

When Chris was small, her aunt, Florence, spoiled her, played with her, baby-sat her and bought her lacy undergarments and expensive pop-it beads to match every dress. When Chris was older they went on trips together—to Hong Kong, London, Tibet. They bought everything of leather, gold, silver and jade that they could carry or ship home. When Chris was eighteen Flo made a down payment on a car for her. A Jaguar.

What she remembered most vividly, however, and missed most painfully, were the letters and phone calls. While Chris was at Princeton, she wrote Flo weekly and called her collect. And Aunt Florence replied—consistently. Chris, studying literature, couldn't believe that her job for four whole years would be reading all the greatest books ever written. She was a straight A student. She loved books, always had, especially Regency and Victorian romances, from Austen to Brontë. And she loved the inexpensive love stories you could buy at the A&P for $1.95. So did Aunt Florence; they agreed that everyone deserved a buck-ninety-five happy ending. They often discussed the books the way other women discussed their favorite soaps.

They had been so close, the best of friends, confidantes.

Florence had never married—the "old-maid" aunt. Except that Aunt Florence was only fourteen years older than Chris. More like an older sister than an aunt, actually. Five-year-old Chris had sobbed for hours the day Flo left for college; she sat by the front bay window all afternoon awaiting Flo's first weekend home. Flo was brilliant, sophisticated, fashionable and rich. She was also bossy, fiercely independent, ambitious and stubborn as a mule. Devoted, sometimes controlling. Loads of fun or a pain in the butt, depending. Such was the deal for an aunt and niece who were more like siblings. Flo couldn't help it that she was the elder.

Chris, her parents and Aunt Florence had always lived on the same street. Flo had kept the old Palmer family home on the upper river drive after her parents—first her father, at the age of seventy-two, then her mother, at sixty-four—died. Flo was only twenty-one then, and Chris vaguely remembered an argument over Flo's living alone in the big house when she could just as easily move in with Randolph's family. Flo, predictably, won.

Chris's mom, Arlene, whom Chris still ached for, was the nurturer of them all. Chris longed to revisit the smells from her early childhood: her father's cologne, her mother's cooking and baking, Flo's furs. Arlene had married Randolph and, she joked, Florence. And indeed, Arlene was like a wife to both of them, representing both Randolph and Flo at charity functions. A society wife—philanthropic, on a number of boards—and caretaker in one. Randolph and Florence had inherited the family business and worked at it. Arlene hadn't "worked" technically, except that no one ever worked harder at taking care of a family. And that was all the family there was. The Palmers of Chicago. Randolph, Arlene, Florence...and Christine.

Then it happened. Arlene and Randolph. Dead. They were in their forties—too *soon*. Chris came home from Princeton to help Aunt Flo bury them, to pack up what they wore and wiped their noses with. It had been black and horrid. She didn't go back to school. What for? For *literature*?

She met Steve at a nightclub. Steve Zanuck—they called him Stever. Hotshot, arrogant, sexy Stever. He was a few years older than she, and Aunt Florence became instantly bitchy, as if she were jealous of him. As if she didn't want Chris to be in love. Flo believed he might be no damn good, as she so tactfully put it. Chris, who needed love, assumed that her grieving aunt had turned mean and selfish. Steve had said that Florence was clinging and manipulative. The pot was definitely speaking of the kettle. So Chris slept with him, married him and sued her Aunt Florence, the executor of her parents' estate, for control of her trust. What had happened? Had she been having an out-of-body experience? Had he drugged her? With sex and flattery. She was so vulnerable and alone she was just a big dope. She had somehow managed to stay asleep for four whole years. Dear God, what an imbecile she'd been.

Trying to emerge from that nightmare had produced some growth and even a little dream or two, like writing, but also immeasurable loneliness. At one time she had had more friends than there seemed time for. The past few years, though, had been largely solitary. Trying to make it on her own, to develop independence and self-reliance, had led to a fundamental absence of people in her life.

She looked at the back of her children's blond heads; they stared up at the television, transfixed by luxury. Kyle's toe stuck out of a hole in the foot of his pajamas. And that was all he had now. So, to prevent their being hurt or further deprived, she might have to call Aunt Flo. For them.

She had hoped, somehow, that she could reverse her circumstances. She could never recover her entire lost legacy, but she could be at least a self-supporting single mother, couldn't she? And so here she was, lying in this bed she had made, because she had to take responsibility for her own mistakes. And because, when Flo was proved right about Stever, her sensitive remark had been, "Well, you just couldn't listen to me, could you? You had to let that slime ball run through everything Randy left for you before you could even figure it out! Will you *ever* learn?"

Probably I will learn, Chris thought. Probably I have.

That was why calling Flo was on the very dead-last bottom of her list of possibilities. She loved Flo, she missed her desperately, but she didn't expect her aunt to be very nice about this.

Of course, she deserved Flo's anger, her scorn, but...

Perhaps Flo would forgive her? Be somewhat kind?

Perhaps she would hang up, like the landlord's wife. Or say, "Chris who?"

"Hi, Ma," Mike yelled as he walked through the living room toward the kitchen. "Ma?"

"Yes, yes, yes," she called back from the kitchen. "I'm up to my elbows in dough. Come in. Come in." She pulled her hands out and turned to look up at him. She frowned. "You look hungry. But good."

He laughed and kissed her forehead. "I weigh one-ninety-five, and I'm not hungry." He took a cookie from the cookie jar. "Not real hungry, anyway."

"You must have had a quiet night," she said softly, quickly looking away from him and back to her kneading. "No bags under the eyes."

"Not so much as a peep," he replied, leaning against the cabinet, watching her back. She glanced over her shoulder, and he smiled. Then his shoulders shook. They both knew she had been awake, stayed awake, and they both liked that to some degree. "Where's Dad?" he asked. But she didn't have to answer. The toilet flushed, the bathroom door opened, and Mike's father, a short, muscular and thick, bald-headed Irishman carrying a newspaper, wearing his eyeglasses on his nose and his leather slippers on his feet, came down the hall into the kitchen. His name was also Michael.

"I thought I heard lies being told," he said. "Mikie, my boy, 'not a peep' went by the house at about the witchin' hour, 'round ninety-five miles an hour, followed by the second bell."

"Oh?" Mike's mother said without turning around. "I didn't hear it. I sleep like the beloved dead."

"We went down Forty-second Street, as a matter of fact, four blocks east," Mike said. "House burned down—one of those little ones over on Belvedere."

"Everyone okay?" his mother asked, turning around. "And the firemen?"

"Everyone is fine, but as a matter of fact, that's the reason I stopped by. Last night's fire. Ma, I've gone and done the craziest damn thing; they just might lock me up for a lunatic. The woman who was burned out is a young divorcée with two cute little kids, just three and five years old. They had nowhere to go, and I loaned them my place. Can I sleep over here tonight? Maybe a couple of nights? Until they get settled?"

"Your house?" she asked. She decided to take her hands out of the dough altogether and wash them. "You gave this family your house?"

"No, Ma, no, I didn't give it to them. I offered them a place to stay until they can make some plans. See, she's pretty young, I'd say about Margie's age, under thirty. And she has no family except the kids. It's so close to Christmas, and the shelters are—" He stopped. His parents were looking at him as though he'd slipped a gear. At any moment he expected his mother to feel his brow.

He didn't know how to explain how it made him feel to think of those kids in one of those crappy shelters. *Or* how it made him feel to think of them in *his* house. Something peculiar and personal had already attached him to them. Maybe he wouldn't have done it if the woman, Chris, had been totally unappealing. He briefly considered her appeal; not a bad-looking woman, and feisty. He had gotten snagged on their helplessness, on them, all three of them, even that stupid dog. No way would they get that dog into one of the shelters, and the kids needed the dog. He had no idea what was happening to him.

"Crammed," he finally said. "The shelters are crammed full."

"They could stay here," his mother said.

"No, Ma, no. My place is fine."

"This divorcée? She's pretty?"

"Ma, she's a little short on houses right now, and I'm hardly ever there. Anyway, I'm sure it'll only be for a few days. Oh," he said, looking at his dad, "do you have an hour or so you can spare? I need a hand; her car is still over at her house. There's been an inspection and cleanup crew going through the mess, and they found her purse and keys. Maybe you could drive my car so I can ferry hers back to my place?"

"Sure," he said slowly, looking over his glasses at his son, maybe considering putting him in a rest home until he became stable again.

"Okay, then."

"Okay, then," his parents replied in unison.

"Anything we can do to help?" his mother asked. "How are they for clothes? Do they need clothes?"

"Well, since you asked, you know that box of toys and coloring books and things you keep here for when the kids come over? I think her kids would love to borrow it. What do you say?"

"And some bread, maybe? Rolls?"

"No, Ma." He laughed. "There's plenty of food. Just some toys for the kids."

"Clothes, then?"

"No, really..."

"So what do they have for clothes, then?" she asked.

"Mattie, never mind," said Big Mike, who was far smaller than his son, whom they called Little Mike. Big Mike stopped his wife as though she was getting personal. Mattie—short for Mathilda—and Michael Cavanaugh looked with deep concern at their eldest son, who stood nearly six foot two and was about as wide as a refrigerator.

"Don't worry, Ma," he said, touching the end of her nose with a finger. "They aren't naked. There are no naked women and children running around my house. I can stay the night here? No problem?"

"Sure, Mike, sure. Let me give you some rolls to take to her. I'll roll a few, and you tell her to let them rise and have them for her dinner. Do you take dinner here, or there, with her?"

Mike thought his mother stressed *her*. After all, his sisters, Margie and Maureen, had brought home plenty of good Catholic women who were not divorced with kids. "She'd love some rolls, Ma. That's nice. I'll bring Big Mike back in about an hour, okay? Then I'm going to go back to my place to make sure that anything kids can get hurt on is locked up—the tools and all that. I'll have dinner here. I'll be back around five. I won't put you out, huh?"

"You never put us out," she said, patting his cheek. Actually, she slapped his cheek, but she did so affectionately.

* * *

An hour later, when the car exchange had been accomplished, Big Mike walked into his house. Mattie came out of the kitchen, wiping her hands on a dish towel. "So?" she asked her husband.

"There is a dog, too," Big Mike said. "A woman, pretty, two kids, both, like he said, cute, and a little dog with no manners."

He walked past his wife to his favorite chair and picked up the newspaper, which he had already read twice. Big Mike had been retired for a year and still had not done any of the projects he had been saving for retirement. "Do you think the dog will hurt his carpet?" Mattie asked.

Big Mike sank into his chair. He shook the paper. It always read better after a good shake. He looked at his wife of almost forty years over his glasses.

"Mattie, four times you saw your boys fall in love and get married. Two times you took our little girls to the bridal shop and took me to the cleaners before you let me take them down the aisle. Why do you act like you don't know nothing about your own kids. That dog could make Tootsie Rolls on Little Mike's head and he don't care. You pay attention then, Mattie," he said, shaking his paper again. "Little Mike's gonna keep even the dog. And it's a terrible dog. His name is Creeps."

"Rolls?" Chris asked.

"Listen, just count your blessings that she didn't come over here to dust you, dress you and feed you with her own hands. All I had to say was you've been burned out, and my mother almost adopted you all, sight unseen."

"That would be nice," she said. "Your dad looked, well, I don't know... reticent. Hesitant." Suspicious.

"Suspicious." At least he said it. "I've never done anything like this before. At least he didn't frisk you." He went back into the garage, brought in two more bags of groceries and put them down.

"Why would he want to frisk me?"

"Well, my mom and sisters have been parading nice Catholic old maids past me for ten years without any luck at all. And then I go and invite you and your kids to move into my house," he said with a laugh. "When I told them what I'd done, the first thing my mother said was, 'So, is she pretty, this woman?' " Mike decided Chris could find out how his mother felt about divorcées later, or maybe never. "I told you, they shake their heads over me. I'm sort of a special project. Since Joanie died, anyway."

He left again, brought in two more bags. "You want me to put this stuff away?" she asked.

"Please," he said, getting still more.

"Gee," she said, "this is because we're here. You shouldn't have done that. I feel—"

"Hungry, probably. The rolls have to rise. Put them in the sunlight—there, on the windowsill."

He brought in more bags. Eight. He felt very big across the chest, bringing so much food into his house. Taking care of people, really. It was not like giving things to his siblings or folks, who all tolerated it very patiently, even gratefully, but, no kidding around, they didn't *need* his giving. They could get by fine without his gifts, his interference. What he gave his family was extra, not essential, like this. Today was the first time since he'd lost his family that he'd stocked so much; it filled him right up.

Next he brought in different kinds of bags. Then the box of toys, which he took into the living room for the kids. In the kitchen Chris was trying to figure out the cupboards. "I can't really tell where things go, Mike. You don't have a lot of food here."

"I almost never eat here. My mom would die of grief if she couldn't feed people all the time. I go over there almost every night. Here, I keep chips, beer, coffee, pop, cereal and eggs. And toilet paper. I don't even get a newspaper." He took out his wallet, unfolded some bills. "I ran into your landlord, and he told me to give you this to tide you over. I bought a couple of things for the kids, so you don't have to take them shopping in their pajamas. I would have picked up something for you, but I didn't know...you know..."

She looked at him in disappointment. "Mr. Blakely?"

"That his name?"

"That's not true, Mike. You didn't run into him."

He didn't seem to mind being caught in a lie. "You sure?"

"I talked to his wife. They're thinking of suing me. They aren't going to be generous about this."

"Suing *you*?"

"It would seem. I'm going to have to fight them."

"The son of a bitch. Here," he said, holding out the money. "You can pay me back out of your settlement. You ought to fry the bastard."

She smiled but hesitated to take the money. "Thanks. Why didn't you just say it was yours straight out?"

"I was afraid you wouldn't take it. You suffer too much, Chrissie. It's almost like you want to."

"No," she said, feeling a slight shiver at the sound of the nickname. Her dad had always called her Chrissie. "No, it's just that I have an extraordinary amount of bad luck for someone who doesn't take drugs or pick up hitchhikers. And I don't want to take so much from you that I feel guilty."

His face lit up. "I didn't know you were Catholic."

"I'm not," she said, confused.

"Oh. You mean other religions borrow guilt when they don't have enough, too?"

"Come on," she said, taking the money.

"I think these will fit the kids," he said, picking up the department-store bags. "I didn't even want to take a chance guessing your size.... You'll be okay in that sweat suit, huh? It isn't high fashion, but it isn't pajamas."

"People shop at Iverson's in worse than this. Why are you doing all this?" she asked him, a gentle inquiry.

"I don't really know," he said, the enormous honesty of it causing his dimple to flatten. He didn't break eye contact with her, even though he knew the heavy brows were probably making him look dangerous. "But I am. I want to. Just let it go. Okay? Please."

"Mike, I appreciate this; it's very generous and kind of you, but—"

"In the closet in the room with the desk, there's a typewriter. IBM Selectric. You might have to buy ribbons. And here's a house key, since you'll be coming and going."

"Mike," she said slowly, "do you have some crazy fantasy about all of this? About these poor, destitute little kids and you're the big strong fireman who—"

"Don't," he said, holding up his hands and looking as though something had just poked him. "Don't, okay? Don't start all that. My family has been dead a long, long time—I don't have a lot of fantasies anymore. It's almost Christmas, for Pete's sake. I'm not trying to make you feel too grateful or too guilty. I don't have any big plan here. It's just sort of happening. They're good kids—they're too young for bad luck. Just get things back together. I don't expect anything. Let it be."

"Well," she said, "it's a lot to do...for a complete stranger."

"Did you find everything? Bedrooms? Bathrooms? Towels? Need to know where anything is?"

"No. You have a wonderful house."

"Well, you have your keys and some clothes for the kids. Go get something for yourself, have a good supper, take a bubble bath or something. Relax. There's some liquor in the dining room cabinet, if you drink. So the heat's off for a while, okay? Your run of bad luck has been replaced by a little good luck, huh? And, Chris? I wouldn't hurt your feelings for the world, but you smell sort of like a ruined brisket."

Chapter Four

In one bag from the department store were three pairs of corduroy trousers, three shirts, pajamas, underwear and socks and a pair of tennis shoes, close enough to the right size, for Kyle. Pants, shirts, undies and tennies for Carrie were in a second bag, these in pink, lavender and white. All the price tags were removed, as was done with presents. "How did you feel, Mike, buying these things for the children?" she had wanted to ask him. But even had he stayed while she went through the bags, she would have lacked the nerve.

She suspected, or imagined maybe, that he would say it felt like something he had needed to do for a long, long time. She remembered how he had looked after the fire, his features rigid from hard work, wet with sweat and smeared with dirt. He had seemed so physical, rugged, dominant, yet there had been this tenderness all along. His kindness and humanity had glowed like a light in his soft green eyes.

It was as though he did things from the heart, not necessarily prudent or logical things. What was prudent about running into burning buildings to save lives?

She had been pulled out of a fire; there was hardly any position more vulnerable than that. He had pulled her out, taken her in. There was hardly anything more masterful.

He had so quickly, so bravely told her about his missing family—not flippantly, not melodramatically—openly. Raw with honesty but no longer stinging with pain. An uncomplicated man who could speak in simple terms; he gave shelter, just like that. Because he was hardly there anyway, because the kids were too young for bad luck and because the shelters were awful... and because he'd had a daughter once. This gave her comfort and hope; her own pain was still fresh, and she looked forward to a time when she could calmly discuss all that had happened as the distant past rather than a current event.

"Here's the deal, Chris, your daughter reminds me of my daughter...."

He had locked up his tools in the garage with new padlocks before leaving again. To keep the children safe. He asked if she would mind leaving him notes on the refrigerator, taping up her schedule so he would know if she was out for errands, working, whatever. He didn't mean to pry, but he would have to stop by for his things now and then, and he didn't want them to be tripping over each other or getting in each other's way, surprising or embarrassing each other. And he gave her his mother's phone number, plus the private line at the firehouse. It seemed to Chris as though she was being given everything, including space and privacy, when he should probably be asking her for references.

She had told him as little as possible about herself, secretive because her life story was so complex and astonishing. Mysterious Chris, so alone with her kids and their mean little dog. Him she had sized up within a day.

His eyes were a little sad, which was easily accounted for. He didn't have a mustache now, but in a photo she had found while looking for a TV schedule he had a thick brown mustache. He had been photographed in a T-shirt that read SACTO #54; he'd been younger, his cheeks shallower, his eyes wider, not yet experienced and crinkled. He'd been prettier, not more handsome. That was the man, she imagined, that Joanie had fallen in love with. A strong, lean, hopeful youth.

She liked his older looks. He had cozied; his manliness, the strength of maturity, even his sadness, gave him a depth a woman would be tempted to sink into for comfort, for pleasure. Every plane on his face reflected seasoning, seasoning by pain and sorrow but also by compassion and abundant love. When Mike Cavanaugh had offered to provide for her and her kids, and then did so, the gesture had settled over her like a warm blanket. He seemed sure, capable, sturdy. Here was a man, she thought, who wouldn't collapse when leaned on. He was a complete stranger to her, but she felt perfectly safe. She hoped she would not become drugged by the feeling.

She had felt safe at other times in her life. She had felt the security of an only child; then suddenly she was an orphan. She had depended on her aunt's unconditional love, then felt betrayed by Flo's rage. And then—three strikes and you're out—she had felt safe because she'd had a bunch of money and a husband she loved and a baby and what could go wrong?

She had obliquely asked Mike if he were trying to compensate for his losses. And he had said, "Don't, okay? Just don't. Just let it be, okay?" And then that little breathy way he had of saying, "Please?"

There was more, Chris knew. She felt a familiar pull. She was attracted to his power, his arms, his tanned face and curly hair, his bright, imperfect smile. The dimple. It had been such a long time since her body spoke to her of needs that she was shaken by this sudden, spontaneous awareness. And she sensed his feelings were not very different. Oh, this was supposed to be for the kids, but he looked at her in a way that made her think he was trying not to look at her in *that* way. She couldn't help but wonder what his motives were. Maybe he wanted a woman. Or a family. He couldn't replace what he'd lost, but he could try to recapture some of those emotions he had experienced when they were alive. The feelings of usefulness, companionship. This he could do by providing shelter. The thing he didn't know was that he was exercising a need to provide on a woman who had a terror of dependency.

"It's a roof," he had said. She would try to remember what it was. And she would remind him, if necessary.

Chris scribbled a note. "Gone to shop, post office, Iverson's, baby-sitter's and burned-down house. Be home all evening. Thanx. Chris."

She hiked up the sweatpants, pulled down the sweatshirt and was grateful her moccasin slippers had rubber soles. On her modest shopping spree she bought two pairs of blue jeans, blouses, some underwear and tennis shoes. Also, typewriter ribbons, just in case. She had purchased the barest minimum, and all on sale, but still the money Mike had given her was nearly depleted.

She stopped to pick up a new smock from Iverson's Grocery so she could get back to work. Her boss and coworkers offered sympathy and help, which touched her deeply but did that other thing, too: made her feel even worse. What right had she, after all, to such concern, such sympathy? She had been an heiress, for God's sake, and she had bungled it. She felt like an impostor. She longed for her mother, as she often did. Her mother would understand.

She dropped by Juanita Jimeniz's house to explain her time off and to plan a new baby-sitting schedule for when she could get back to work. Then she went to the old house, which was roped off to keep the neighborhood children out. Her own children stayed in the car. The typewriter was hopelessly destroyed, but some of the books that had been shoved in the refrigerator had survived. She took them back to Mike's house but left them in the garage to air out.

She fixed herself and the kids a simple, cheap dinner; she didn't want to use up too much of the food Mike had bought. She would repay him, in any case. Then she soaked off the burned-brisket smell and washed her hair with Ivory Liquid—she had been too cheap to buy shampoo. She borrowed very little of what belonged to Mike and was not fooled by the appearance of new, unsqueezed toothpaste in the bathroom he probably never used. In fact, there were many new, unopened items in that bathroom, while he had a bathroom off the master bedroom full of half-used things. She didn't think he had much call for Jergen's Lotion or baby powder, yet it was available for her.

She scrubbed the kids, gave them ice cream, snuggled them for a while. She tucked them in early. Then she lounged, indulging in a weak bourbon and water. She wore her jeans because she wouldn't spend her limited funds on sleepwear. The soft, deep velour sofa was decadent; the movie channel was as entertaining as a producer's screening room. And she waited.

For Mike. Because she had left the note, she wondered if he would stop by. To see how she was holding up? To see if she needed anything? To see if she had ripped off the TV? To see if the kids were okay?

But he didn't come by. He might not even have been there to read the note.

Her next day's note said: "Out for errands, home by six. Will be here all evening. Thanks for everything. Best, C."

But again there was no evidence that he had come home. And the phone didn't ring while she was there. It felt very odd. Being in his house was somehow intimate, as if he surrounded her and was everywhere she looked but still was far away and hard to reach. Like Santa Claus. Or God.

She looked for something to read and found a small library in the master bedroom, which she entered guiltily. She was afraid to intrude, to invade. His books, in a bookcase by the bed, were almost all men's adventure and spy novels. Cussler, LeCarré, Ludlum, Follett, Shaw. Some horror by Stephen King. The book that was open on the bedside table was Tom Clancy's latest bestseller. The books gave her a good feeling about him; he read by choice and for fun, entertainment, to imagine, to widen his vision. She wrote for similar reasons. Then she went to the study, where she made her bed from the couch. She opened the closet there. "Well, what do you know," she said out loud.

The ten-year-old IBM Selectric sat on top of a small bookcase that held some very different titles. Collections of Dickens, London, Melville, Tolstoy, even Austen. There was an old copy of *The Jungle Book*, a children's edition of *Tom Sawyer*, and other classics. There were hardcovers and paperbacks. *The Little Prince*, and *Illusions*, by Richard Bach. Did he read them, or were they here for another reason? Had they been his wife's? She finally picked up a copy of *Moby Dick* and, caressing it, went downstairs to luxuriate in the living room again. And to wait.

For him. What kind of guy can do this? she asked herself again. Give a complete stranger, who's obviously in a mess, a key to his house? And be so unworried? It was pretty hard not to like this guy. She liked his house, his generosity, his soft spot for a couple of unlucky kids. The thing that bothered her the most was that she couldn't quite tell if she liked him as a friend . . . or a man.

Then it was Friday, her third day in Mike's house. She knew she shouldn't complicate things. But she wanted to know about the man who owned interesting books and clothed and fed them because it was "just happening." Her note said: "Will be at the library today until 2:00 p.m. Appointment downtown with landlord at 2:30. Do you like tacos? We'll eat at 5:30-6:00 or so. Join us if you can. C."

She was back at the house by four. On the bottom of her note were some pencil scratchings. "I'll bring beer. M."

She showered and washed her hair. She was eager for his presence, for his approval and his concern. She would promise not to take up his space for long, and maybe she would learn a little more about the man who locked the tool cupboards to keep the children safe, the man who kept classics in one room and new fiction in another. The man who would bring beer, even though there was already beer in the refrigerator. He had been here, but his presence had flowed through without leaving a mark. Had he been here every day? Waiting for just such an invitation?

No way could he flow through her life without leaving a mark; already, she would never be able to forget him. He had touched them all in a permanent way. The way life can be forever changed by the smallest act. A man gives a quarter for a cup of coffee, but instead of coffee the recipient makes a phone call for a job and ends up being president of the company, makes millions, tells the story in the *New York Times*.

When he arrived he rang the bell. Carrie let him in, and Cheeks growled.

"Hello, Mr. Cabinaugh," Carrie said. "Mommy, Mr. Cabinaugh is here for tacos. Our mother is being very careful with your house, Mr. Cabinaugh."

"Carrie, you can call me Mike," he said, picking her up. She was light as a feather. A six-pack in a brown paper bag was under his other arm. "Are you feeling better?"

"Was I sick?" she asked him.

"No, but your house burned down."

"Oh, that wasn't our house, we were *renting* it. We had a 'partment before. Are you feeling better?"

He smiled broadly. "Was I sick?" He liked the games precocious children played.

"No, but our mother says we've taken your house."

He laughed, delighted. His laugh rumbled through the house, and Cheeks nearly lost his composure, seriously growling. "I loaned it to you because I wanted to. Have you told *him* yet that this is *my* house?"

"Maybe if you give him part of your taco, he'll start to like you."

"No way. He can like me or not, I don't care."

"Maybe he'll bite you if you don't share," she said.

He looked at her in such shock that her giggle exploded. Both her hands came together in a clap; she'd teased him good.

"He won't bite you really," she said.

Mike wished that adults could look at one another the way children looked at people. A child's look was so unashamed, so blatantly invasive. They wanted to *see* you. They looked hard. Without flinching or feeling self-conscious, looking you square in the face to see what you were made of, what you were about. And they didn't care a bit that you saw them looking. If adults could do that, friendship wouldn't take so long.

"Maybe we should have a fire tonight," he said. "It's cold and rainy outside."

"Our mother says the fireplace is brand-new."

"It's been used. Come on," he said, even though he carried her into the kitchen where the sound of meat sizzling indicated Chris was working.

Tacos were not fancy by anyone's standards, but Mike thought the kitchen smelled wonderfully homey; she might as well have been baking bread. And she might as well have been wearing an evening gown; she cleaned up real good. But it was only a pair of jeans. His eyes went right to her small, shapely rear, although when she turned around to greet him he shifted his gaze guiltily to her face. She smiled and said hello, and he began to color because he had sex on his mind and was afraid she would know. It had been a while since he'd had that reaction. He hardly knew this woman, but he couldn't wait. He was somewhat ashamed, somewhat relieved. He had hoped that part of him wasn't all used up. He also hoped he wasn't going to be terribly disappointed when he didn't get things his way, which he suspected he wouldn't. He handed her the bag. "Smells good. Can we have a fire? The screen is safe, and I'll watch the kids."

"That would be good. I don't want them to be afraid of safe fires."

He cocked his head to look at her, impressed. "I thought you might be more nervous about it . . . after losing everything."

"I have them," she said, smiling. "The other stuff wasn't that valuable."

Kyle was sitting on the counter by the sink, and Mike grabbed him with his free hand. Holding a kid on each hip, he hauled them off to the living room to get the fire started while Chris fixed tacos.

She heard him talking to her children, and she peeked around the corner to see what was going on.

"We're going to stack the logs very carefully, like this, so they won't fall. What would happen if a log fell off the grate while it was on fire? That's right, it might fall right out of the fireplace and onto the rug. Uh-huh, we have to put some paper underneath, here, like this, to start the fire easier. Yep, the wood would burn without the paper, but the paper makes it hotter quicker. Paper burns very easily. Now, Kyle, is that very hot? Yes, you must not go closer than this. The screen will be very hot, too, while the fire is burning. There, isn't that warm and pretty?"

Chris handed him a cold beer. "Thanks," he said.

"About ten minutes for tacos."

"The kids want a drink, too, Don't you?" Both kids stared at him hopefully. "Chocolate milk?" Their eyes became wider, more hopeful.

"Uh, Mike, they should come into the kitchen. . . ."

"They can't see the fire in the kitchen." He saw Carrie and Kyle holding back gurgles of desire.

"What if someone spills?" Chris persisted.

"So? We want chocolate milk by the fire. Don't we?" He looked at one, then the other, and they nodded very carefully. Carrie's tongue was poking out of her mouth, and her eyes beseeched her mother's sense of adventure.

"All right," she said. She heard them laugh, all three of them. When she was safely in the kitchen stirring chocolate into glasses of milk, a smile ran through her body. He was spoiling them, giving in. Thank you, God. He was gentle and giving and fun, and they would remember him forever. Chris had been worried about the total absence of male role models for them, but she had lacked the time, energy or courage for even the most innocent of relationships with men. Also, she had thought it necessary to keep them safe from her poor judgment. She had really messed up when she picked Steve. This was good; they needed a decent man to think about, to remember. As did she.

She brought them their drinks, a beer for herself. "I turned the meat off for now. It looks like we're going to have a cocktail hour here," she said.

"Good," he said, passing the milks. "Relax. Enjoy yourself."

She sucked in her breath and flinched as her younger child sloshed his drink to his mouth. Before long Kyle's indelible mark would be on the fireman's rug.

"I said, relax. I could throw a cup of chocolate on the carpet right now just to get it over with if it'll help you calm down. Don't be so nervous."

"It's just that everything is so nice. Practically new."

Mike knew, as he had known the very night her house burned down, that although she seemed to own almost nothing of any value, she was not a person who had done without all her life. She didn't come from poor people. He didn't know how he knew, but he did. *He* had come from poor, blue-collar Irish Catholics transplanted from the East Coast. His mother had fried round steak on special occasions; his father had said, "Chewy? Good for your teeth." The way Chris talked, or walked, or held her head, or something, he knew she had grown up differently. "It's new because it's hardly been used, Chrissie. That isn't necessarily good." That won him a grateful smile. "What did the landlord say?"

"He said he'd get back to me."

"What?" That made Mike a little angry.

"Actually, he offered me a few hundred dollars—my original deposit. But he wanted me to sign a paper that promised we were uninjured and wouldn't seek a larger settlement. I wouldn't sign it. I told him that I lost several thousand dollars' worth of stuff—none of it new, but none of it stuff that we could spare. It's not as though it was my fault, really, although I should have had some insurance. I would have expected him to be a bit more compassionate."

"Son of a bitch. Sorry," he said, glancing at the kids. "Now it'll only go harder on him. Sue him."

"I'm not really the suing kind," she said, and thought about adding, *anymore*. "But I will try to get a little more money out of him."

"A bunch of money. The fact is, you could've all been killed."

"I know," she said, shuddering. "I've given a lot of thought to that."

She had condemned herself for the risk she had exposed Carrie and Kyle to, living on pride as she was, struggling to be independent. Renting a cheap, crummy house in a questionable neighborhood when Aunt Flo would have taken them in—probably after a mere tongue-lashing and Chris's promise never to disobey again. Her kids could have more, be safer. It only meant admitting that she had been a fool, a senseless fool, and she had already been punished plenty for that.

But having more had never been the issue. Even though she had grown up rich, she didn't miss luxury all that much. She wanted to recover, not beg forgiveness. She wanted to make herself safe, not sink into someone else's provisions. She wanted to call Flo and ask if they could make up, *not* call Flo and ask for plane fare. She didn't want to be completely beaten, a total victim. She had been teetering on the edge before, ready to pick up the phone and call Chicago collect, but she always managed to steal one more day of independence. Pride. Her father's gift to her. Fierce and unyielding. And sometimes quite tiring.

"I haven't called my aunt yet," she said apologetically.

"No hurry on that," he said. "Did you find the typewriter?"

"Yes. And books—wonderful books."

"My brother," Mike said. "I'm the oldest one in the family and wasn't interested in college. I just wanted money and a man's work—my father's son, all right. The other kids are all hotshot brainy types. Tommy—he's about twenty-nine, I guess—is a professor. Big-shot professor. And a coach. Every time he was working on a book with his class, he wouldn't shut up about it. You'd think he was gossiping about the neighbors, he was so wound up and chatty. He'd always give me a copy." He laughed at himself. "I never let on that I read them, but I read them. Hell, with Tommy carrying on for weeks, it's like taking the class."

"I had a little college myself," she said. "Two years. I studied literature."

"Then you know," he said, as if there were a club for the few people who cared enough to discuss the little-known secrets about things that happened inside books, a small group who entered these classic stories, lived in them briefly but were forever changed, deeply touched.

During tacos they talked about Chris's writing, even though she usually tended to be secretive about that, too. She was slightly embarrassed about her novice status and the enormity of her ambitions. She wanted to be the next Judy Blume. Her love of books had begun these dreams, but it was the way creating a story of her own could take over her life, consume her thoughts, charge her with energy, that kept her enthusiasm so high. It took her away from her petty, surface concerns, while at the same time making her probe more deeply into her inner self than was possible to imagine.

She especially liked stories for kids; there was something magical about them, and she identified so closely with the emotional impact of their experiences.

"I don't think everyone remembers details from their childhood the way I do," she offered in partial explanation. "I remember what I was *wearing* the day Barbara Ann Cruise pushed me out of the lunch line; I remember the exact feeling of being third-to-the-last picked for the soccer team. It might as well have been last to be that unpopular. And the first boy-girl party, sixth grade. I *know* I was the only one not invited, and I was so miserable and hurt that my mother let me sleep with her. I remember those feelings so exactly that it's almost scary."

And, she explained, she loved kids in general. Loved what they had to build on, endure, traverse, overcome, become. Had she finished her degree, likely she would have chosen a field in which she would be working with children—probably teaching at the elementary level.

She was amazed at how she went on and on, how natural it felt, and how nice it was to have someone encourage her to continue.

"Do you want more children?" he asked her.

"I'd like to concentrate on doing all right with these two. I've got no real job skills, but I'm a good writer. Eventually I want to stay home with the kids and write for a living. Writing for kids is the only thing I've ever done that feels right."

Carrie and Kyle asked to be excused and ran off to play quietly.

"How about if you remarry?" he prodded.

"No chance of that," she said emphatically. "My ex went on a business trip and never came back. Before Kyle was even born. Now my future is in these two hands," she said, holding up her palms.

"Never say never; gets you into trouble."

"I'll be fine. I land on my feet. When times get real tough, I work overtime, or I clean houses. If I clean for people who are away working, I bring the kids along. And with that schedule, I can write. As long as I take care of the kids and do enough writing so that I feel I haven't given up every little dream I ever had, then I'm as happy as I expect to be." She watched his face. "Maybe I won't write great books," she said. "I'll write a few good books if I work very, very hard—books like the kind you have in your bedroom, books that entertain, that help people imagine, get away and expand a little. The kind you have in your study, people are born to write."

He smiled a small smile.

"I didn't sleep in your bed," she said.

"I know," he replied quietly.

They shifted their eyes away. She wondered how he knew, wanted to ask, but had too much fun with the fantasy. Had he rigged something? Left a pencil on the bed? Positioned the bedspread just so?

He had glanced away because he was embarrassed by how he knew. When she was gone, doing errands, he had lifted the pillows from his bed, hoping to smell her on one of them, disappointed when he had not. He had thought about the pillow on the hide-a-bed but had restrained himself.

He was relieved when the children chose that moment to interrupt. They all played a game of Candyland in front of the fire and watched a thirty-minute Muppets special on TV. Mike scratched Cheeks behind the ears, inadvertently creating a slapstick routine with the terrier. Every time he reached toward the dog, Cheeks snarled blackly, then allowed the scratch anyway. The game made the children laugh with uncontrolled passion.

At eight o'clock Mike turned off the television. The fire was dying down. He turned on the light behind his recliner, pulled the kids onto his lap, and opened a big Richard Scarry picture book. He began to read.

At eight-thirty Kyle was asleep on Mike's chest with his thumb in his mouth. But Mike was still reading. His shoes were off; his voice was growing slower and scratchier. Chris stood and hovered over them. "Come on, Carrie. Bedtime. I'll help you."

"Not yet, Mommy. I want to fall asleep here, like Kyle did."

"It would be better if you brushed your teeth and fell asleep in your bed," Mike said gently, kissing her forehead.

"Okay," she said, "but first finish the story."

"I'll read to you again next time. Let Mommy put you to bed."

Chris lifted Carrie out of the recliner. "Let me get Carrie settled, then I'll come back for Kyle."

"Okay," he said. He didn't offer to carry Kyle. He wanted to be left alone with him for a few minutes, alone in the dim evening with a child in his arms. Mike embraced the little boy tightly. He inhaled the smell of his hair, the redolence of child. Tangy. Sharp. Kyle snored when his thumb came out of his mouth. Mike put it back in. Childhood was so short.

Too soon, Chris took him away. Mike felt a choking sensation in his throat and something binding his chest. He reached behind him to turn off the lamp. The living room was bathed in firelight, glowing but dark. When Chris returned to the living room she said "There," in that way a mother does when her duties are done, even though she's still on call. Joanie had said it that way when she finally tucked rambunctious Shelly into bed; that kid wanted to go all night.

Then Chris sat on the sofa and looked at him. He knew he was caught in the shadows and that she might see the tear that had slipped down his cheek. He decided he wouldn't wipe it away because then she would know for sure. He wasn't ashamed of emotions like these, but crying was so intimate, and he didn't want to invite her in any farther yet. He wasn't all that sure this was something she could share. She must have known, however, because she gave him a few moments of respectful silence while he suppressed his emotions. She did, after all, know of his losses.

"Did you read *Out of Africa*?" he finally asked her.

"Years ago. Way before anyone considered a movie."

"Me too. It was Holden Caulfield's favorite book, remember? I read *The Catcher in the Rye* with my little brother Tommy's class. Then I read *Out of Africa*. This part wasn't in the movie, anyway. There's a place in the book where she tells about the veldt-sores you can get in Africa. If you're not careful, the sores will heal on the outside, but inside they get worse; they get infected and runny and full of poison. The only way you can get rid of them is to open them up, dig them out at the roots, leave them open on top until they get the proper scabs and scars."

He brushed off his cheek.

"You don't just get them in Africa," Chris said.

"Don't call your aunt yet," he said. "Please."

"It might be better if I called her right away."

"Please," he said again.

"Look—"

"There's plenty of room here. There's no hurry."

"But—"

"You need a place for them. For you. For now."

"It's not mine though. It's hard to—"

"You wouldn't exactly be taking charity, Chrissie. This works as well for me as for you."

"Mike, what's happening here?"

"Stay a while. Just a while. I gotta get a scab on this, so I can scar. I'm way behind. I didn't do it on purpose, but I waited too long."

"Oh, jeez," she said through a sigh.

"Maybe I can grout the veldt-sores. If I can't, it's not your fault."

"What if staying here only makes new ones?" she asked him.

"No. I don't see that happening."

"Just what the heck *is* happening?"

"Nothing bad, I don't think. Big Mike calls things like this 'unconscious plans'—when you do something that looks to the whole world like it's crazy as hell and totally coincidental and you don't think it ran through your brain for one second first, but unconsciously you knew all along you were going to do it. Like I wasn't looking to help out anyone, for a family to move in here—there have been lots of burned-out families over the years—and I didn't know I was going to offer you a place to stay even when the shelters were full, and I sure as hell didn't know I'd ask you to hang around longer than you have to, but—" He stopped and shrugged. "But Ma says Big Mike is full of it."

A huff of air escaped Chris—it was almost laughter.

"I don't talk about my feelings very well," he apologized.

"You're doing fine."

"If things had been different, if I'd met you at the zoo, I'd just do something normal, like ask you out to dinner or offer to take you and the kids to a movie."

"You would?"

"But it isn't that way. You got burned out. You need a place to stay. Feels like it oughta be this way, like this is the natural order. That's all. I haven't brought a lot of food into this house before. I don't have to be quiet when I get up early. No one messes anything up; it's pretty quiet all the time. And it has one or two advantages for you and the kids, too."

"But—"

"Not just the kids," he added in such a way that she thought he felt he should be completely honest.

"Oh."

"I'm not making a pass," he said.

"This is crazy," she said, leaning an elbow on her knee and cupping her chin in her hand.

"Yeah, the whole world is crazy. Your ex left you when you were pregnant. Your only family hates you. Your house burned down. And some lunatic wants you to hang around a while because..."

She waited for him to finish. When he didn't, she prompted, "Because why?"

"Because, why not?"

"Look," she said, taken aback a bit. What kind of reason was "why not?" "You've been very generous, you seem like a nice guy, but really, Mike, I don't know you, and you don't know me, and—"

"This is crazy, Chrissie, but I'm not. I'm pretty safe. I mean, I pulled you out of a burning house, for Pete's sake. You want some references? Want to meet my mother?"

"I just want to know what you're after."

"An extension. Of tonight. It was a fun night, huh?" He grinned, proud of himself.

He had a contagious smile that made you smile back even when you didn't have a smile ready. It *had* been a nice evening. She had even had the fleeting thought that she liked him, desired him, felt comfortable and secure for the first time in a very long time. What she had *not* had was the slightest notion of this kind of invitation.

"And that's all?"

"That's all I have the guts to ask for."

"You're making me nervous," she said.

"Don't overthink it. Men say more daring things than that in singles' bars, right?" Again he grinned. He knew. She knew. He knew she knew he knew. "Won't hurt anything if we're friends."

"How long?" she asked him.

"How about Christmas? It isn't very far away. It could be fun, huh? For the kids, anyway. Maybe for me and you, too."

"Christmas?" she asked doubtfully.

"Shelters and places like that, well, they're sometimes... pretty dangerous. Dirty, a lot of unsavory types hanging around... people get hurt. It wouldn't be a good idea. Really. If you don't like the idea of staying here, you should call your old-maid aunt who hates your guts. I think it would be lousy for you to go to Chicago because then we wouldn't find out if we like each other—all of us, I mean—but all things considered, it would be no fun at all to visit you at one of those awful shelters."

"Christmas?"

"It might be nice for the kids to know where they're going to be for a while. To have something to look forward to."

"I find this a little scary," she admitted.

"No scarier than sleeping in your car."

"True. But—" She couldn't think of any buts. Even though she hadn't expected him to ask her to stay, she had known almost instantly why he had done so. Because he missed his family, because he wanted his home to be less lonely, because Carrie reminded him of his daughter... because he was attracted to Chris.

"But you understand." He looked at her with easy, unbrooding eyes, relaxed, trusting eyes. She'd have to be nuts herself not to understand that they'd started something. "Don't you?"

"Are you going back to your mom and dad's?" she asked.

"Yeah," he said, sitting forward and reaching for his shoes.

"You don't have to." He stopped. "If you'd prefer, I understand, but it's your house." She curled her feet under herself, Indian style. "If what you're looking for is some noise, it'll break loose at about seven."

He leaned back, leaving his shoes where they were. "Thanks. Sure you don't mind?"

She shook her head. "I'd just like you to remember that this is temporary."

"I know."

"Don't get yourself all caught up in it."

Too late. "I won't."

"I appreciate the generosity."

"I appreciate it, too. Your part, I mean. I understand why this would make you a little nervous. You probably don't trust men."

"Not a lot, no."

"Well, that's understandable. It'll be all right."

"Roommates. This is really astonishing."

"Probably nothing like this ever happened before," he said.

"Never."

"That hide-a-bed is okay? Comfortable?" He lifted one eyebrow.

"Perfectly," she said.

"I could take it. Or—"

"Don't even think it," she said.

This time his eyes sparkled with the grin. He was feeling a lot better. "Come on, Chrissie. You can't make me not *think* it."

She threw a couch pillow at him. And, in spite of herself, she laughed at him. Or at herself—it was hard to tell which. After all, she'd been thinking the same thing almost since she met him. It just scared her, that was all. But not enough to run for her life.

It was the middle of the night, and Mattie Cavanaugh was sitting up on the edge of her bed. She reached toward the bedside table.

"If you touch that phone," Big Mike said, "I will break your arm."

"Shouldn't we know he wasn't in a bad accident?" she asked.

"No, and I don't care if you don't sleep for a month. You leave the boy alone. He had a hard time of it. Some things his mama can't take care of."

"But we don't know this woman, this *divorcée*."

"Both arms," Big Mike said. "I'll break both arms."

"I hope he's all right, is all. I hope he's all right."

"He ain't been all right for ten years now. Lay down. Come on, here," he said, pulling her back into his arms. "If we're going to be awake thinking about what Little Mike's doing, maybe we should fool around, eh?"

"Fool around? How can I fool around with some old man when all I can think about is my son, maybe lying in a ditch somewhere?"

Big Mike laughed and kissed Mattie's cheek. "That isn't what you're thinking about, Mattie Cavanaugh. The priest is gonna get an earful at confession, eh? Nosy old woman. Come here. Closer." He was quiet for a long time. "It ain't the woman worries me so much as that dog, Creeps. That dog's gonna maybe take Little Mike's toe off."

Chapter Five

Chris had pulled out the sofa bed at 10:00 p.m. She left her door ajar to listen for the kids, although they always slept soundly. She had left the desk lamp on, propped *Moby Dick* on her knees and trained her eyes on the page. But not a word of it soaked into her brain.

She could hear the sound of the television downstairs. Also she heard him make two trips into the kitchen and slam the refrigerator door once. She heard water in the sink, lights clicking on and off and, finally, at eleven, the squeaking of the stairs. What in the world have I gotten myself into? she asked herself.

She heard his shower running. She had never heard of a man showering before bed. Unless... Just what was he cleaning up for? She heard a blow dryer. So his wet hair wouldn't soak the pillow? His mattress creaked softly, his light clicked off, and before very long she heard the purr of a soft snore that hit an occasional snag and tripped into a brief snort. Her shoulders began to ache from the tension of listening.

Chris's imagination always worked best late at night. For someone who was struggling to make it alone, she was the last person who *should* be alone. Night noises always grew into monsters; melodramas unfolded in her mind at the slightest provocation. Once the sun came up she was remarkably sane. It was, however, nearly midnight before she began to realize that as long as she could hear him snoring, he wasn't tiptoeing down the hall toward her sofa bed. What kind of guy wanted to have kids—someone else's kids—in his house? No, no, surely not *that* kind of guy! He seemed like a nice, normal fella—pretty good-looking, too. Just what unusual habits had prevented his remarriage?

At one she put down the book, of which she had read four paragraphs, and turned off the light. She got out of bed and peeked down the hall. He had pulled his door to, but it was ajar a few inches, which was why she could hear him snoring. She got back into bed, but her neck was stiff and her nerves were taut. What if he *was* crazy? If she and the children suddenly disappeared, would Mr. Iverson, or Mike Cavanaugh's Irish mother, demand an investigation?

At about two, rather bored with the rapist, pedophile, murderer fantasies, she began to indulge another kind. He was a nice guy, a decent and friendly man who'd had his share of troubles but had not been destroyed by them. Only wounded. Chris had not had to listen to him long before she could actually feel his desire to heal himself. He had accomplished a feat that Chris still felt was slightly out of her reach—he was managing on his own—but it hadn't made him whole. He hadn't asked that much of her, she reflected, and a small part of her was even relieved not be the only needy one.

She wanted to drift off to sleep, but his presence down the hall overwhelmed her. It was so long since she had shared her space with anyone but the kids. All she could think about was him—what he wanted from her and what he'd done with the past ten years. Why hadn't he found a fire victim with two little kids five years ago? Would his "unconscious plan" have fallen into place with someone else in similar circumstances?

At three Chris tried putting her pillow at the foot of the bed. Steve had never read to Carrie. He'd rarely held her. He wasn't at the hospital when she was born, and he only visited twice; he said he was in the middle of a deal. He didn't care what they named their daughter; Carrie was fine, he said. A person's name for a whole life... fine. After he had been missing for quite some time her lawyer finally found him in Dallas, living, she was told, very modestly. Struggling. Staying with acquaintances, friends. Driving a borrowed car. Wearing last year's clothes.

"What about my money?" she had asked the lawyer.

"He doesn't seem to have it anymore."

"But it was *mine*!" she had exclaimed.

"Did you have a prenuptial agreement, Chris? An account number somewhere? Anything? We could sue him, but you should be aware of the cost, and the consequences of losing... or of finding out there's nothing left anyway. So, Chris, did you do *anything* to protect yourself?" the lawyer had asked her.

The lawyer had then asked Steve if he would contest the divorce.

"Absolutely not," had been his answer. "Chris deserves better than me," the lawyer reported Steve as saying.

What a generous bastard he was.

"And the custody of the two children?"

"Two?" he had countered.

"Since you don't want to sue him for support," the lawyer had said to Chris, "I imagine it doesn't matter that he questions the paternity of the second child."

Oh, hell no, why would a little thing like that matter?

She turned her head. Her pillow had become somewhat damp from remembering. If she hadn't been used the first time around—lulled away from her home, tricked into betraying her own family, abandoned and humiliated—then maybe she would walk down that hall and curl up against that strength and power and comfort, just as her kids had. Because they weren't the only ones who needed to feel some of that. And they weren't the only ones who missed having a man around. Life was very big. Everyone needed a top and a bottom, a right and a left, a masculine and a feminine, a full circle that connects. Wouldn't it be nice, she thought, if she hadn't been so thoroughly educated in the perils of trust?

At three-thirty she noticed that Mike wasn't snoring, but she had decided he wasn't dangerous a couple of hours earlier, so she wasn't worried that he was sneaking down the hall. She hadn't stayed only because it was safe and comfortable for the kids, and she hadn't been afraid of him for one minute, not really. After those few hours of wild sleeplessness she had finally remembered that the only person she was frightened of was herself.

She fell into a jerking sleep, every muscle taut from insomnia, her brain throbbing from vacillating between the idea of reintroducing sex into her barren life and running away with her kids before she became tempted.

* * *

Morning had been around a while when Chris awoke. She heard her kids talking quietly, and she sat up with a start. Her back was sore, and her head ached. An insomnia hangover. By the time she had fallen asleep she must have been in a double pretzel position. She rubbed her eyes; they were swollen from crying. She tried to smooth her wavy hair and reached for her jeans to pull them on. Then she heard *his* voice. He was up taking care of her kids. This was going too far.

Distracted, she failed to glance into the bathroom mirror to see how the night had worn on her. She immediately began looking for the kids. She could hear their voices coming from his bedroom. She stood at the door, listening.

"Do you shave your legs, too?" she heard Carrie ask him.

"Women shave their legs. Not men."

"Why?"

"No telling. Want shaving cream on your legs?"

"Yes. Then you'll shave them?"

"Nope, we're just practicing today. You have to be older."

"Kyle? Carrie?" Chris called, not entering his bedroom. "What are you doing in there?"

"Mommy, come and see us shaving."

"Shabing. Vrooom," Kyle added.

She thought about it for a second. "Mike? Can I come in?"

"Well," he said, dragging the word out, "I don't know if you should, but—"

She shot into the room. What had she expected? That he would be naked? She shook her head at them. Carrie sat on the closed toilet seat with shaving cream on her legs. Kyle sat on the sink beside where Mike stood shaving. They had their own bladeless razors to scrape shaving cream off themselves, and slop it into the sink. They smiled at her, all three of them. Mike met her eyes in the mirror.

"What are you kids doing?" she asked, looking at the biggest kid of all.

"Got anything you want shaved?" he asked. He turned around to face her, and his brows drew together a little. "Didn't you sleep well?"

She peeked around his shoulder to look in the mirror. Ugh. It must have been a worse night than she remembered. How did you apologize for waking up ugly?

"I've never slept on that bed," he remarked, turning back to the sink. "Is it terrible? Maybe I should take it. Or try the couch downstairs. Or maybe one of the kids, being pretty light, would be able to—"

"It wasn't the bed," she said, feeling stupid. "It was one of those nights, you know, when you're being chased all night long and wake up exhausted." And then she made a decision that the next time she heard rapists and murderers in the night, they were just going to have to get her in her sleep; she wasn't waiting for them anymore. It wasn't the first time she had resolved this, but maybe from now on she could make it stick.

"Chased? As in nightmares?"

Kyle had scraped off all his shaving cream and was ready for more. He grabbed the can and gave it a squirt. Bad aim. It snaked toward Mike's ear. Chris grimaced. Then she laughed.

"Not exactly nightmares," she said, reaching for a towel and wiping Kyle's face. "No more," she told her son. "You're done." She wiped Carrie's legs. "More like a vivid imagination."

"You overthink everything," he told her, starting to shave the other side of his face.

"Want some breakfast, Carrie?" she asked.

"We had pancakes already. Clown pancakes."

"Oh. Okay. Go watch TV."

He wiped his face clean. He turned around. "So, what chased you all night?"

"Just your basic neurotic fantasies."

"You want a lock for your door? Think you'd sleep better?"

"How'd you know?" she asked, amazed that he had seen through her that quickly, that easily.

"Well, to worry about things that *have* happened is one thing, but to worry about things that *might* happen . . . well, you seem to specialize in that. But you have a long way to go to catch up with Mattie."

"Mattie?"

"My mom. Guilt and worry. She's got a Ph.D. Dr. Ma."

"Well, gee, we're strangers, you know. All you have to do is read the newspapers to—"

"Chrissie," he said solemnly, touching her nose and leaving a little spot of shaving cream. "We're not strangers anymore. And we almost never were." She looked into his green eyes. "Chrissie, Chrissie, maybe you have good reason to be careful. Me too. But honest, there isn't any reason not to get a good night's sleep. Take it easy. I like you guys. I'll take good care of you."

"I don't want to be taken care of," she said, though not very vehemently. It was, in fact, something she still wanted very badly sometimes, something she hadn't grown out of naturally before her parents were suddenly killed. But she'd spent four years remembering that such wants were immature, grounded in ignorance, *and* double-edged. Let someone take care of you, and they might just take care of you.

"Fine," he said, smiling. "So, wanna chat a while? Or can I take a shower?"

"But you took a shower last—" He smiled more deeply.

"I think I'll go eat something," she said, turning away.

"I have the day off," he called after her. "Wanna rent a movie for the kids or something? I left two clown pancakes for you in the kitchen. There's coffee, too. Chrissie? Chrissie?"

She leaned against the wall outside his bedroom door, arms crossed over her chest. She didn't answer him. She wanted to eat the clown pancakes. Rent a movie. She wanted all of it. Oh, please, God, don't let me wake up for a while. Please.

There were a lot of things besides men and sex that Chris had given up. She had simply been too busy to notice. Leisure time had been the first thing out the door behind Steve. Things like walking around the mall, or sitting at a picnic table tossing popcorn to ducks. Things like sitting down to a meal *with* her kids rather than cooking something for them while she ate out of a pan over the sink. And friendship—having someone reach for your hand or give you a hug at precisely the right moment. These were the kinds of simple things that made life satisfying.

"I didn't think I was smart enough for college," Mike told her when they were walking around the mall. "I missed that gene the other kids got, the one that made them ambitious and convinced they were smart enough. I worked construction for a couple of years out of high school. Then I drove a truck until I got hired at the department. Like I said, I always just wanted physical work and a solid paycheck. That's all."

"But what kind of gene does it take to never doubt, not for one second, that you're going to get out of that burning building?" she asked him.

"I doubted it once or twice," he said.

"Too scary."

"Wanna know what's scary? Fear itself. I've seen two guys, in my twelve years, get scared. Too scared of the fire to do it anymore. They all of a sudden couldn't go in. Whew."

I can relate, she thought.

"That's why I try not to think too much."

"If you don't think about it, it won't happen?"

"Sort of. Ever read any of those books, you know, the how-to-get-through-anything, or how-to-love-someone-who-loves-someone-else, or—"

"Pop psychology?" she supplied.

"Yeah. Well, I went through about fifteen of them in the two years after Joanie and Shelly. *Love Yourself First. Grief Management. Living Alone Happily.* Think, think, think."

"Didn't they help?"

"Yeah. They gave me something to do while I was letting time tick away. I'd be right here, right now, doing exactly what I'm doing if I hadn't read a word. In fact, most of the ones I read about grief said you just have to admit your feelings and feel them. Hell, I couldn't *help* that."

She laughed sympathetically.

"How many of those books have you been through?" he asked her.

"Oh, twenty or a hundred."

"And did it ever turn out that your husband hadn't walked out after all? Did you ever slam the cover shut after the last page and find your life any different?"

"You're an analyst's nightmare," she suggested.

In the park, tossing popcorn to the ducks, she told him a little about herself and her divorce, though she remained cautious of the exact circumstances.

"He said he was going to a business meeting in San Diego," she explained. "Then the phone started ringing—people were looking for him. He didn't call. I was afraid he was dead. I called his office. They hadn't heard from him, his secretary said. I called the police; he wasn't missing long enough. I started dialing every hotel in San Diego. It was horrible. It was two weeks, then four. I started to find out how little I knew about him and his life away from me. I realized I was pregnant, and even though I had a little money and could pay some of the bills, I didn't know how to go about finding this joker.

"When I started calling some business acquaintances I'd heard him mention, I found out he'd done a lot of lying. The big wheeler-dealer was a con artist, and he'd skipped town. Literally." She decided not to mention that she herself had been conned.

"What did he do for a living?"

"He said he was a lawyer. I'm even starting to doubt that."

"And you never found him?"

"Once I had myself convinced I wasn't a widow but an abandoned wife, I hired a lawyer. The lawyer found him in another state. Do you know what I asked the lawyer to do for me? I asked him to ask Steve if he would please come home, for the children." She turned her head and looked at him. Tears filled her eyes. "He said, 'Children?' He didn't even know about Kyle."

That was when he reached for her hand. He gave it a squeeze and did her the courtesy of saying nothing.

"After he walked out on me when I had a one-year-old and was pregnant, I asked him to come home. Can you beat that?"

"Course you did, Chrissie. Whenever something bad happens, the very first thing you want is for it not to have happened."

"The kids don't even know him."

"Kids. They're always the lucky ones, huh?"

He put his arm around her shoulder. Carrie and Kyle hopped around while ducks chased them for popcorn.

"What I've been trying to figure out for the past four years is how I could have been that stupid. I believed everything he told me. I trusted him completely, even though he did all these things that should have signaled me he was a liar. Not being where he was supposed to be, not getting home when he was expected, not following through on any of his promises, not showing any real affection. He was so good-looking and entertaining and funny that I, big dope that I was, went right into a coma and didn't wake up until he left me."

Mike squeezed her shoulders. "I don't mean to butt in, Chrissie, but aren't you blaming the wrong person?"

"I don't ever want to be that stupid again, know what I mean? Hey!" she said when he pinched her upper arm. "What was that for?"

"Just making sure you're wide-awake," he said, grinning.

Later that evening, after the kids had gone to bed, they stayed in the living room, Mike in his recliner and Chrissie curled up on the couch. He had made them each an Irish coffee. And they talked. About what he'd done with the past ten years. About his women.

"My mom thinks I've been celibate for ten years. That's fair, since I think she has. She's always worried I'm alone too much, but she has to know where I am every second, so I can't really be alone *with* someone, right?"

There had been only a few women in his life over the years. Sometimes he knew right away it wasn't going anywhere, and he'd end it after a couple of dates. No one-night stands; he'd never understood how people could do that. Men did it all the time, he knew, but it didn't appeal to him. There was a guy, Stu, he worked with, for example, who seemed to be hot to trot every minute. A married guy, no less.

Then a few years back there had been two women at once; he dated them both on and off for a whole year. One was a flight attendant who was out of town a lot, and with his twenty-four-hour shifts at the department, it was hard for them to connect. They seemed to get bored with trying. The other one he liked pretty well, but he knew she was on the rebound. She'd broken up with a guy she had really been in love with, then ended her affair with Mike when the guy came back. "My sister Maureen found out about me seeing two women at once and gave me a book about fear of intimacy. She's the family counselor. I told her to shove it."

"Well, that was a nice thing to tell her."

Then there had been the woman in Tahoe. An artist. She threw pots, painted, sculpted, did incredible and beautiful things, things no one would ever think of doing, and lived in a small adobe house furnished by her own hands. She had made the rugs, furniture, wall hangings... everything but the toilet.

"When I first met her I thought I'd died and gone to heaven. She's a little older than me—she's over forty. After a year of driving to Tahoe every time I got a few days free, if she had a few days free, too—she traveled and taught, gave workshops and all that—I started to figure out there was something missing. I *admired* her. *Envied* her. That talent, skill. Those ideas. Like a pioneer. I couldn't wait to get to her place and see what she'd done. I was actually surprised to realize I didn't love her. I *liked* her a lot—still do.

"She's one of the neatest people in the world. But you know what was missing? She needed absolutely nothing from me. There were things I could give her, like friendship, or like, you know, the physical stuff. But she never suffered without it, either. The last time I was in Tahoe and gave her a call for the first time in almost a year, she said, 'Mike!' real excited like. 'You're back! Come on over!' Then I realized she had never once, in over two years, called me in Sacramento. A real free spirit. She needed herself, period. Amazing."

"I think that's where I want to be," Chris said.

"Would that be good? I don't know. What if everyone was like that, really? Totally without needing other people?"

"There might be a lot of people who were in places they *wanted* to be, not trapped in places because of need," she suggested. "Need weakens you."

"Lip service," he scoffed. "You say that because you had a bad experience needing somebody you shouldn't have trusted. But you were pretty young."

"Well, yeah, but—"

"I'm not talking about that trapped kind of needing; that's no good. I've never been trapped by anything, but I know it would be no good. I'm talking about give-and-take. Like, I could get by just fine without my family butting into my business every single minute, but there's not a one of them I could give up. Plus, I complain, but if they didn't butt in, I'd probably feel ignored. Do you know what I'm talking about?" he asked seriously, his brow furrowing. "If nobody needs you, then when you're gone, you just slip through the cracks and disappear, and everything stays the same. You've had a whole life, and you've made no impact."

"But your Tahoe friend has," Chris argued. "Her art!"

He drained his Irish coffee. "*I* don't have any art."

"You've saved lives in fires! That's impact!"

He got out of his recliner. "People I've rescued don't call me Sundays and say 'Come and watch the game.' They won't know I've gone when I go. I'm just doing my job, and that's not the same thing, is it? I sort of felt as if I was just doing my job with the artist—that she didn't need me for anything and wouldn't know I was gone if I was." He flipped on the TV. "Wanna see who's on Johnny?"

"Sure," she said, after a moment. "But did you need her, the artist?" she couldn't help asking.

"Yeah. I guess. I think that's why it ended as undramatically as it did; she didn't need me back. No connection."

No wonder he'd told his sister to shove it when she gave him the book. He wasn't as afraid of intimacy as he was of never having it again. That real, vulnerable intimacy of needing another person. And having that person need you back.

Chris couldn't dispute its worth. She had two little people depending on her, really needing her, and often that was what kept her going, kept her from self-pity. But, she wanted balance—to be able to lean on someone who wouldn't betray her or control her or collapse under the weight of her need. She knew, unfortunately, how unlikely it was she would find such a person. Thus, she was on her own.

Maybe Mike wasn't afraid of needing because he hadn't been let down. He'd been tricked by fate. There was a difference.

Many times she had asked herself, if Steve had been honest, loving, devoted and dependable but had died, would her loss and pain have been terrifically different? She never answered herself, because the answer seemed almost as shameful as what had happened to her.

"More Irish?" he asked.

"Yes, please." Maybe it should be a double, she thought.

Chris worked three six-hour shifts at the grocery store during the week before Thanksgiving. Mike worked two twenty-four-hour shifts. That left a lot of time to be filled with chores, cooking and watching movies or television. They shared the cooking, but Mike had her beat by miles; fire fighters were great cooks, she had learned. There was time to talk—not only the kind of talking that's done when all is quiet and dim, but also the kind of casual talking you do while one of you is sweeping the kitchen floor and one is loading the dishwasher.

"What about that book of yours?" he asked her while she was folding some clothes. "Shouldn't you be working on that book?"

"I have sort of missed Jake—he's the twelve-year-old I've been writing about. He's had a rough year—seventh grade."

"Well, why don't you work on Jake while I make dinner. It's my turn, right?"

They had done it, as he'd said. They'd stopped the clock. She hadn't worried about the burned-down house or the kids or anything. She slept well; the sound of his snoring had become as comforting as the purr of a well-tuned engine. She threw his shorts in with her dirty clothes. He washed her old Honda when he washed his Suburban. He brought doughnuts home with him in the morning when his shift was relieved. She brought ice cream after work.

Chris turned off her brain. She refused to analyze. She scorned common sense. She was briefly, blissfully content. The dog ate Mike's socks, the kids spilled on the floor, there was warmth and an extra hand to wipe off a chocolaty mouth, to hold a tissue and say, "Blow." And in the eyes, the smile, the occasional touch of a hand, there was a pleasant tug-of-war of sexual possibility.

Chris knew that the past seven years of her life constituted a trash heap of problems that should be sorted out, organized, settled and resolved. No way she could make that mess go away. She should contact her estranged Aunt Flo; she should reaffirm her goals and sense of direction.

But she waited. She couldn't bear to upset the applecart, couldn't bring herself to spit in the eye of good luck. In fact, if real life would be so kind as to not intrude for a few short weeks, she had the potential to be disgustingly happy.

Chapter Six

There was nothing to prepare Chris for the Cavanaugh family. After having met Mike's father, she had been afraid to meet his mother. The prospect of meeting them *all* simply terrified her. But she couldn't think of how to refuse. She was scheduled to work until two o'clock on Thanksgiving day, and Mike suggested that, since he was not working, he would baby-sit until she was finished, and then they would have turkey dinner with the Cavanaugh clan.

Clan, indeed. What would they ask her? she wondered. Would they ask if she slept with him? Should she say no politely? Or indignantly? Or disappointedly. Would they ask her how long, precisely, she would be staying with him? Should she say: "Look, Mike is a good and generous man, and he needs my little family for a while, to complete his grief, as I need his strength and friendship, and you must not interfere''? Or should she say, ''Until December 26''?

''So this is Chrissie,'' said Christopher Cavanaugh, the brother closest in age to Mike. ''Glad you could come over. Well, you don't look too badly singed. Everything going okay since the big burnout?''

''We're getting it together, I guess,'' she said, weak-kneed and shaking inside.

''My wife, Stacy. Stacy, here's Chrissie. Palmer, isn't it? My partner's name is Palmer. Rusty Palmer. You know any other Palmers in Sacramento?''

She didn't.

Christopher Cavanaugh was an orthodontist. His wife, Stacy, managed his office. They had three children, the oldest in braces. Next came Matthew, about thirty-two. Wife, Maxine. Three kids, aged four, six and eight. And then Maureen, whom they sometimes called Mo, and her non-Irish, non-Catholic husband, Clyde. Maureen, a nurse, was in uniform because hospitals, like grocery stores and fire departments, did not close for holidays. She was a petite, feminine version of Mike: curly brown hair, bright green eyes, that notable, crooked Cavanaugh smile that seemed so perpetually full of fun. Then came Tommy, the professor-coach, his wife, Sue, and their two little kids. And finally Margaret, the twenty-six-year-old baby of the family, who was a graphic artist, and her husband, Rick, and her huge stomach, which would soon provide Cavanaugh grandchild number eleven.

Ten children. Fourteen adults. Mattie, on her feet the whole time, getting some trouble from the daughters-in-law about how hard she worked. They called her Mother, but her own children, to the last, called her Ma. It was an experience in itself, hearing an orthodontist say, ''Ma, hey, Ma—we have any beer to go with this ball game?'' And the kids called her Gram, like a metric measurement, nothing so precious or pretentious as Mimi or Grandmother. Everyone called their dad and grandfather Big Mike, and of course they called the bigger Mike, Little Mike.

Chris should not have bothered to worry about what they would ask her. They talked so much, all of them, that they could easily have ignored her presence, except that they included her quite naturally.

"The *prints*?" Margie howled. "Did Little Mike pretend he had something to do with the McKnights? What a hoot! He didn't even buy the ashtrays! I did the house. He wouldn't let me upstairs, though. I bet he doesn't even have a shower curtain."

"I have a shower curtain, brat."

"Oh, yeah? What color?"

"Never mind the color. You don't need to know the color. I'm not helpless."

"I bet it's brown. Or green. Come on, is it green?"

"It's red," he supplied.

Margie laughed and held her big belly. "Red? In a blue bathroom?"

"It looks good. It looks fine. Tell her, Chris. Doesn't it look fine?"

Chris had a vision of them—six of them born within ten years—growing up here, in this four-bedroom, one-bathroom house, fighting or laughing, yelling all the time, the way their kids were doing.

Mattie managed them all. She placed them where she thought they would be most comfortable. She set up a card table and put children with coloring books there, at the end of the living room where her boys—her men—watched the game, so that arguments over crayons could blend with shouts over a touchdown. The women stayed around the dining room and kitchen, talking about their houses, their kids, their work. That was where Chris felt she belonged, yet didn't belong. The bigger kids were in the garage-converted-to-a-family-room with games and Atari. The family room had been added, Chris learned, after the first three of Mattie and Big Mike's kids had left home.

Carrie had been intimidated at first. She held back, but Maureen swept her in with her five- and three-year-old. Soon Carrie was playing hard, behaving like a normal child rather than a whiz kid. And Kyle talked. Carrie was too busy to speak to him, so he spoke to the others, snatched toys away and alternately offered them, negotiating his terms. Here, among so many Cavanaughs, no one looked askance at the things children did, whether sweet or mean.

The small house became hot, close, with so many bodies that Chris felt at once trapped yet never more alive. They touched, this family, hardly ever speaking without hands on one another. Even the men. Except, perhaps, Big Mike, who sank into the role of patriarch, letting them come to him. The children came readily and often. "Big Mike, will you get this apart?" "Big Mike, what color is this color? Is this color red or *rose*?" They climbed on him, asked of him, sought comfort from him. He attempted to look a little aloof, a little bored, but he wiped four noses with his own old hankie.

Chris, who had been afraid they would be suspicious of her, saw Big Mike draw Carrie in, and she had to look away before she wept with longing. Carrie, who had watched all the other children take their minor accomplishments and miseries to their Big Mike, had approached him holding a picture torn from a coloring book. She stared at him; he had a newspaper in his lap, which seemed natural for him, even with his entire, huge family around him. As if he might read it, hide behind it, while they carried on their intimate family relations.

"Does Big Mike mean Grandpa?" Carrie asked him.

"Around here," he said, looking at her over his glasses.

"I don't have any Grandpa. Or any Big Mike."

He stared at her for a long, gloomy second. Then he said, "You'd better come up on my lap, then."

She went very easily, as if she had climbed onto that lap many times before. Together they looked at the picture she had colored. As if she was one of them. With so many, there were no favorites. Or they were all favorites.

It took three tables for the Thanksgiving meal: the dining-room table, fully extended, pockmarked and burned from many such dinners; the kitchen table for the smallest children, where their spills would create fewer problems; and two card tables in the family room for the not-so-small children. Christopher and Little Mike took sides against Tommy and Clyde in an argument over unions that went as far back as the air traffic controllers' strike. Rick and Margie tried to convince Big Mike about some investments that would yield him more from his retirement, even if there was a risk. It was perfectly clear that Big Mike had no concept of what they were suggesting, would not change anything about his retirement but loved their frustrated interference.

Watching them, Chris ached. She wanted to share with them the way they shared with one another—advice, arguments, concern, love. It was a family so tight, so enmeshed, so interdependent—original Cavanaughs and in-laws alike—that there was barely enough autonomy here to fit a gasp of surprise into. But no one seemed to mind. Not at all.

She wondered how they had done it, how so many people could achieve this kind of intimacy. But their closeness, so involved and intense, seemed to be a thing they simply had, not a thing they strived for. It was too effortless to be contrived.

Through snatches of conversation and questions freely answered she had figured out who was responsible for whom. Christopher had gone to college on a football scholarship. Dental school had been made possible through loans Little Mike, probably a young widower by then, had cosigned. Matt had borrowed for college with brothers cosigning, then Christopher had paid for nursing school for Maureen. Tommy had gone to school on Little Mike's and Christopher's money, and Big Mike and Mattie were able to manage for Margie. They had all done it together. Whoever had, gave. Whoever needed, took.

On the buffet were the pictures. A few studio portraits, six wedding couples in tuxedos and lace—yes, Joanie and Mike, too—but mostly school photos in their traditional tacky cardboard frames. And there was Joanie and Shelly, the same picture Mike had on his desktop, only larger. The young mother, the little blond angel.

All things considered, she thought, the Cavanaugh family had held together pretty well, lost little compared to what they had. The Palmers had been a family of four, after all, and had lost two, leaving the two survivors estranged. Half gone, half broken. Still, Chris felt a twinge of despair over Mike's losses.

Mike. He seemed to need little. Chris had been surrounded by ambitious people: her father, her scheming husband, her aunt Flo. Her mother alone had loved her gently. For a man to be content with simple things—some work, some play, some family, some privacy and some companionship—seemed to Chris to be of the highest virtue. He did not seem to long for easy money so much as comfort he had earned. Nothing too fancy, nothing too complex, nothing too frivolous.

The Cavanaughs had no idea how different she was, had no idea of her secluded, privileged childhood. She had gone to Tibet when she was fourteen, for heaven's sake. She had had none of what they had and probably much of what they longed for. Despite the differences, though, they did not allow her to remain an outsider. They drew her in, delighted to have an audience.

"So, the big shot, Chris, says to me, 'If you go down the clothes chute, I'll go, too. I've already done it three times,' he says. And he says, 'Come on, Tommy, you're skinny, you won't get stuck. Chicken?' And of course I didn't get stuck, but the big shot, who had never—I mean *never* done it himself, got stuck. And I had to go to the church, where Ma was doing volunteer work with the League women, and get her and bring her home to try and unstick him from the clothes chute."

"Yeah, sure. As I remember, *you* called *me* the chicken and said you'd tell about the names I'd carved in the dresser top, under the doily...."

"And how do you s'pose he got out? You think Ma got him out, Chrissie?" Tommy went on. "Oh, no, nothing so nice and neat as that. Ma had a fit, and I thought she was going to die of a heart attack, because the big shot had turned his head inside the clothes chute and couldn't turn it back."

"I called the police," Mattie said. "What could I do but call the police?"

"You shoulda called the undertaker," Big Mike said.

"Almost had to after you got home," Little Mike said.

The had to tear out the wall to get Chris out of the clothes chute. When Big Mike got home and the wall had been torn out, it was almost murder. But that was nothing compared to the time Little Mike was kissing his girl—Joanie, probably—in the front seat of his car in her driveway, thought he had his foot on the brake when it was on the gas and plowed through her dad's garage door and into his car.

The banter continued throughout the meal, through cakes and pies and ice cream and coffee, engulfing Chris, making her laugh, making her forget herself.

Preparing to leave the Cavanaugh house, however, stirred up her original anxieties. In this intimate, nosy family where everyone minded everyone's business but their own, wouldn't someone mention the new housekeeping arrangement Little Mike had introduced into his life? She fairly shivered with nerves as she cloaked her children for the trip back to Mike's house.

"Goodbye, God bless you, go to Mass. Are you going to Mass?" Mattie quizzed her brood as they departed from the Thanksgiving gathering.

"Yes, Ma," each of them said. Even Mike.

Chris wondered what Mattie was going to say to her. Go to Mass, perhaps? Are you Catholic? Where, exactly, do you sleep?

"You come again sometime, Chrissie," Mattie said. "And the kids. Don't make them be too good, now. They're good enough, those kids."

"I won't. I mean, yes, they are. Thank you. Very much. It was lots of fun."

Big Mike said to Carrie, "Take care of that dog, now. You make Creeps behave himself."

"Cheeks," she giggled. "I keep telling you his name is Cheeks."

"I know, I know. Creeps. Good name for that dog."

During the quiet drive back to Mike's house, with the kids nodding off in the back seat, Chris knew what was going to happen later. She wanted him. She wanted to be part of something again.

She put her good-enough, happy, exhausted children into the twin beds in the fireman's house. They went to sleep instantly, but she waited a moment to be certain. She tried to warn herself about the danger of getting more deeply involved with this man, but she was drunk on family, on hope and life and pleasure. Lonely, weary, needy. A little afraid, but not afraid enough. All her alarms were malfunctioning; she could not summon the least ping of warning. She couldn't remember a time in her life, even way back when she had had a family of her own, that she had felt this secure. Mike's embrace was so wide. Had he known, she wondered, that by taking her to where he had come from, she would find the surety and peace of mind she needed to touch him, hold him, invite him in?

Downstairs, the house was quiet. A light was still on in the kitchen, but Mike was sitting in the living room, on the couch, in the dark. Waiting. He had known. Or hoped.

It would be a holiday from real life for them both, Chris decided. For just a little while there would be no tangled, complicated pasts for either of them. Nor need they consider their uncertain futures.

She went to the couch, knelt beside him, put her arms around his neck, kissed his lips. She meant for it to be light, preliminary, but he had little patience. He was a man, as he had said, who didn't think for a long time about things but simply did them when they were right.

"Oh, God, oh, Chrissie."

The arms that pulled her close were so caring. Powerful, caring, needing arms; this was the embrace she had wanted to fall into, to disappear within, where she would feel forever loved. His mouth, hard in wanting, covered hers with such heat that she felt wild inside.

"Mike," she whispered against his open mouth. "Mike."

They couldn't simply kiss for a while first, Chris realized, as if on a date. She lived in his house; she had come to him and put her arms around his neck. It was not a seduction and could not be misconstrued as one. It was surrender. Until now they had both reined in their desires, knowing it without speaking of it, until they were ready for all of each other. She would not have played with his delicate restraint; she wouldn't lean toward him, inviting, until she was prepared to take him into her body, and this unspoken fact was understood by them both. That was why his hands were fast and greedy under her blouse, her bra.

"I want to touch you," he said. "Every part of you. Every part."

His hands on her were desperate yet considerate as he squeezed her small breasts. He held her waist, his thumbs and fingers almost meeting. He pulled her onto his lap, across him, and her hands worked on his shirt, tugging open buttons, as frantic as his hands but less careful.

One of his big hands went under her, between her legs, his palm flush against her, pushing, rubbing. She wished she had come to him naked, saving time. Beneath her thighs and buttocks she felt him grow; she ached so deeply, wanted so much to be full of him, full of passion and love.

He lifted her. He carried her. She had never before been carried to bed. With her arms around him she kissed his neck, licking in the taste of him, floating in his arms up the stairs. As they approached his bedroom she lifted her head, glancing anxiously toward the bedroom where the children slept.

"Mike?" she whispered.

"We'll close the door," he said, entering and doing so.

They tumbled onto the bed together, their hands moving wildly over each other, struggling with clothing, desperate to get it out of the way.

"Do you want me to use something?" he asked her.

"Can you?"

"Yes," he said. "Sure." But he didn't stop kissing her or pulling at her clothing. He tugged at her jeans, her underwear, burying his head in her breasts, her belly, kissing, licking. She found the hard knot of his erection and unfolded him, rubbing him through his underwear, then beneath. He moaned. Then her jeans were gone, her legs kicking them away. Her panties flew off in pursuit. She tugged down his shorts, and he sprang out into her hand, large and hot and impatient. She folded her hands around him. She opened herself.

Mike rolled away a little, jerking open the drawer by the bed, retrieving a hard-to-open cellophane packet. "I can't wait. I can't wait, Chris."

"Me either," she admitted taking it from him and using her teeth to open it. "Is this ten years old?"

"Four days. Ahhh."

"You knew?"

"I don't think about things too much," he said, rising above her, sheathed, waiting.

"Don't think now," she whispered.

He pressed himself in, slowly, very slowly. Then, lowering his head slightly, he tongued her nipple. She locked her fingers together behind his head, holding him to her, and it happened. That fast. That wildly fast. Almost without motion, almost without any movement at all. She felt a pulsing heat and could not tell his from hers. Five minutes, maybe less. The moment they came together, tightly fitted to each other, wham. Incredible.

"That," she said when she caught her breath, "is almost embarrassing."

"Yeah? Well, what did you expect? A warm-up game?"

"Warm-up game?" She laughed.

"To tell the truth, I'm lucky I got up the stairs."

"You bought rubbers," she said, her tone accusing when it should have been grateful.

"Yeah," he said. "The eternal optimist."

"All along, you knew we would? You wanted to on that first night you invited me to your house?"

"Nope. Oh, wanted to, yeah, just about right away, but I didn't offer you the house because of that. And I didn't buy the condoms because I wanted to or because I knew we would. I bought them because things are complicated enough. And because if we got it into our heads we were going to, I didn't want you to say no at the last minute because there wasn't anything. So, what a Boy Scout, huh?"

"Yeah," she said, snuggling into the crook of his arm, not really wanting to discuss complications and what-ifs tonight. She had started to think responsible behavior was a thing of the past. Then Mike. "Thanks. I don't need any more problems."

"Who does? So, what do you need, Chrissie? Tell Little Mike."

"Ohhhh," she moaned, a laugh trailing on the end. "Little Mike... now maybe."

That was the sex and the brief conversation afterward. Then came the lovemaking, which was, like Mike, generous and serious and very physical. As with all things he did, he used earnestness and strength. He had power and control but was so soft and loving that Chris couldn't tell whether she was giving or taking.

She hadn't ever thought of herself as a little woman before this night. His hands turned her so deftly, so artistically, that she felt small, lightweight, almost fluid. And cared for, always cared for, as this man she had come to think of as quiet, a man of few words, spoke to her, comfortable with words that usually embarrassed people. "Like that?" he whispered to her. "Here?" "Now?" Or in giving her instructions. "Yes, here. Like this. Please, here."

He took his time. She, to her surprise, did not have nearly the stamina or patience he had. When she frantically begged, desperately squirmed, tried to stop his playing around and pull him into her, she could feel the smile on his lips against hers, and he said, "Okay, baby, okay. This is for you, and you owe me one."

His manner and tone were as sincere and good-natured in bed as at any other time in his day-to-day living. He seemed not to notice how skilled he was. She was astounded by his talent; she had not guessed at his abandon, the shameless fun he had making love. It intrigued her, for she had little experience and had never considered that men had such a good time with sex. It had seemed to her that men were driven by some need that, once fulfilled, was forgotten. She had not thought of men as giving of their bodies, until Mike. Mike was the only man she had ever known who was so completely sure of his feelings that, as a lover, he trusted himself and her completely.

Chris had thought of lovemaking as give-and-take; one gave, one took, alternating perhaps. With this man she was a participant. He pushed her up, up, up, ruthless in his determination to push her over the edge, relentless in his stubborn wish to blind her with pleasure, and then he held her tenderly in her shuddering release. And again. Sometimes there was a little request for himself. He had, after all, earned that much. "Come up, here, like this. Yes, just like this. For me, my way. *Oh, God.*"

Deep in the night, while she lay on her back beside him, he on his side with one large hand spread flat against her stomach, he whispered, "I love you, Chris."

She was silent. She bit her lip in the blackness but turned her face toward him. She had never felt so much love in her life as she had today, yet the words wouldn't come. Not even now.

He turned, fell onto his back, removed his hand. In the silent darkness, still humid with the past hours, he sighed deeply, with hurt.

"Mike..."

"Never mind. No big deal."

"I'm afraid to say—"

"What you feel? Come on. I didn't *ask* you for anything!"

"Didn't you?"

"No! Saying what you feel doesn't mean you're promising anything."

"I love you, too," she said, her voice small and terrified. "It's just that—"

"Shh," he said, calmer now. "It wouldn't be a good time to talk. Anyway, I already know what it 'just is.'"

She was awakened in the morning by the sound of Mike's moving around in the bedroom. She opened her eyes, and, as if he felt her awareness, he turned toward her. He had showered and shaved, and he was putting on his pants and fireman's T-shirt. He smiled at her, and she saw that his joy had survived the hurt of her reluctant words.

He came to sit on the edge of the bed. "I have to go to work," he said.

"I know."

"Stay here and sleep. The kids are okay—I checked them. Want a T-shirt?"

"Yes, please."

He fished one from a dresser drawer, held it for her when she sat up to put it on. He playfully pulled her hair, wild and woolly, through the neck, then kissed her lightly on the lips. "You taste like a good night of it."

"I feel like I fell down the stairs."

He laughed, proud of himself.

"Mike, yesterday was wonderful. The whole day. And night. Your family is... well, they're just plain incredible."

"My *family*?"

"And you," She smiled.

"Thanks. Any time."

"I think I should call my Aunt Florence. Let her know I'm all right. That the kids are all right. I haven't even contacted her in years. You understand."

"Family is family." He shrugged. "You gotta be good to 'em. You can't let family slip away. She deserves to know you're okay."

"Yeah, she does. Don't worry."

"One thing? Don't surprise me. Please."

His eyes were begging her, his brows furrowed over his nose. She thought about the long-ago phone call telling her that her parents were dead. She thought about the call Mike might have gotten. She remembered her shock and dismay when Steve had not come home. For the past several years she had put so much energy into deciding whether or not this person or that could be trusted, she seldom wondered whether she, herself, was trustworthy.

She summoned courage. She bravely faced the fact that she had crossed a certain line with him. Not ignorantly, perhaps foolishly—time would tell—but not unknowingly. Even if she remained afraid to trust, she must prove trustworthy. Must. If she wanted to be able to live with herself.

She touched his eyebrows with her fingertips, trying to smooth them out. "I won't do that to you. I'll make plans and talk to you. You won't come home and find me gone. I promise."

"That's all I ask."

Chapter Seven

She could not help making the comparison. If Mike knew her thoughts, he would say she was overthinking it. But the last time Chris had made love, Kyle had been conceived. Sexy old Stever, the last of the red-hot lovers, devil-take-the-hindmost man of the world . . . had not really liked sex all that much. They had not made love often; he was busy and preoccupied. He had been talented, not sensitive. Expressive and creative, not tender. Chris had been drugged by his sexual skill, for he could satisfy her quickly and efficiently, but the satisfaction was fleeting; she always felt unfinished. There was a lot left undone. Orgasm and fulfillment, she now realized, were not the same thing. Maybe that was why she hadn't really missed that part of her life. Maybe it simply hadn't been that great. Perhaps her body had felt Steve had not really loved her long before her mind knew it.

She got out of Mike's bed before her children awakened. She went down to the kitchen, poured herself a cup of the coffee he had made and stepped out onto the patio in the T-shirt and bare feet. And breathed. Down to her toes. Feeling wild with life, positively smug with gratification. She thought about the differences between then and now, the differences between Chicago and Los Angeles and Sacramento. The sun was brighter here, the air crackling clean, cool, clear. If she looked over the fence she would see the mountains. Los Angeles, on the other hand, would be balmy and thick with humidity and smog, sort of like a dirty piece of crystal. She would be happy never to see Los Angeles again. Chicago would be dank, dirty, old. Like a woman planning to start her diet on Monday, Chris decided she couldn't face Chicago before spring. Today—and maybe for one day only, but maybe for a week, or a month, or many months, who knew?—she felt she was where she ought to be. That was almost a first, at least since she had buried her parents.

Feeling she belonged prompted other comparisons, as well. Though she suspected she was not extremely clear-headed—she was, after all, nearly limping with pleasure—she remembered how wrong she had felt during the years of grappling with Steve and Aunt Flo. Clearly she hadn't felt right about what Steve talked her into doing; not only had she cried a lot, but she had frantically sought alternatives to suing her aunt, options other than completely estranging herself from Flo. Nor had Flo's suggestions given her a feeling of warmth and safety; she had ached at the thought of giving up Steve, only to be managed by Flo.

She had had to choose. Between her only family and the only man she had ever loved. And the move to L.A. had been so painful and scary that she cleaved tighter to her man, her husband, in loneliness and fear. It had felt so wrong that she had struggled even harder to make it feel right. She had had to slam the door on her own feelings, her instincts. Now, barefoot on the fireman's patio after a wonderful night, she realized that when something is right, it just is. You couldn't make it so.

Then she heard the sirens. All her life she had ignored sirens, unless they made her pull off to the side of the road. Now, because Mike rode the engine, she took sirens far more personally. She had never realized there were so many emergencies in a quiet, residential part of town. Four times she heard that trill, that scream. Because the big fire fighter had crept into her body and heart, she sucked in her breath in fear when she heard the sirens.

The nurturer in her wanted to keep Mike out of harm's way. In that and other ways she was like her mother. She had been certain nothing could satisfy her as much as to live the kind of life Arlene Palmer had lived. That was what had prompted her to fall in love with Steve; she had wanted someone to whom she was so intimately connected that his life became her life, and together they would create more life. That tendency helped make her a good mother; it also made her miss the aunt who was now her only family, even though Flo could be an ordeal in herself.

And then, of course, there was what she had done last night with Mike, which made her shiver in aftershocks this morning.... She nested well.

And all of this made her hate the sirens. Mike went into burning buildings. Still, he was experienced, right? He'd been a fire fighter for more than a decade. A fireman had not been killed in a fire in Sacramento in years. Years?

"We'll turn your show back on in a minute," she told the kids. "I want to see if there's any local news." There wasn't—at least none pertaining to fires. Not satisfied that there wouldn't be, however, she played the local radio station while she got ready for work.

She had only been at her cash register for thirty minutes when it happened. The event that overturned all the safe, peaceful, nesting feelings she had decided to indulge for the past week, especially the past twenty-four hours. She had been in a better mood than usual, joking with the customers, bagging groceries quickly, clicking those old buttons like a demon. Then she pulled one of those gossipy rags past the cash register between a box of Tampax and a pound of hamburger, rang up the price and saw the tabloid cover. Her face stared back at her.

Missing Heiress Speaks from the Grave.

No! She picked it up, stricken. The customer held a pen poised above a check. Chris threw the tabloid after the other groceries. Please, God, no. She rang up the total, and the customer, unaware that Chris's life had just flashed before her eyes, wrote out the amount. Chris stood frozen, panicked, paralyzed. Just when she started to think things were going to be okay, she tripped over some major event. Like smoke pouring out of the vents. Like this.

On automatic pilot she bagged the groceries, then checked two more shoppers through her aisle. At the first lull, she spoke across the partition to Candy, a college student who worked weekends and holidays. "I have to take a quick break. I'm closing for a minute, but I'll be right back."

She locked her register and grabbed a copy of the scandal sheet. Her face stared out between equally poor pictures of Robert Goulet and Dolly Parton. Good Lord. In the worst of times life had not seemed as grotesque as this. She raced to the bathroom, closed the door and read.

"You should never be surprised," Aunt Florence had once said, "at what you read about yourself in the newspaper if you have a lot of money. Or fame. Or whatever." Chris wanted no part of money or fame; she had simply wished to disappear and recreate herself. But it looked as if she were stuck with her past.

In Chicago, where the Palmer family had been considered among the upper crust of local society, their names had occasionally appeared in the society column. They had had a minor scandal once, too—a manager of one of their stores sued Randolph for wrongful firing—but it hadn't come to much. And of course Chris had had a debutante's ball, there had been the death of her parents, and then her horrid suit against her aunt and the estate. But that had been the extent of press coverage on the Palmers.

Now, however, someone had written a book about her and Steve Zanuck. Steve, her ex-husband, was apparently dead. As was his wife, Mrs. Zanuck. Months ago a luxury yacht headed for some Caribbean island had left Miami and never been seen again. Recently a piece of the vessel with the name of the boat on it had been found. The authorities suspected an on-board explosion.

Chris was not that Mrs. Zanuck; yet, she realized, not everyone knew that.

According to the article, Aunt Florence was not certain whether or not it was her who perished. *"The last time Florence Palmer talked to her niece was in 1984, when Christine Palmer Zanuck, then a Los Angeles resident, was discussing divorcing Zanuck."*

In 1980 Chris had married Steve in Chicago. A small ceremony with only a few friends. Florence had grudgingly gone along with this; she was even a little relieved that they didn't want a big wedding, since she didn't expect this "fling" to last. Chris had been twenty. And absolutely dumb with passion.

She had gotten pregnant instantly. Was pregnant, in fact, when she turned twenty-one and Steve insisted that the hundred grand per year she received from her trust fund would simply not do. Not when there was a million, at least, to be had, and he was an attorney, for goodness' sake! They had very politely asked Aunt Florence to fork it over, please, so that they could get on with their lives. She had said no.

It had taken a while for Chris to be completely convinced by her charismatic, con-artist husband that it would be logical to sue the executor of the estate, the trustee, for that money. And it had taken two years for them to win the lawsuit. Chris had already had precious little Carrie when she was given $1,750,000. And they moved to Los Angeles, where Steve was going into business.

The high life, then. What had she been high on? She lived in a palatial house on the side of a hill and went to many parties and opening nights. They went on cruises—Steve more often than she because she wanted to make a home with her child. Steve invested in films and other things and, according to his secretary, had a legal practice. Oh, Chris had seen the office and staff on occasion, but Steve didn't like to discuss business with her. And she, big dummy that she was, had plopped her entire fortune into a joint account. She trusted him. Why wouldn't she? In her grief and loneliness, he was all she had.

She began to suspect him of having an affair that year, for his attention toward her, his desire to keep her perpetually happy, had started to flag. Affair? That would have been easy by comparison. So she asked him to set up a trust for Carrie, and he said, "Sure, babe, we'll get that taken care of pretty soon." He was very busy with clients;

he had a lot of socializing to do. She became pregnant with Kyle. Steve had to leave town on business. The phone calls began to pour in. Where was Mr. Zanuck? Bills had to be paid. The mortgage was due. The office had been closed. The secretary had vanished. The film company he claimed to be investing in had never heard of him.

Too ashamed to ask Flo for help, Chris had not known what to do besides call a lawyer. The long and short of it turned out to be that, during the first three years of marriage, the degenerate monster had lived on the hundred grand a year from her trust, and during the last year he had been busy either losing, spending or stealing her money. She had never been entirely sure whether he had converted it, moving it out of her name and into his, or whether he had actually *lost* it. But it was gone. Out of all that money she could only lay her hands on one account of around thirty thousand dollars. Was this an oversight? Or had he left her a few bucks purposely so she could take care of herself while getting a divorce? The rest was really and truly gone.

Kyle was born, and when she came home from the hospital, her house was locked against her. For the next two years she rented one tiny apartment or another, working as a receptionist, housekeeper or waitress, living mostly on the goodwill and generosity of friends she had made since moving to L.A. But those friends had been lied to, if not swindled by, Steve Zanuck, too, and, burned, they drifted away from her. The attorney stuck by her for a while, believing he was eventually going to get a big hunk of dough out of either Steve or Aunt Florence. Instead, he got most of the thirty thousand.

Steve Zanuck never reappeared in Chris's life. Though he was found, the money wasn't. Chris was left exhausted, afraid, weak. Once she understood what had been done to her, she committed the unpardonable sin in her lawyer's eyes. She wanted the divorce, period. The jerk she had married didn't even know or care that he had a son. She wanted to be Chris Palmer again. She refused to ask Flo to bail her out, refused to have Steve Zanuck prosecuted, refused to hire detectives to track down the money. "Let me out," she had said.

Though she couldn't ask Aunt Flo for help—not after what she had done to her—she did call her right after Kyle was born. "Yes, Flo, I'm all right, I guess," she had said. "And you were right; I married a real scumbag."

"Are you coming home?" her aunt had asked, her voice tight.

"Maybe when I can get myself together a little bit. I just had another baby."

"When are you coming?"

"I don't know. As soon as I can."

"Are you going to divorce that bastard?"

"Yes," she had said, and cried. Cried her heart out. And for what? For grief; he was gone, and she wanted him back. For fear; she was alone, all alone, unless you counted Flo, who was very angry. For shame; this was her fault, really. And maybe for love; though he made a mockery of that, she *had* loved him. "I am. I will. And . . . I'm sorry."

"I should think so."

She had hung up on Flo then, not answering the phone when her aunt rang back.

She should have gone home right then. She should have taken the little money that was left, gotten on a plane and told Flo to do whatever she wanted to do. Hire the lawyers, lock Steve up, have him knocked off, anything. The broken bird should have flown back under Flo's wing. Her aunt might have been angry, bossy, outraged, but she loved

Chris. It wasn't Flo's fault that she didn't know how to give the unconditional, selfless kind of love and caring that Arlene had found so natural; that didn't mean it wasn't real love. And Flo would have forgiven her, eventually. But Chris had screwed up so badly and wanted so desperately to salvage something, she had only made it worse.

Every day since Kyle was born, for three long years, she had lived day to day, barely able to afford anything, but had not called on Flo for help. She had tried to find a way to rectify her mistake, to pull herself out of it. She wasn't sure she even knew why. Pride, maybe. Guilt and humiliation, probably. Also, a deep wish not to have Flo take care of her, which meant Flo would run her life.

Now this article. Someone had written a book about her, and within the book were dozens of little-known facts about her husband. It said that Christine Palmer was one of possibly four women he'd married. Wives with money. Wives who had disappeared. They didn't disappear, Chris wanted to say, they only ran out of money and became clerks and housekeepers. She ought to buy a copy of the book, find out what that weasel had done with her money.

But first she had to talk to Mr. Iverson. And Florence.

"You mean I gave you a hundred bucks and you're worth millions?" Mr. Iverson said. He held the paper in his hand. She sat across from him. He had an office, sort of. Two walls in the shipping area in the back of the store. A cluttered desk. An adding machine.

"Read a little farther," she said. "I was ripped off. I married this jerk who took me for my inheritance, and I am now a destitute grocery clerk with two fatherless children. That's who you gave the hundred bucks to."

He read farther. "Says here you're probably dead."

"Well, I suppose that's the *current* Mrs. Zanuck."

"Jeez. Who wrote this book?"

"I haven't a clue."

"Maybe you ought to read it."

"I was thinking that myself." She watched while his eyes roamed the page. "Look, I'm really sorry about this, Mr. Iverson, but I didn't exactly do it on purpose, you know? I'm going to have to get in touch with my aunt—I can't have her thinking I'm dead. I'm probably going to have to go home. Chicago." She swallowed hard.

"You want some time off? Jeez, you don't want to work here. You're an heiress, for crying out loud. What are you going to do? What about my hundred bucks?"

"Oh. That. Look, don't worry about that, okay? Here," she said, digging into her purse frantically, trying to pay her debts and retain her dignity. She stopped suddenly. This was what she'd been doing for more than three years. Trying to assure people that she wasn't a no-good, taking-you-for-a-ride con artist. She slowed down. People had helped her, had always said don't worry about it, but in the end they worried they might not get their loans back. They were, in fact, more suspicious of her when they found out she'd come from money than when they believed her to be poor, pitiful and down on her luck. It was as though she had no business being so stupid if she was so rich.

Well, they were probably right about that.

She pulled sixty-three dollars out of her purse. "Okay, here's sixty. And I worked the other day—six hours. That's forty-two. And I'll ask Aunt Florence to send me something. But that's one-oh-two, right?"

"There's taxes."

She sighed and gave him the three she had left. "Let me know if I owe you," she said quietly.

"How do I reach you?"

He instantly thought she'd run out. Would Mike see the paper? Would *he* think she'd run out? Would he *want* her to run out, now that she was someone else? People got crazy when they found out there was more to you than what was on the surface. And here was this terrifically nasty article, plus a book. Mr. Iverson was looking at her as if she were Patty Hearst.

"You can reach me at the same number," she said even more quietly. "I'll let you know if it changes."

She picked up the kids at the baby-sitter's and went back to Mike's. She told Juanita not to expect them unless she called, paid her in loose change from the bottom of her purse but didn't quite say goodbye. She never had, she realized. To anyone. Anywhere. She always acted as though she was just going down the block to buy a candy bar and would be right back. And if she didn't do that to people, they did it to her. She was going to have to stop that. At once. Stop running, stop pretending that she would have this fixed in a minute. It was now officially bigger than she was. She would have to either fold her hand or learn to blame the right person. She didn't *do* this. It was done to her. Help.

That was her thought as she placed the call. She was thinking hard about it, about her promise to Mike, when she dialed direct rather than collect. She wanted to negotiate with Aunt Flo, if possible.

But when she heard Flo's voice, when she felt the tie that bound them tighten around her heart, she forgot negotiations. What she said, through her suddenly rasping tears, was "Oh, God, Flo, I'm sorry. I'm so sorry! I never meant to hurt you like I have. Never!"

"Chris! Chris, where *are* you? Are you all right?"

"I'm all right; I'm in shock. I just read about myself in the paper, and I'm in total shock. I didn't know I was missing, didn't know I was the subject of a book, didn't know that Steve—I'm in California,'' she said, not mentioning Sacramento.

''California? We tracked him as far as Texas.''

''Oh, I've been alone for years, Flo. Years.''

''Where in California? I have been looking for you *forever*!''

''Flo, I didn't know that... honest. I thought you were still mad, which you have every right to be. I wasn't hiding, I was trying— Listen, listen, one thing at a time. I'm not going to hang up in the middle, I promise. But first, is he dead? Is he really dead?''

''Oh, who knows? Who cares? Three years, Chris! Good God, how could you? Even after all we'd been through, you had to have known that I...'' Flo's voice caught and drifted away. Chris couldn't quite imagine her aunt crying. Flo could be angry, wildly happy, or her usual—completely composed. But cry? Make her pillow wet and wake up ugly, like Chris did? Was she in pain?

Chris, the nurturer, tried to comfort. ''Oh, Flo, I kept trying to get it together, to salvage something. He wiped me out, naturally. And I have two little kids; Carrie is five now, and Kyle is three. I've been working, trying to get on my feet so when I did go home I wouldn't feel like such slime. I was wrong. I should have called you. But I... just couldn't get up the nerve.''

''What about Steve? When was the last time you saw him? Did he leave you anything? Anything at all?''

''I haven't seen him since before Kyle was born. He ran out on me, left me holding the bag. I don't know what he did next. I hired a lawyer who tracked him down, finally, in Dallas. I got the divorce. I never got anything back. Except my name. I got my name back.''

''Your name? Palmer?''

''Yes,'' she said through her tears.

"I guess that explains why I couldn't find Christine Zanuck."

I screwed that up, too, she thought. Figures.

"Come home," Flo said. "I'll send the money. I'll wire it. I'll come and get you. We can deal with this. We can—"

"Wait. Hold it a second, Flo. I'm coming. I'm coming home, I promise, but—"

"But? You said that before. You said 'as soon as I can,' and weeks went by. Then I couldn't find you. Then—"

"No, no. No, I won't do that to you again. No, Flo, but listen. It's a little complicated."

There was silence, then a short laugh. "How is it that doesn't surprise me?"

Chris started to cry again. "I'm like a bad penny. Why do I do this to people? I never meant to hurt anyone. Never."

"All right, all right, calm down, Chris. Try not to be childish. This isn't the worst thing, God knows. At least you're all right. First, give me the number where you are—the real number. Please don't lie to me."

Chris grabbed for a tissue to blow her nose. "No, I won't lie to you." She sniffed again and recited the numbers. "Now look, Flo, listen, I want to come home, I mean it, but I'm not ready yet. I can't just pick up and run. I won't. For the moment, the kids are more comfortable than they've ever been. I don't want to jerk them out of here. They're—"

"Out of where?" Flo interrupted.

"I'm living with a man. He's been very good to us. I can't run out on him."

"Who is this man, for goodness sake?"

"His name is Mike. Mike Cavanaugh. It's real complicated."

"I bet. So bring him, too. Who cares? Or I'll come there. Chris, after all this—"

"Let me try to explain." She took a deep breath. "I moved from Los Angeles to Sacramento in August. I rented a house and got a job. The house caught fire and burned to the ground. Mike Cavanaugh was the fireman who carried me out of the house, and he let the kids and me move in here with him until we could get resettled. Since then it's gotten kind of, well, kind of—"

"Oh, God."

"He's a wonderful, generous man. He's calm. Sensible. He's good to the kids, and they adore him. It's the very first time a man has— He's been very good to me, too. I'm not going to stay here forever, but I promised him that I'd stay for a little while. See, he lost his wife and daughter in a car accident about ten years ago, and he's been all alone since then. And here I was, all alone with my kids, and we—"

"God Almighty."

"This is important, Flo. For both of us. It's as if we're both in some kind of recovery. This is the most comfort and safety I've felt since before Mom and Daddy were killed. It's not necessarily permanent—we don't have any long-term commitment, but—"

"Chris, listen to me. Here's what you do: tell this nice man you appreciate everything he's done and you'll write him as soon as you get to Chicago. Tell him—"

It was all coming back to her. *Chris, here's what you do....* Chris, you wear the beads on the outside of your blouse, but on the inside of your sweater. Chris, you don't study only literature, you have to have a few business courses. Chris, you don't just marry the first man you—

"Are you listening to me? Tell him you'll call him every night, all right? Visit him. Let him visit you! You've been *missing* for three years, and I am your only family! He'll understand. Do you hear me?"

Chris started crying again. "I'm not telling him that," she said. "I don't want to."

"Chris, now listen to me. . . ."

"Flo, please, don't. Stop making my decisions for me!" She blew her nose again. Carrie found her, in the kitchen, pacing with the phone in her hand, crying her eyes out. Carrie tugged on her jeans. "Flo, listen, I haven't made this mess on purpose, but ever since Mom and Daddy died I've been bouncing between people who want me to do things *their* way, to take sides, to choose. Like now."

"Chris, you're getting—"

"Just this morning I told Mike I was going to call you so you'd know where I was and that we're all right. He thought that was good, but he asked me not to surprise him, you know, like run out on him without any warning. Don't you understand, Flo? His wife and baby—they were *gone*, without warning! And I know how that feels because Steve... Oh, please, try to understand. He saved my life. And I . . . I told him I was going to stay a while. Just a while. I can't keep doing this, Flo. I love you. I want to see you desperately. I want to make up for hurting you so much. I just don't want to hurt him, too. I'm sorry."

And she hung up. She blew her nose. "Mommy?" Carrie asked, her little chin wrinkling. Carrie would cry if Chris was crying; children didn't need to know the reasons.

Damn. She had hoped to find Flo tractable, reasonable. She had wanted Flo to be glad to hear from her, relieved to know she was safe and happy, period. She had wanted Flo's humor, generosity and spirit, not her commands. She *needed* Flo; Flo was her only link to her roots. She even liked Flo's take-charge manner on occasion; it sure came in handy in foreign airports. But that was where she wanted Flo to stop. She didn't want Flo to keep taking charge of *her*.

The phone rang. Chris laughed through her tears. "Hello."

"Dear God. You really are there. I don't know why I try. You are the worst brat."

"I really wanted to talk to you, you know. But I want to talk when you start listening and stop ordering that *I* listen to *you*." She was amazed at the strength in her voice. Yes, this was why she hadn't called before. Yes, she was sorry she'd hurt her aunt so deeply, frightened her so much. And she did love her, but she wasn't going to be pushed around anymore. By anyone. "I shouldn't have hung up, but I was upset. I would have called back. Do you want to talk a while now? If you can listen and I can keep calm?"

"Please tell me exactly where you are. Tell me I can fly out there and see that you're all right, that you're alive, and well, not living with some lunatic. Or some jerk like that Zanuck masterpiece. Please. I deserve some peace of mind, after all."

"Sure. But, Flo, you're going to have to hold back a little. I want to see you very much, but you're not going to keep telling me what to do. I'm going to make my own mistakes and pay for them myself."

"That," said Flo, "is the understatement of the year."

"Will you give me a couple of days, please?" Chris asked patiently. "Before you come? So I can get Mike ready for this? So I can explain what kind of mess I've made?"

"Two days?"

"Yes. And, Flo, you're going to have to understand that I have business to finish here. I might be ready in a day or in a couple of—"

Flo sighed heavily. "You want my promise that I'm going to leave you and the children with this—this fireman?"

"Flo, do you know anything about that book? *The Missing Heiress*?"

"I just read it."

"Is any of it true?"

There was a moment of silence. "Only the really bad parts."

Mike was hoping to run into Chris at the grocery store when he and the guys went shopping for dinner, and he couldn't hide his astonishment when he inquired about Chris's whereabouts and the clerk said she was gone. Quit. Poof.

Well, he thought, maybe Aunt Flo had come through, wired money. Then, back in the rig, Jim handed him the newspaper. "Isn't that your Christine Palmer?" he asked gently.

My Christine Palmer? So I had thought, briefly.

Back at the station Mike took the paper into the bathroom with him. He read it. Christine Palmer Zanuck, heiress to a multimillion-dollar furniture empire, possibly dead—one of four women Steve Zanuck had married and swindled. The Palmer fortune, excepting Chris's inheritance, was still sound and in the possession of Florence Palmer, who did not know where her niece was but had been actively hunting for her for three years. Even after the horrible ordeal of their lawsuit, Aunt Florence longed only to know that her niece was alive and well.

He left the bathroom.

They had two alarms in a row. One turned out to be nothing—a smoking stove. The other was a burning car, no injuries. He kept quiet, doing his job, straining his muscles, his mind elsewhere.

"Well," Jim said. "That her?"

"I guess so. Yeah, must be."

"She still at your place?"

"She didn't say she was leaving."

"You seen her lately?"

"Yeah, I saw her. Before I came to work." Jim probably knew, Mike figured, that he'd left her in his bed. The other fire fighter knew how early they reported for their shift. It was pretty unlikely that Mike had gone from his parents' house to his house for coffee at 6:00 a.m.

"Think she's still there?"

"Well, I suppose so. I'm not afraid she's going to rip off the television, if that's what you mean. Especially now."

"Want to call? Take a couple of hours of family-care time to run home?"

Want to? Oh, did he want to. So bad he could hardly stand it. But if he rushed home to check on her, what did that say about *him*? That he had not known what he was doing when he asked her to stay with no strings. That he could talk about love and trust but couldn't act on it. "Nope," he said. "She's a big girl." It's her life.

He lifted weights that afternoon. He thought it through. Long and slow.

He believed in people. He believed in love—in saying it, showing it, trusting people. And when he loved, he loved hard, totally and with faith.

He had known right off that Joanie was the one for him. The second time he'd felt that way was with Chris. With Chris he hadn't felt giddy the way he had with the flight attendant, desperate the way he had with the woman on the rebound, or entrenched the way he had with the artist. He had felt secure and strong and exact. So he had done what he had done—given everything he had. He didn't hold back a little, save a little, like for a rainy day, in case he had been mistaken. Nope. He'd plunged in with everything he had—every tear, every passion, every possession, every hope.

Kind of stupid to think you'd be more relieved to find out she'd kidnapped her own kids than to find out she was rich. *Stinking* rich.

He didn't want to push his own needs onto anyone. He didn't want Chris to save him, exactly. He just wanted her to tell him the truth or refuse to answer. That simple, two choices. Don't say it if you don't feel it. When he had asked her to stay a while and she had said okay, even though she'd been afraid of what it would mean, what it would become, it had meant she'd stayed because she wanted to. And when she said "I love you," it meant she did. Oh, he knew she was reluctant to say that, and he knew why. Maybe he shouldn't have pushed her, but he had, and she'd said it. Simple. She didn't say she would stay forever, he didn't ask her to, and unless something happened to change her mind, she would probably go. But not without saying goodbye.

No alarms through the night, but he didn't sleep. He almost picked up the phone to call her about fifty times. But she had the number. He'd *told* her to call if she needed him. You can't be any plainer than that.

Long and slow, he thought about it. By morning he thought he knew what he felt. He wanted to take care of her, protect her and love her because it felt good. He wanted to have some time with her and those two little kids because if he could remember what it felt like to be loved and depended on as a man, a provider, a lover, maybe he could get on with his life. Finally. He wanted to hold her without holding her down.

He didn't hang around the station for breakfast. He drank a quick cup of coffee and went home. The old Honda was in the driveway, but he didn't breathe a sigh of relief—not yet. If Aunt Flo had recited the numbers on her American Express card, there might be a note on the refrigerator telling him to sell the car for his trouble. Please, God, no. Please, God, all I ever wanted was the straight line.

He unlocked the door. They might still be asleep; it wasn't even seven.

But Chris unfolded herself from the couch, already dressed. Her eyes didn't look a whole lot better than his. She picked up the tabloid that lay on the coffee table and carried it toward him, her lips parted as she was about to speak. She was going to tell him the whole thing. But he didn't want to hear it right now. He didn't care about anything now. She was there.

"Come here," he said, opening his arms, so relieved he was afraid he was going to shout. "Come here and fall on me. I didn't sleep all night."

"Me either," she said, and a sniffle came. "There's so much to tell you."

"You're here. Tell me later. There's lots of time."

"You saw this, then?"

"Oh, yeah. Kind of hard to miss. And they told me you quit Iverson's."

"But you didn't call here?"

"You said you wouldn't surprise me. I had to believe you."

"How could you believe me? Especially after all this?"

"You maybe left a few things out, but you haven't lied to me. I would know."

"Oh, Mike. Oh, hold me. Please."

Which he was glad to do. Ah, that was relief. To believe and find that you were right. "Any of it true?" he asked.

"Some of it," she said. "Like the part about me being dead. That part's probably true. I'm probably just watching this film in purgatory."

He laughed at her. He squeezed her tighter. "Naw. If purgatory felt this good, there wouldn't be any Catholics."

Chapter Eight

Fire fighters do not think in rainbow shades of many possibilities but in simple light and dark. Hot and cold. Perhaps good and evil. Chris began to understand that Mike Cavanaugh lived in a yes-or-no world that he laboriously kept neat and uncomplicated. It began to make perfect sense to her, the way he thought, even if she didn't think that way herself.

Fire fighters don't stand around the outside of a burning building and draw straws to see who goes in, who climbs up on the roof, or who drives the rig. Everyone has a job; he does it. They are decisive, with practiced instincts about safety and danger. They do dangerous things that no one else would dare, but they know it and they know how. They are men and women of skill and strength. They *never* overthink things.

On the Saturday morning after the tabloid story broke, they curled up on the sofa with cups of hot coffee, talking until the kids woke up. He heard the whole long story about Chris's marriage, lawsuit, divorce and Aunt Flo's desire to come to Sacramento if Chris would not go immediately to Chicago.

"I told her I was staying here for a while, that the children are safe and comfortable here. She doesn't understand, of course, because the kids would be safe and comfortable in her house, but—"

"Did you tell her why you were staying?" he asked.

"Because the kids—"

"Did you tell her you love me?"

She looked at him for a long time. "In the past," she explained, "I haven't used the best judgment based on that emotion. My instincts, which I'm only just beginning to trust, say we're safe here. It isn't very logical, and it probably isn't fair to you, but if you still want us to stay a little while—"

He was either acting on instincts that told him he was safe, or he was using his skill and expertise to enter a danger zone. "I want you to stay."

"Aunt Flo wants to fly out, see me, make sure I'm all right. She's a pretty forceful person, Aunt Flo and—"

"Chris, if you want to be here and I want you here, old Aunt Flo will just have to live with it. All that other stuff, about your instincts and your judgment, well, I think you ought to take your time with that."

"Well, she'll come here, then. Monday."

He shrugged. "I can't blame her. She's family. She's worried about you. We'll manage."

"My family, Mike, is nothing like your family."

"That's a relief," he said with a laugh. "I have the weekend off," he said. "Why don't we take the kids to the cabin? It's nice and cold in the mountains; it's snowing. It's quiet. Monday, huh?"

But no more running away or disappearing. That was another thing about firemen. Maybe they didn't borrow trouble, but they liked to face the fire, not have it hiding in a basement or behind a closed door. Sometimes it came at them from above or behind or beneath. When they walked or crawled into a smoky, stinging, blinding problem, they liked to know where it was. So he suggested to Chris that she call Aunt Flo and tell her that she was going to the cabin, that she would be away from the phone, and give Mrs. Cavanaugh's phone number in case there was any emergency. And find out when, on Monday, Aunt Florence should be picked up at the airport.

Then they drove for two and a half hours to the mountains, to a place called Pembroke Pines, just north of Lake Tahoe. At Mike's cabin in the woods they could talk and play and worry in peace.

Mike swung Kyle up onto the back of the mare. "Hold on here," he told him, placing the boy's hands on the saddle horn. "Hold on, now."

Chris held the reins of Carrie's horse. Mike's nearest neighbors, the Christiansons, had loaned him the horses. Mike and Chris walked together, leading the small, gentle mares on which the children were perched. Cheeks trailed along, barking and snarling. They trudged down a sloppy dirt road in the Saturday afternoon sunshine, talking more like old friends than new lovers.

"Big Mike once saw that movie, *It's a Wonderful Life*. My dad gets an idea about something and makes it into a whole philosophy. Hurray for Hollywood, huh?"

"I liked the movie, too," Chris said.

"So that was how he handled us. Every single problem, from the fumbled pass during high-school football to death and despair. 'So Little Mike, what one thing would you go back and change, huh? What one thing that *you* could do would make it all turn out different?' And I would say, 'Well, I woulda studied for the test, that's what.' 'There you go,' he'd say."

"I should have paid more attention to the movie," Chris said.

"So, Chrissie, what one thing would you go back and change?"

"Ah! What wouldn't I change!"

"Your lousy ex? Wouldn't have married him, huh?"

"Starting there..."

"No Carrie and no Kyle. See, that's how this little game works. You go ahead and change something in your past, and you remove a big hunk of your future. That's the trick. You have to be real careful what pains you're going to trade for what pleasures. This is not as simple as it sounds."

"So what about you? What did Big Mike tell you?"

Mike laughed. "Oh, he had me so mad I thought I might deck him. Big Mike hasn't always been a little old man, you know. Even ten years ago I couldn't beat him arm wrestling. Yeah, he put me on the spot with Joanie's death. 'So what would you change? Never having met her? Never having married her? Never having Shelly...for even a little while?' For a long time I believed that would have been easier, better. Then I decided that if I could change anything, maybe I would have gotten up at night and changed the baby's diapers more. Or maybe I would have fought with Joanie about money just a little bit less. Maybe I wouldn't have asked her to join the Catholic church just so Ma would relax about the whole thing. But I don't know. I try to think, would that have made losing them feel any different? Easier? Harder?"

"And what about this?" she asked, taking his hand. "Starting to wish you hadn't been on duty that night my house burned down?"

"Oh, heck no. No, I really needed this; it shook things into place. I'm thirty-six. I had a bad deal, and I gotta get past that. I hadn't been with a woman in a long time. And before that I'd been with some without really being with them, you know?"

"Terrible waste," she said.

"In case you're interested, I feel like a big dope about it now. I was afraid of what I wanted from life. I want a lot, Chrissie. I want a family again."

"Whoa, boy," she said, shivering.

"You get worried when people tell you what they want, don't you?"

"If I think they want it from me, I do."

"No, that isn't it, I bet. You want it, too, and it scares you half to death. That's just what was happening to me. For ten years. I wanted a family again, but what if I tried to get one, got it and lost it again? After about ten years you decide to either play the hand you're dealt or stay out of the game."

"So," she said, "you're getting back in the game?"

"Me? I shouldn't have tried so hard to be alone. So, now that I remember, I'm not giving up on it again."

"I don't think you should."

"You're my first choice," he said, grinning at her. But he did not ask her to make him any promises. "Just having you around has been real good for me. It's like waking up."

"But will it always be good?"

"Chrissie, you'd make a great Catholic, no kidding. You borrow more trouble than Ma does. Never thought I'd meet a woman who could compete with Ma for worry and guilt."

The cabin, one open room with a large hearth and shallow loft, was equipped only with the necessities. But while the wind blew outside, the fire was hot. All four of them had to use sleeping bags in the central room. The loft wasn't a good place for the kids to be alone, in case they woke up in the night and began to wander. And downstairs alone, with a fire that had to burn all night, was an even worse idea.

"Why didn't you tell me the whole thing right off?" he asked her late in the night while the kids slept nearby.

"Because it's so shocking," she said. "People find the whole thing just plain incomprehensible. I told a couple of friends I met after Steve was gone, trying it out. The first thing they can't understand is why I didn't go after Steve, have him at least put in jail. People think you can do that, no sweat. You can't. He'd lost community property; proving he did it on purpose or stole it might have been impossible. Next, they wondered, if I had this rich aunt, why I didn't just call her right away. Say, 'Send a few bucks, you can afford it.' But a few bucks wasn't the thing I needed most. Pretty soon people look at you strangely, like you've made it all up. I began to feel weird, like a fraud or something, so I stopped telling anyone, which made me a real impostor. I might have had acquaintances but fewer and fewer real friends. With real friends you share personal things about your life. And my life was becoming more and more impossible to believe."

"But you decided to call Aunt Flo. Before the newspaper story," he pointed out.

"I wanted to call her because of the Cavanaughs. I had family once—very different from yours in a lot of ways, but tight, close, intimate family. Once Flo and I were very, very dear to each other—we were like best friends, in a way. There had been lots of other friends in my life, too—friends from high school and college—but I lost touch with some once I married Steve and moved, and the rest after the divorce because I was so embarrassed about how stupid I had been. When things settle down, I should probably try to get in touch with some of them.

"But first I have to deal with Flo. We didn't start to butt heads until my parents died and she took over as my parent. She began telling me what to do, what to feel, I guess because she felt responsible for me. Probably half the reason I married Steve in the first place was because Flo told me I couldn't.

"But I'm not really like you were; I'm not afraid of what I want. I'm more afraid I want all the wrong things. I'm afraid that I really and truly lack judgment. That I am really and truly incompetent."

"All you lack is confidence. It'll come back. Give it time."

"We're not talking about climbing back on a horse here, Mike. We're talking about lives and futures. Mine. Theirs."

"Ours."

"Don't," she said.

"You can hurt yourself more than one way, Chrissie. You can hurt yourself by making a wrong choice and loving some creep who just wants to use you, or you can hurt yourself by not loving someone who would be good for you."

Loving or not loving, she thought, was something she seemed to have no control over. But she had to try to have control over her *life*. "I'm not too worried about what's going to happen to me," she told him, "because I'm going to take my time and not rush into anything. But I would hate myself forever if I somehow hurt you...or them." She glanced at her children.

"One of the first things I noticed, Chrissie, is that you take good care of them. You're a good mother. That doesn't sound incompetent to me. I think," he said, pausing to kiss her nose, "you can be trusted with human life. I'm not worried about what you'll do to me."

"When Aunt Florence comes, Mike, would you like me to go stay with her at the hotel, or stay with you?"

"I would like you to stay where you want to be. But remember that your aunt has been through a lot, Chrissie, and you have to be careful with her. She's your family, and you gotta be careful with your family. You be nice to her, be gentle. But you can also tell her that you're a grown-up woman, a mother yourself, and you have to be where you have to be."

"She said almost the same thing about you."

"Oh?"

"She said, 'Oh, Chris, you just tell that nice man that you're very grateful for everything and that you'll write him and call him, even visit.'"

Mike frowned his dangerous frown. "Well," he said with a shrug, "even if Aunt Florence turns out to be a real bitch, we can handle it."

Yeah, Mike could probably handle just about anything, she decided as she tried to fall asleep.

She had always been attracted to independence and mastery. Her father, her lousy ex-husband, ever her Aunt Flo. Mike was like them all in many ways.

The next morning Mike wandered off, returning with firewood. Later, Chris heard a noise behind the cabin and found him repairing the pump. He puttered quietly, but when there was something to talk about, he opened up. It was all right when they didn't talk, too. One of the things that Chris learned was the kind of quiet she could have with intimacy. She had never had that in her marriage.

Mike took the kids for a nice long walk after breakfast while Chris cleaned up the dishes and rolled sleeping bags. They held on to his hands and toddled off, asking a million questions as they went out the door.

This was why she didn't leave. Not because she had any illusions about happily ever after, but because she was briefly visiting with her desires, the ones she was afraid were stupid and impossible.

For a short time she could indulge the fantasy of having a man for herself and for her kids. A man with enough love and caring to embrace a family. That was what she had thought she saw in Steve, but what she had seen was a lot of energy, not a lot of love. She had been too young and filled with grief to know it.

She had given her kids plenty of love and nurturing, even though she had been bereft herself, but they had lacked some vital things. A happy mother, for starters. She worried about that a lot; what had they learned from her loneliness? Were there hidden emotional scars that would hinder them later, making it tough for them to form critical relationships? Would they not know how to make a family of their own because in their formative years all they had seen was their mother's tired, frustrated struggle? The absence of a father figure? Deprived of the sight of adults touching each other, showing easy and natural affection that came of love? What about a smile on their mother's face because a good man had made love to her?

There was no kidding herself, after making love with Mike she had felt different—relieved, soothed, fulfilled.

And when a woman felt good, she mothered better. Did they pick up on these things?

And Mike provided. It wasn't just the things he provided, like cable TV or the new jackets, boots and mittens they had needed to go to the mountains. It was also the zone of calmness, sanity. His trust and confidence. She could see that they sat differently on his big lap, more secure because of his size and self-possession. They had hungered for a father, and for now they had a big fireman to show them what it might be like.

She wanted a life like the one they were pretending. To cook while he worked and to surprise him with something special. Or to not cook and have him complain. She wanted to be there to talk about the fires with him and take a casserole to Mattie and Big Mike's. She wanted to take her kids to the park, be a room mother, buy a chair she didn't need and argue over the expense, complain about the way he never wiped out the sink, and make love regularly. Then she wanted to work on her books and maybe have another baby. And be up through the night and nag that he took her for granted and have him say he was sorry and never would again.

She wanted a stupid, happy 1950s marriage that was fraught with give-and-take and pleasure and trouble, and sensible women did not want that anymore! Especially women who had jumped into that bonfire and been badly burned. She did not make any sense to herself.

He hadn't asked her to stay forever. She hoped he wouldn't too soon, but she knew he was sneaking up on that. She felt it. The fact that she would be tempted only made it worse. But she couldn't stand to think about leaving him, either. She was in love with him. And she knew it. If only she could have a little time to think.

But Flo was coming. Better think fast, Chris.

* * *

Late on Sunday night, when they were back in Sacramento and getting into bed, he asked her, "What time are you picking her up?"

"Noon."

"Bringing her here?"

"No, I made a reservation at the Red Lion."

"I'll be at work. Till Tuesday morning."

"The kids and I will spend the afternoon and evening with her, but we're coming back here, if that's all right."

"Stop acting like I'm going to change my mind. Old Aunt Flo doesn't worry me nearly as much as she worries you."

"That's because you don't know her."

"What's she going to do? Punch me out? Come on, relax. You call me if you need me. If she tries to kidnap you or something, we'll take care of Aunt Flo."

"Make love to me," she said. "Please. And don't make love to me like it's the last time."

"Is it? Is there any chance it's the last time? If it is, don't lie to me, that's all I ask. Just tell me the truth."

"I don't want it to be," she said, but tears came to her eyes. "I swear, I don't want it to be."

"That's good enough for me."

The Sacramento airport was small, tight and busy. Chris parked her car as close to the terminal as she could, but it was still quite a walk. She held hands with Carrie and Kyle. They were solemn, though they didn't exactly know why. They had been told about Aunt Flo, Mama's aunt from Chicago whom they had never seen before, whom Mommy hadn't seen in five years...since court. She didn't tell them that part.

Chris was so nervous about the reunion that she didn't even indulge in people-watching. She simply found them seats at the gate and waited. And waited.

The plane was late, but Flo got off quickly. She would have flown first-class. Naturally.

And there she was, more stunning and powerful than Chris remembered. She was five foot eight and still wore heels. She was dressed in a mauve suede suit and a low-cut lacy blouse. She wore boots—probably eelskin. Her coat, slung over her arm, had a white mink collar. Flo wore as many dead animals as she pleased. Her diamond stud earrings glittered behind her short auburn hair. She was gorgeous, aristocratic. Forty-one years old. Good old Aunt Flo. Be nice to her now.

Chris saw her aunt spot them: she in her blue jeans, T-shirt, ski jacket and tennis shoes, no makeup, her hair pulled back into an unsophisticated ponytail; and two little kids who wore practically new but nonetheless rumpled clothes. Not a designer label among them.

The two women rushed toward each other and embraced. Chris was reduced instantly to tears. It was like meeting her past, her longed-for, frightening, grievous, essential past.

"Chris!"

"Flo! Oh, Flo!"

A camera bulb flashed.

"Oh, hell!" Chris gasped.

"Ms. Palmer, how long have you waited for this reunion?" "When did you first discover the whereabouts of your niece?" "Who died on that yacht, Ms. Palmer?" "Where will you be staying?" "Was any of the fortune recovered, Mrs. Zanuck?"

Chris grabbed her kids, one with each hand. She took only two steps before she looped an arm around Kyle's waist, lifted him onto her hip and headed down the concourse. Flo trotted after them.

"My God, Flo!"

"You think I invited them?"

"How did they know you were coming?"

"How the hell should I know? They know everything. Ever since that damn book came out!"

"Can't you get rid of them?"

"How, exactly? Let's just get out of here. Where's the car?"

"It's in the parking lot! Did you think I pulled the limo up to the curb?"

"You had to wear jeans? And those . . . shoes?"

"What do you think? That my designer is all tied up? Jeez, my house burned down! Anyway, who cares what I'm wearing? I didn't know it was going to be a damn press conference."

"Stop swearing. They'll hear you swearing."

"*You're* swearing."

"My luggage. Oh, forget the luggage. I'll send someone for it later.

"What if *they* get it?"

"Oh, they can't get my luggage. Later," she said to a reporter. There were only about six, but it seemed like six hundred. "I just want to spend some time with my niece. I'll give you a statement later."

"You will not!" Chris said.

"Just come on, all right?"

They were followed to the parking lot. They were half running, dragging Carrie along.

"Get a shot of the car! Get a shot of them getting into the car. Man, will you look at that car!"

They were not followed from the airport, but by the time they had Flo settled in her suite—after warning the manager about reporters, having someone sent to the airport for the luggage, and making various other arrangements for Flo's comfort—Chris was exhausted. And disgusted. She began to remember the photographers at the courthouse. When she won, she had had tears in her eyes, sensing if not admitting her betrayal. But Steve had been whispering in her ear, "Don't cry, for God's sake. Smile. Tell them you have no hard feelings, that you love your aunt, you know. Come on, we won."

We. There had never been any *we*.

Flo hadn't cried. "There should be no question of my motives or my relationship with my niece; I only attempted to protect her future as was spelled out in my brother's will. She didn't sue *me*, after all. I happen to think that it's a mistake for her to contest her father's wishes, but the court has made its decision, and we'll certainly abide by it." To Chris, later, Flo had said, "I am too angry to even talk to you. You just don't know how foolish you are."

In Flo's suite, Kyle bounced on the big round bed and Carrie carefully manipulated the buttons on the television. Flo spoke on the phone, ordering room service. Chris slouched in the chair.

"Well, they're sending up some sandwiches and sodas for the kids, salads for us, and I ordered a bottle of wine. We should toast this occasion, hmm? Then I think we should go shopping. I'm renting a car, and—"

"Tell me about the stupid book."

"Well," Flo said, sitting down gracefully, sliding into the chair and crossing her long, beautiful legs, "the 'stupid' book is exactly that; it is contrived almost solely from old newspaper articles and gossip and isn't nearly as revealing as it claims to be. I'm sure a great deal of it is made up. And I think it's been thrown together and rushed to print in the few months since that yacht has been missing. All of the pictures are previously published photos, and—"

"Pictures?"

"Oh, yes. How they got a baby picture of you is beyond me. Stole it, probably."

"Who did this? And why?"

"The author's name, Stephanie Carlisle, is a pseudonym. This is her third such exposé; she writes a decorator column for a Miami newspaper. The Miami paper ran a small piece about a missing yacht, a missing woman and an investigation of a man by the name of Steven Zanuck, the name under which the missing yacht was chartered. And I think I can tell you how this all started. That weasel's third wife, not his fourth, was the daughter of a Texas millionaire. Naturally. Her father began investigating him, not liking in the least who his daughter had fallen for. I think it's pretty certain that Steve took her off to Miami when things were getting a little hot in Dallas. We think, for example, that he might have married her before he was divorced from you. And we also suspect that he didn't divorce his first wife at all—a woman he married when he was only twenty-one and living in San Francisco. Precocious little devil."

"What? Who was that?"

"Sondra Pederson, daughter of a rich Swedish shipper. But that one wasn't as messy as the other ones. He managed to get a bunch of money before Daddy flew from Sweden to San Francisco and simply collected his broken-hearted daughter. She's alive and well and living with her family in Stockholm. That hasn't been mentioned, however. It would probably hurt book sales."

"Jeez. It figures."

"He wasn't a lawyer. No record of his ever having attending law school or taking the bar exam."

"Why didn't we know any of this sooner? When I was stupidly trying to win my fortune?"

"Believe me, if I had been able to find one thing on him, I would have used it. He checked out; there was a Steven Zanuck who passed the bar after graduating from law school in New York. There was even a yearbook picture that resembled your husband. He was pretty good at this little scam. And, although I thought he was a weasel and a creep, I didn't know the worst of it. It was that Texan, Charles Beck, who dug up the real dirt. And I think it's possible his family paid the biggest price."

"You think they're really dead, then? Steve and his—"

"Fred."

"Fred?"

"His name wasn't really Steve Zanuck. In San Francisco his name was William Wandell, and in Texas he was Steven Wright. He kept a place and a small business under the name Zanuck for a while, kind of living a dual identity. It probably had something to do with monies he had received as Zanuck. His real name is Fred Johnson. And the real Steve Zanuck, a nice young tax attorney with a practice in Missouri, isn't real happy about all this, either."

"Fred?"

"Terrific, huh? Well, I always knew he was no damn good. Just couldn't prove it. I hired detectives and lawyers, and they didn't figure him out, either. Real slick, this lizard. I ought to sue them. Incompetents."

"Is all this in the book?"

"This business about his aliases is our little secret so far. We're going to have to do something about that hair." Flo reached across the small table and plucked at Chris's hair.

Chris withdrew. "You know you shouldn't wear your hair all the same length."

Chris put her forehead in her hand, leaning her elbow on the small round table. "Fred," she moaned. "This is simply impossible."

"It'll blow over. There's a little money, I think. The Texan found some money, but maybe it's not in this country. I wonder what the scum was saving up for?"

"Does he have a lot of children, too?"

Flo glanced at Kyle, bouncing, and Carrie, sitting entranced in front of the big TV. Her features softened. She looked back at Chris. "Not that I know of," she said gently. "You should have called me so much sooner."

"I know. I know." But then I wouldn't have been pulled out of that fire, she thought. She almost told Flo about the philosophy behind *It's a Wonderful Life*, but she held her tongue. Sophisticated Flo, who'd climbed to a mountaintop in Tibet to learn about meditation from the masters, would have a tough time swallowing something as effective as playing the hand you're dealt. "Well, I figured you were pretty mad, Flo. I was trying to make it on my own, I guess. I've been working, taking care of the kids and writing."

"Writing? What?"

"Never mind that. Not my life story, I promise. I was trying to take care of myself, trying to figure out what I really wanted to do. I'm getting a little tired of feeling stupid. I just wanted to make it on my own for a while. I thought I'd done enough damage. I wasn't planning to *never* call you."

"Well, you should have called me. I was worried sick. Now, when are you coming back home?"

Chris began telling her story. She tried to explain how for the first time in so long she felt free but cuddled at the same time. This wonderful man and his lovely family had embraced her, and though they didn't have many luxuries, within their tender assembly there was such a rich intimacy, such love.

Room service arrived. They set up the kids at the table, and Flo brought the wine to the sitting room where Chris was telling her tale, knowing she sounded like a romantic fool. Yet another chapter in Chris's novel of misguided fortunes, fantasies and foibles. Flo poured wine and sat listening, pulling a long, slender cigarette from her snakeskin case, inhaling, the smoke curling up past her perfectly enameled nails, past her rose-colored lips, over her artistically fashioned copper hair. Listening to this story of love and woe.

"I always wanted to have a family," Chris said. "A family like my family was. Even before Mom and Daddy died, I always figured that whatever I ended up doing, I'd be doing it in a home with a husband and children."

"Well, you have children," Flo said.

"I should have listened to you. I shouldn't have married Steve—I know that. But I did, I have them, and in Mike's home and in his family the kids have a sense of belonging. For the first time. I can see a change in them already—they feel more loved, more secure, at ease."

Flo did not comment.

Chris told of parks, ducks, movies, stories read. "Imagine Carrie not knowing that men don't shave their legs! And they love his cabin, the horses they rode. The cousins at Mattie and Big Mike's."

"I can't come up with cousins," Flo said, "but the horses shouldn't be a big problem."

"It's more than horses and cabins and movies. As for me," Chris said, "I had been lonelier than I realized. I had let myself become friendless. I hardly even noticed that I had lost touch with old friends who probably would have stood by me. Then, meeting the Cavanaughs, I saw the potential to have family and friends again." She smiled almost sheepishly. "They liked me. Right off. Without knowing a thing about me.

"And Mike," she went on. "Logically I knew that all men aren't men like Steve... Fred. But I had stopped believing it was possible for someone to care for me, no matter whether I was rich, poor, smart or dumb. This guy just opened up his heart and his home, no questions asked. It had nothing whatever to do with my bloodline or checkbook balance. I can't tell you how it feels to have this man not give a damn about all that."

Flo stamped out the cigarette. She sipped the wine.

Then, Chris tried to explain, he had needs, too. He wasn't asking her for anything, really, but because his life had not been a picnic, this unit they had formed, the four of them, was helping him, too. He was finally getting in touch with what he had lost, what he could have, and was thinking in terms of having a real life again—one filled with love, people, give-and-take. Before Chris and her kids, Mike had cut himself off, afraid to feel, afraid to be involved.

"The long and short of it is, I'm simply not ready to leave him. That doesn't mean I'm planning to stay forever—I haven't made commitments—but the four of us, well, we're comfortable with one another when none of us has been completely comfortable for years. We're recuperating from past hurts. It might not sound very practical, but it's a good feeling to be needed."

Flo lit another cigarette.

"I love you, Flo. I know I haven't been very good family, the way things have gone. First the lawsuit, then disappearing like that. I'm sure you've been at the end of your rope with me, and I want to patch things up. I want to have our old relationship back. I want to be friends again. You're the most important person in my life, my only family. But I'm not going to do everything you tell me, and I'm not going to leave Mike's house until I'm ready. Until we're healthier. All four of us."

Flo swirled out the smoke. Her eyes were locked tightly on Chris's. Chris realized Flo probably thought her niece still had a screw loose, as though she had moved from one absurd situation to the next. But for the first time in seven years Chris felt sane. And—another first—she felt tough enough to deal with Flo. She lifted her chin, waiting.

"Well," Flo said, as composed as ever, putting her cigarette in an ashtray and lifting the wineglass, "how long do you think this is going to take?"

Mike had finally talked about it. He had told Jim some of this incredible tale. He had come right out and said it, that though he probably sounded like a lunatic, he had fallen for this goofy woman and her kids. And it was true, like the story in the paper said, she had been pretty well kicked around by that jerk she had married, but she hadn't known it was all a scam from the start. Young, you know, grieving over her dead parents, no one but her old-maid Aunt Flo, and then along comes this good-looking, fast-talking lawyer, and bam! Before you know it the whole family falls apart over money. Figures, huh? Money and sex, the biggest problems in America.

And yes, he had said, he'd told her to stay for as long as she wanted. He hoped it would be for a long time because he liked it; it was good to take someone to his mom and dad's, not go alone. They loved the cabin, all of them. Especially the kids. For a few years now he'd been thinking of building a room on. Maybe this spring he'd get started.

These complications from her past? Well, he had said, who didn't have a past, huh? His past, for example, wasn't very tidy, all things considered. She had to try to reconcile with her aunt, keep her family together somehow. She hadn't taken any of her aunt's money, of course, only her own. She didn't need money right now, but everyone needs family. So he had encouraged her to be as patient and kind with old Aunt Flo as she possibly could. This would all work itself out.

The afternoon paper arrived. Mike had been playing Ping-Pong with a couple of the guys. Jim walked in and stopped the game, spreading the paper on the game table. At least it wasn't the front page. The headline said *RE-UNION*. The airport scene. Blue-jeaned Chris was being embraced by a tall, fashionable woman who looked to be about Mike's age. She wore jewelry everywhere, *big* jewelry. She carried a fur coat and a briefcase.

"Old Aunt Flo," Jim supplied.

"Holy shit," Mike said. Then he picked up the paper and took it into the bathroom.

Chapter Nine

Mike entered his house quietly. He peeked in at the sleeping kids. Cheeks, the great watchdog, asleep on the end of Kyle's bed, didn't even greet him. Cheeks was exhausted from spending the entire night eating a pair of Mike's socks. He was sleeping with the remnants still under his chin.

When Mike found Chris in his bed, still asleep, he felt his chest swell with pride. He felt as though he were in possession, as if he had won. He didn't mean to feel that way, but he did. He wondered how many more mornings he'd leave his shift wondering what he'd find at home. He sat down on the edge of the bed, gently, and kissed her. "Hey, sleepyhead," he whispered.

She moved a little, moaning. "You had fires," she sleepily informed him. "I can't sleep through those sirens."

"I can't sleep through them, either." He laughed. "I'm going to have to sleep today though—I'm bushed. I saw Aunt Flo."

"You saw her?" Chris asked, coming awake, sitting up. "Where?"

"In the paper. Your picture was in the paper."

"Oh, yeah, I should have thought of that. There were reporters at the airport, but we ditched them. Was the story awful?"

"There wasn't much of a story, no quotes or anything."

"That's a relief. They didn't make anything up."

"Any particular reason you didn't tell me that Flo wasn't some crotchety old bat?"

"Is *that* what you thought?" she asked with a laugh. "Well, don't worry, I won't tell her. No, Flo is everything every woman dreams of being. Intelligent. Sophisticated. Independent. Beautiful. Rich. Successful." And a few other things, she thought, like belligerent, possessive, domineering.

"How old is she?"

"Oh, about forty. Maybe forty-one."

"Jeez. I had no idea. I was expecting this little old lady, like from *Arsenic and Old Lace*, just a rich old biddy who couldn't understand true love because her libido had dried up."

Chris laughed again.

"How was it? The reunion?"

"There were three things we had to get out of the way: first, how ashamed and sorry I am for having sued her, abandoned her and worried her half to death; second, this business about my ex-husband and that stupid book; and finally, how I'm not getting on a plane with her this afternoon. Then we had a lot of fun reminiscing. I've missed her so much; we had such fun together when I was growing up. My mom would say that she had married Randolph and Flo; we were a famous foursome. And Flo was always there, spoiling me, pumping me up, taking my side. Auntie Flo," she said sentimentally, shaking her head. There had been affection, such hilarity, such joy in their relationship—so much lost since the death of her parents and the lawsuit. Chris longed to have it back. "My best friend while I was growing up. She's more like an older sister than an aunt."

"So. Not this afternoon, huh?"

She kissed him, quick and cute, on the lips. She wrinkled her nose. "You stink. Awful. Smoke?"

"And a bunch of other things. I would have showered at the station, but we had a shift relief in the middle of a fire."

"What other things?"

"God knows. Sweat. Mud. Good old Jim ought to take an emesis basin into a fire with him, for starters."

"A what?"

"You know, that curved little pan they give you in the hospital when you have to throw up. It's amazing—everything hits your turnouts, but you still come away smelling like all of it. Jim shot me with the hose to clean me off, but I still need a scrub, huh?"

"Oooo. I guess I thought only the victims threw up."

"Bet you also thought only the victims swallowed a lot of smoke, huh? I'll take a quick shower."

"Were they bad fires?"

"One was at a paint store. Those are almost the worst—chemicals and all. That one will be on the news—horrible mess. It took hours in the middle of the night, but it was just about over by the time I left. The other two were pretty good fires."

"Good fires?"

"Manageable fires, no injuries, easily contained."

"Do you like fires?"

"I like to put water on fires."

She watched while he stripped off his shirt and pants, heading for the shower in only his briefs. She remembered the young fireman in the photo she had found, the leaner, trimmer man. But though he was thicker now, he was firm and graceful. He walked with such purpose, even without clothes on.

"Mike, have you ever gotten hurt in a fire?"

He shrugged. "Not bad."

"This is really dangerous, what you do. You could be killed."

"Don't overthink it. I know what I'm doing or I wouldn't do it." He yanked down the briefs.

"*Overthink* it? What about fire fighters' families? What must they go through every time they hear the siren? What if you—"

He stood in the bathroom doorway, hands on his hips, not in the least distracted by his nudity. "Chrissie, being born is dangerous. Joanie and Shelly were driving to the grocery store. If you're going to worry for a living, worry about something you can control, for Pete's sake. I'm going to shower. *I* can't even stand the way I smell."

While the shower ran she thought about those two things. One, he could get killed in a fire. Two, if she were paid for worrying, she'd be a millionaire.

"Tell me about Aunt Flo," he said, standing in the bathroom doorway with a towel wrapped around his lower body, using another to dry his hair.

"I invited her to dinner. Is that okay?"

"Here?"

"Would you rather not?"

"No, it's okay. But—"

"She is not going to relax until she looks you over, Mike. She simply can't believe I'm planning to stay here for a while. And I thought we'd all be a lot more comfortable here than in a restaurant or something. I'm cooking."

"I'm getting into bed," he said, moving to close the bedroom door and then tossing the towel to the floor. "When did you tell her you'd go back to Chicago?"

"I didn't say when."

"What did you say?"

"Want to know how I sold you, huh? Well, I told her you were this big, handsome brute who—"

"Actually," he said, pulling back the covers to climb in beside her, "I want to know how you sold her on not dragging you off to Chicago."

"I said we were getting healthy here," she replied, her voice soft, her words serious. "All four of us. Is that true?"

He thought about it for a minute. "Yeah, I think that's true. Yeah, that's okay." He pulled up the covers. His eyes looked bright, but dark circles hung under them. Fires. His eyes, scorched but excited, tired but revved up. She wondered how long a man could do this work before it took its toll. "But you never told her that you love me."

"She thinks I'm crazy as it is."

"Well, in that case, I hope this is a long illness," he said.

"How long do you think you'd like it to be, Mike?"

"Oh, thirty, forty years. I want to keep you."

"Forever?"

"If I can."

"I can't make that kind of commitment. You know that. It's way too soon."

"Well, it's an open invitation."

"How can *you* do that—ask us to stay here permanently? You mean you want to marry us after knowing us such a short time?"

"Are you going to hold that against me?"

"No. But I'm not rushing into anything."

"Just so you're not rushing *out* of anything."

"You haven't even met my family. My 'family' will blow in here at about six-thirty tonight with twenty-two midgets carrying her train and polishing her crown. I think the term *formidable woman* was invented to describe Flo. Then you might add some conditions to this not-very-romantic proposal."

His hands went under her T-shirt, which was his T-shirt, and he squirmed closer. "You want romance, Chrissie? I'll give you romance."

"Mike, why would you bring up marriage so soon? Really, why?"

"It's what I want. I think it's what you want. I think you want to be a real family. I want to take care of you."

"If I wanted taking care of, I could call the Red Lion. Flo would be thrilled."

He squeezed her breasts and moved against her thigh. "Oh?"

"That's not enough, wanting to take care of someone."

He shrugged. "We can think about it for a long time, or a short time. But, Chrissie, life is short. You just never know how short. And I love you. I haven't loved anyone like this in a long, long time."

"What if you don't feel that way in another month?"

"Look, if you're not sure how *you* feel, that's one thing. You had a hard time of it, I know, so take your time and decide how you feel, okay? But I know how *I* feel, and I know that this kind of feeling doesn't come and go that fast. They trip around a little from time to time—every marriage on record has ups and downs. But love is love, and I'd rather live it than give it lip service."

"And you didn't feel this way about the other women you've been with?"

"Nope. I wanted to, but I didn't. Boy, when it hits you, it about knocks you over." He smiled. It was a feeling he liked.

"I'm afraid of being in love," she whispered.

"Really? Afraid of being in love? Or afraid of loving someone who's going to hurt you?"

"Isn't that the same thing?"

"Depends," he said, shrugging, his eyes getting that tired, drained look. He was going to nod off. "Are you afraid of me?"

"You know I'm not."

"Then it's not the same thing." He put his head on her shoulder, holding her close, snuggling up tight.

"Actually," she said almost to herself, "what I'm really afraid of is depending on someone too much. Really needing, *counting* on, someone. Giving in so totally. Because the next stage seems to be taking it all for granted, expecting it will stay safe and satisfying forever until the only thing about yourself you're sure of is who you are in relation to the person you feel you belong to. Whether he's a great guy or a jerk, it could—whoosh—disappear, leaving you suddenly on your own. Do you know what I'm talking about, Mike? Mike?"

He had fallen asleep.

"Marriage!" Flo said, in a combination of shock and distrust. Chris sat in the beautician's chair, Florence stood behind. The kids were with a sitter, a *bonded* sitter at the hotel. "Are you even close to seeing how ridiculous this is

becoming? Marriage! Layer it,'' she instructed, pointing a long, polished fingernail at the back of Chris's head. ''But leave some of the length. No bangs. Brush it *back*, so.''

''I can tell her how to cut my hair, Florence.''

''Tell her then,'' Flo said, hands on hips.

''Well, I'd like you to cut it shorter around the top and take only about an inch off the length so that it still touches my shoulders, and—''

Flo smiled. ''That's what I thought.''

''I wish you wouldn't tell me what I want to do all the time.'' Especially when you're right, she almost added.

''Marriage, huh? He suggested marriage this soon? You certainly didn't accept?''

''Not because I wasn't tempted.''

''Chris, you're going to have to be sensible at some point in your life, and now would be a good time. A little shorter on top, here,'' she instructed the stylist. ''You're on the rebound; you can't enter into another marriage.''

''Rebound? I've been alone for nearly four years!''

''Yes, but you haven't really recovered from that yet. In fact, you don't know for sure if you're divorced, widowed or still married.'' The stylist stopped, eyes widening. Flo dismissed her curiosity with a hard stare. The comb moved again. ''There,'' Flo told the technician, ''that looks good. Real good.''

They shopped for clothes and accessories. Makeup, nail polish, files, perfume, bath oils, shampoos and rinses. Chris turned before a full-length mirror in the department store. She looked very different in tailored dress slacks, a loose angora sweater, heels and hose, makeup, a sculptured hairstyle and even a necklace. A thick, curving gold collar. Very chic.

"I'm not on the rebound. I've been on my own for four years. I haven't had any kind of serious relationship, but that doesn't mean that I didn't meet and know men. I've worked several different jobs in the past few years. I even had a couple of dates. And Mike hasn't met anyone he wanted to marry, but that doesn't mean he doesn't know women. You've got this all wrong."

"What kind of a guy offers his house for the night because a woman is burned out, and then, lickety-split, asks her to marry him?"

"Oh, you're right, only a real pervert would do a thing like that!"

"What if this has something to do with your money?"

"I don't have any money, Flo."

"*I* have money. And what's mine is yours."

"No, it's not, Flo. We aren't the same person, remember? All my money, which was Daddy's money, hit the trail."

They walked between the shops in the downtown Sacramento open mall. As they were passing a window, arms laden with shopping bags, Flo drew Chris up short. "Look," she said, standing behind Chris and taking her parcels, giving her a full view of herself. "Do you feel any different? You look great."

Chris looked at herself in the shop window. She fingered the necklace that cuffed her neck—not solid gold, but a very nice piece of jewelry nonetheless. Classy, like Flo. "Yes, Flo," she said, meeting her aunt's eyes in the glass. "I feel different. I look more like your version of me than mine. And your version looks better." She turned around, staring into her aunt's eyes. "I don't quite know what to make of that."

"Why don't you simply enjoy it?"

But Chris had had plenty of time to think about what she needed to be happy, and it wasn't fancy clothes. She needed family. She needed to be connected to people she loved, people who cared for her and counted on her. She also liked to sit behind a typewriter and imagine. She imagined best in a sweat suit or jeans or a man's T-shirt. Grubbies. It might be nice, she thought, to dress up after a grueling day at the keys, but it wasn't necessary in order to become whom she was becoming. What she needed a lot more than a nice pair of slacks and a necklace was someone to talk to about the book she was working on—and for that it didn't matter what she was wearing.

Who wouldn't enjoy nice things? Oh, boy, there it was again. It was difficult to maintain an idea of what you could do on your own when you were being taken care of. That she would enjoy nice things so much more if she could get them for herself and also give them was difficult for people like Flo to understand. And there was no way to refuse Flo's generosity, for Flo spending on Chris was part of their history. But it was already starting to feel loaded. She kept waiting to hear the bait line: "After all I've done..."

You suffer too much, Chrissie, he had said. *It's almost like you want to.* No, that wasn't it. Chris hated to suffer. She wanted balance. Give-and-take. Take *and* give.

"Why haven't you ever married, Flo?" she asked.

"I never saw the need."

"Need? Is that what marriage is? Something you need?"

"You tell me. You're obviously thinking about doing it for the second time."

"I'm not really ready to make any long-term commitments; I only said I was tempted. And Steve...I mean

Fred, doesn't count. I was a victim of temporary insanity."

"Nothing counts *more* than Steve, or Fred, or whoever the heck he was, because you should have learned something from that—something about how impetuous you are when it comes to this kind of emotion. Lord, running back into a thunderstorm again before you're even dried off."

"I think you mean jumping from the frying pan into the fire," Chris supplied, laughing. "Almost literally. Don't worry, Florence. I learned far more than I bargained for." What she did not add was that she was finally *un*learning some of the suspicion, distrust and paranoia Steve had left her with.

"In fact, I know a lot of women who marry regularly. And dreadfully. Like a bad habit. I don't know what moved you to marry the first one any more than this second one, whom you've known for less than—"

"Don't change the subject, Flo. We both know you have a low opinion of my choices. I want to know about *you*. Do you have any kind of personal life these days? You look like success personified—wealth, beauty, intelligence et cetera. I met some of the men you dated, or rather 'attended functions with,' but that was years ago. What's the deal, Flo? Are you a lesbian?"

Flo gasped and stopped walking. "Christine!"

It made Chris laugh to have shocked her aunt, but this was more of their history. Chris would be daring and in need of discipline, and Flo would be sensible and ready to give it. Big and little girl. Teacher and student. Yet as much as Chris admired Flo's composure, her command, her savoir faire, Chris neither envied nor wished to become Flo.

"Are you lonely?" she asked her aunt.

"No," she said. "Certainly not. I've missed *you*."

"But when you're not either fighting me in court or hunting for me, what is your life like?"

"You may wish to remember, dear, that my older brother died and left me a horrendous business when I was only thirty-four. The next several years were a tad busy with very demanding work and trying to figure out what to do about you."

"It might have been better for you if you'd written me off as a loss."

"Ha! The only family I have—a young woman who is in perpetual trouble, my brother's child, once my dearest friend. Why would I write you off? I knew we'd be together again someday."

"But who do you spend Christmas with?"

"Usually with friends."

"Ah. Do you have a lover?"

"Chris, believe me, if I thought it were any of your business, I would—"

"Come on, Flo, you know all *my* dirt. Come on, what do you do when you snake out of all that eelskin? Do you have anyone special and dear? Has your whole personal life been on hold so you could manage Palmercraft and Palmer House and the Perils of Pauline?"

Flo sighed. "I have the same friends I've always had. I've been seeing the same man for years. Literally years. We're both very busy, but we do quite a lot together. We're very good friends. We travel together sometimes."

"Who?" Kate said.

"Kenneth Waite."

"Kenneth Waite? Isn't he the president of some big advertising agency? What is it? Multimega—"

"He's the owner now. Waite Commercial Resources, Inc."

"How long?"

"Oh, I think he's been the owner for—"

"No," she laughed. "How long have you been seeing him?"

"Forever. I don't know. Fifteen years."

"But isn't he married? Wasn't his wife a friend of Mother's? Wait a minute. . . ."

"As I said," Flo went on, "we are two busy people with a great many commitments. There's not a lot of room in either of our lives for romance. There never has been, although Ken has been divorced for years—seven or eight, I think. We're simply very good friends."

"You were having an affair with a married man!"

"His marriage left a good deal of room for that. And my responsibilities have never left room for much more."

"How well organized, Florence," Chris said, shaking her head. "Are you going to get married? Ever?"

"It doesn't seem necessary, even since Ken has been divorced. We're pretty independent people."

"It sounds so distant. So. . . uninvolved."

"Not everyone has an overactive libido."

"Come on, don't make any cracks about my poor old neglected sex drive. Stever might have awakened it, but he certainly left it in a coma. I couldn't even fathom an interest in sex for years. Have you any idea what it's like to be absolutely insane with passion and then find out the lousy creep probably didn't even *like* you? Talk about impotence! Or frigidity, or whatever. It comes as a real blow. Here you are, willing to do anything short of crawling through cut glass for one more kiss, only to learn he was just using you. Honestly, I bet Steve, or whoever, didn't even *like* me. Whew."

"Well, I tried to tell you, but you—"

"But what about you?" she asked as they reached Flo's rented Eldorado. Chris leaned on the roof, looking across at Flo. "What's your excuse? How come you never fell in love? Dumb, embarrassing love?"

Flo tossed her bags into the back seat and put her elbows on top of the car. She rested her chin on her forearms and looked at Chris. "What is it, huh? What do they offer you that I don't understand? No kidding, what does this big, dumb fireman have that has made you gunky with devotion? A schwanz as long as a fire hose?"

Chris erupted with laughter, covering her mouth.

"This big?" Flo asked, putting up her hands, indicating something of inhuman proportions. "Or is it their vulnerability, the things they need from you? Old Stever needed a few bucks, and this guy needs to play house for a while. Or is it really just some primitive man-woman thing, some bonding that I didn't get the gene for? Come on, tell old Aunt Flo, you little slut."

How she loved her! There weren't many people who knew this Flo. The people who read the society pages expected a Princess Diana sort. But Flo operated a huge furniture business. That meant she could speak many languages; she could communicate as well with the governor's wife as with an upholsterer with an eighth-grade education. She was tough, slick, sassy. No way Mike was ready for this dame.

"Regardless of how utterly stupid I was to have married Steve," Chris said, "it's important to remember that it was a simple mistake. It's important to remember that I was young, vulnerable, and he wasn't just a bad choice—he was a criminal. Mike is a decent man.

"It's risk," Chris said. "Not the kind of risk you take to sneak to a hotel behind your husband's back, or the kind of risk required to put your money in his account, for that matter. It's the risk of your emotional self. It's exposing yourself to a person who will accept you as you are, embrace you as you are. It is the risk, Flo, of being naked in an emotional way, and betting that you won't get cold." She was quiet for a second. "I feel nice and warm," she said softly, "all the time now."

After meeting her aunt's eyes over the roof of the car, Chris opened the door and slid into the passenger side. Flo stayed above for a few moments before getting into the driver's seat.

"Christine," Flo began seriously, "would it not be just as good to buy a nice, thick parka? Mink, perhaps?"

Mike had napped and then gone to his folks' house. When he walked into the kitchen through the garage door, Chris was stirring something at the stove. He looked her over and smiled. "Wow. You look different. Gorgeous."

She turned her lips toward him for a kiss. "I let Florence have me 'done.' "

"She didn't change anything on the inside, did she? When's she coming?"

"Any time now. And, Mike, listen.... Oh, forget it, there's no point in trying to prepare you. Just try to roll with it, okay?"

He took a beer from the refrigerator and walked into the dining room. He looked at the table. "What's this?"

She followed him. "I hope you don't mind," she said. He lifted a new plate. "Flo gave me a bunch of money after she shopped me to death and told me to get something I wanted, something frivolous. It's no big deal for Flo, and it made her feel good to give me the money. And this was how I wanted to spend it. On you, sort of."

His table wore a new linen tablecloth. New ceramic plates in lavender, royal blue and beige sat between new flatware and linen napkins in china rings. There was a new lavender vase filled with fresh flowers. Wineglasses. Mike felt funny inside, a little dizzy maybe. New dishes—because she was staying and wanted a nicer set? Or was his slightly imperfect, chipped set of ironstone too flawed for this event? But he said, "Looks nice."

The kids called his name and ran to him, and his dizziness went away. He picked them up, both of them, and went into the living room where they had things to show him—toys, books and gadgets. He was relieved to see that they wore the clothes *he* had bought them. Cheeks wandered over, tail wagging, and nudged him for a scratch. I got to *him*, Mike thought. If I can impress this mutt, I can handle Flo. Can't I?

And the doorbell rang. He remembered something. He remembered Joanie's dad saying hello but looking at him with that if-you-touch-my-daughter-I'll-kill-you look. Mike had been a mere boy. He had gulped down his nerves. He wanted to kick Cheeks in the ribs for not growling at Florence.

"So, this is the fireman," Flo said, smiling very beautifully. "Well, there's hardly anything I can do to repay you for saving my family."

Yes, you can. Leave. Go away and turn into a surly old woman. I'm good with cranky old ladies. They love me. "Just doing my job," he said, taking the proffered hand.

"And thank God you were," she added, gliding past him into the living room. She had packages. She probably didn't go anywhere without presents. She was dressed casually—gray wool fitted slacks, a fuzzy red sweater, gray pumps out of some kind of skin and a rich leather blazer. Rings and things. She smelled heavenly, expensive. But she did crouch to receive the children. "There are my angels; I have presents. It must be your birthdays."

"It isn't our birthdays." Carrie giggled, reaching for a bag. "And you know it isn't our birthdays."

"Is it Christmas?" Flo asked.

"No," they laughed.

"Then somebody must love you. No, no, you have to give a kiss and hug first."

Mike ached. He wanted to be happy for them, for them all. What was wrong with him? Where were his heart, his convictions about family? Where, for gosh sakes, was his courage?

"Here you are," Chris said, coming from the kitchen. "And you've met Mike?"

Chris kissed the cheek Flo turned toward her. They looked alike, suddenly. None of their features, for Chris was small and fair, while Flo was big and bronze. It was their style. Chris, in expensive clothes and pumps, was very different than she had been in a T-shirt and jeans, hair pulled back, no makeup. She was now more like her rich aunt.

The kids were being fed something simple in the kitchen, after which they would be excused to play or watch television, while the adults sat at the newly appointed dining-room table. Mike sat with the kids while they ate, playing with them, talking to them, watching Flo and Chris in the kitchen together. They were like his sisters and sisters-in-law when they got together around the pots. They lifted lids, gossiped, laughed, helped each other—like good friends, like family. Flo and Chris recited a litany of names he had never heard before—old family acquaintances, friends from high school and college. They were still catching up. But he felt like an outsider, something he had never felt when the women in his family played this companionable game around the food.

For the first time he wondered if he should have gotten himself into this. He was scared of this woman. He was afraid he was going to lose Chris and Carrie and Kyle....

* * *

"Wine?" Chris asked him when they were all seated.

"Sure. Thanks."

"Well, Mike, Chris tells me you had a dangerous fire last night. No one was hurt, I hope."

"No, no injuries."

"But it must be very dangerous, this work."

"We're trained for it," he said. He saw that he wasn't helping. Here she was, trying, and he was so suspicious, he was going to hurt his own case. You couldn't come between family. Chris had tried to blend into his; until now he hadn't known how hard she might have had to try.

He had to concentrate not to shovel food into his mouth too fast. Fire fighters know the minute they sit down to a meal, the alarm will sound. He was going to try to be more refined. He would eat like an accountant. "Fire is dangerous and unpredictable, but our training, which is ongoing, prepares us to make intelligent decisions. We don't take risks foolishly is what I'm saying. But still, there are times..."

"Like in saving people, I suppose. Rushing into a burning building to rescue someone. Don't you ever stand there, looking at the fire, and think 'Wait a minute, here'?"

"That's the thing we don't do, as a matter of fact. Number-one priority is protecting life; number-two is saving the structure. But we don't go in looking for people unless there's a reason to believe someone needs to be pulled out. Usually the person who calls in the alarm informs us on the scene."

"And you wear gear? Like oxygen masks?"

"Air packs," he said, "if there's time."

"And if there isn't time?"

"Look, that's the job." He shrugged. "Time is the only advantage there is, and we don't waste it thinking things over a lot. Fire fighters don't rush into a wall of flame because it's fun. We all have our jobs at the fire; we take informed risks. We've been trained to recognize possible and impossible situations. We only get into trouble when something unforeseen happens—part of the structure collapses, or an on-site explosion occurs. That's the danger."

"So," Flo said, lifting her fork, "you pretty much rush into things, huh?"

Chris gulped. "Mike's been a fire fighter for twelve years," she said. "He's very experienced." She took another sip of wine. "More wine?" she asked. They shook their heads.

"It's always an informed decision. Rapid but experienced."

"Have you ever been wrong?"

Mike stared at Flo for a long moment, using his heavy, brooding brows in that frightening look of his. But Flo met his eyes as if to say she was every bit as tough as he was. Tougher. This lady had played ball in the major leagues.

Chris drained her glass and refilled it.

"Everyone has been wrong, made mistakes. But if you fold your hand after your first mistake, you fail to learn anything, how to do it right the next time."

"You should meet Mike's family, his brothers and sisters," Chris attempted. "They—"

"So," Flo continued, ignoring Chris, "tell me, Mike, does this job require . . . um . . . a college education?"

Mike's cheeks took on a stain. "No," he said. "At least half of the fire fighters in our company have degrees, but I don't."

"And if you had some disability? If you couldn't fight fires anymore?"

His mouth became grim. "I'm sure I'd manage."

"Really, Flo..." Chris said.

"Hmm," hummed Flo. "I suppose it must be the big-city fire fighters who have the most precarious careers. Out here in the suburbs, it can't be as bad."

"Not as many bells as in, say, Chicago. But—"

"But this matter of doing dangerous work and the disability situation must be a major factor when you consider, for example, taking on a family."

"That would certainly be a consideration, Flo," he said evenly. "But usually not the first one."

Flo leaned an elbow on the table. "And what would the first consideration be?"

"Whether or not I could stand to be under the same roof with the other person, I guess."

Chris could tell he was trying, answering Flo's most prying, unreasonable questions with patience and honesty as if this were his steady girl's father. She wanted to tell Mike that he didn't have to prove anything to Flo. She wanted Flo to shut up, to let Mike off the hook. But it was bedtime for Carrie and Kyle, so she excused herself to take them upstairs and tuck them in, reluctantly leaving Mike and Flo at the dining room table.

She heard snatches of their conversation: intelligent decisions... danger is danger.... There are challenges that won't get you killed....

She returned to the table to find it was Mike's turn. He had been trying, but now he was getting mad. He asked about furniture.

"The Palmers began selling furniture more than forty years ago. We started manufacturing a specialized line of indoor/outdoor furniture only twenty years ago—Palmercraft. It's been very successful.

"That's what I hear. Lots of money. That must make life pretty easy."

Chris grimaced. "My grandfather didn't have much when he started. He built the business from his garage and—"

"I don't dislike success, if that's what you mean. But it is hard work. Chris herself has a vested interest in the business."

"Oh? She never mentioned that."

"Because I don't!" Chris said, but she might as well have told Cheeks. These two were not listening to her.

"Well, you already know that business about the will, but there's more to it than that. The will was written before Chris was of age, and it provided for her. The family business was given to me because it was understood that I would always take care of Chris's needs should anything happen to her parents."

"Take care of her needs," he repeated. "Her needs before she became an adult, I trust."

"My thinking is that the furniture company is half hers."

"Really? I suppose she'd have to go to Chicago for that."

"Chicago is her home, of course."

"Oh. I thought her home burned down."

"More wine?" Chris asked in frustration. They ignored her. She filled her own glass and stared into it.

She wanted to stop them. Flo knew Chris was not interested in the furniture business. Flo would happily take care of Chris forever; in fact, if Chris showed up at the factory one morning to take an executive position, her aunt would probably give her a title, plenty of money, and have her emptying wastebaskets to keep her out of trouble. Flo controlled everything. But it was moot; Chris would never even consider it. After all, she had run through almost two million dollars indulging a naive passion for a thief. She didn't want to be responsible for any more family money. The only money she wanted was money that belonged to her.

If these two stubborn people would stop sparring over her for a few minutes, she could probably explain her position better than either of them could. She would return to Chicago at some point soon—maybe not permanently; time would tell—but she did want the kids to see where she had grown up, and she wanted to reacquaint herself with some of her past. But she didn't want to move in with Aunt Flo and have her life managed. She also didn't want to live with Mike if he was going to insist on telling her what her priorities should be. What she wanted was simply their love, as they had hers, while she reconstructed a life that belonged to her. You couldn't share your life with anyone unless you had one of your own.

"There is a lot of unfinished business in Chicago that—"

"—could probably be handled by a good accountant," Mike interrupted.

"There's nothing wrong with a lucrative business, but I was talking about home, family—"

"Home is where the heart is."

Chris refilled her glass as their conversation grew more competitive. Thank God for the wine.

"I think you're suggesting, Mike, that Chris ignore who she is and where she came from to stay here with you, when you hardly know her and can hardly provide for her in the manner she is accustomed to."

"Oh, *that* manner—a crummy little firetrap in a rotten neighborhood, struggling to make ends meet because she's too proud or too scared to call her rich aunt? I can probably compete with that life-style. Yeah, I'm suggesting—"

"Stop it," Chris said, but she slurred it. They looked at her as if she had just arrived on the scene. Their images swirled before her eyes, but she got up from her chair with as much dignity as was possible, given the fact that she was completely sloshed. "When I make up my mind what I want, I'm sure the two of you will let me know."

She walked a crooked line from the dining room. "I'm going to bed. I accidentally got drunk trying to ignore the two of you. G'night."

Chapter Ten

When Chris awoke she had the headache she deserved. On the bedside table was a note under a bottle of aspirin. The fireman had gone off to fight fires. The note said, "I'm sorry. I had no right. Love, M."

After two aspirin and two cups of coffee she called Flo. "Shame on you," she said to her aunt.

"Chris, I'm sorry. I didn't realize we were talking about you as if you weren't even there."

"Yes, and it was awfully familiar. I felt like I was in the middle of a custody battle. I'm not going to do this with the two of you. I'm furious."

"Come and have breakfast with me. I want to work this out."

"Well, as long as you're ashamed and sorry, let me dress the kids. Give me an hour."

"An hour?"

"I have a headache."

"I can imagine."

No, you can't, she wanted to say. She didn't know how she had managed to delude herself that there was any possible way Mike and Flo would hit it off. It wasn't that they were so terribly different—in fact, they had much in common. But in their strength, possessiveness and competitiveness, each seemed to have what the other wanted. Her.

And what did she want? The thought of giving up either Mike or Flo was excruciating, but...

Chris drew herself a bath, the water as hot as she could stand it. She hadn't been in the tub long before Carrie woke up and wandered in. "Morning, sweetie. Want to have breakfast with Auntie Flo?" Carrie nodded, rubbing her eyes, and positioned herself on the closed toilet seat to take waking up slowly. Chris leaned back in the hot water and closed her eyes.

When Chris was six years old she had wanted to be a singing ballerina. A star. She had wonderful fantasies about wowing her friends with performances—Shirley Temple fantasies with full production sets.

At twelve she had wanted to be a chemist. She saw herself in a lab coat and glasses—and when she took the glasses off she was beautiful, a gorgeous intellectual smarter than all the handsome young scientists around her. Soon she discovered that chemistry involved math. *C'est la vie.*

At sixteen she hungered for travel and decided to be a flight attendant. Flo took whole summers off two years in a row to accompany her around the world, to help her fill that need for expansion, appalled by the prospect of Chris's serving drinks on an air carrier.

At eighteen she was in college, reading her heart out. Flo bought every book that Chris wanted to discuss. They talked on the phone for hours each week. Flo traveled to

New York often to take Chris and her friends to plays, museums, art galleries and on plentiful shopping trips. All Chris's friends idolized Flo. Chris was not interested in business, but she wanted desperately to be like her Aunt Flo.

Carrie wandered over to the tub and started playing with her bath toys. "Carrie, I'm taking a bath."

Carrie was now pushing an empty shampoo container under the water, filling it and pouring it out. "I won't get you wet, Mommy."

Chris laughed. "Move down by my feet then," she said, wondering how she'd come to have such a headache over the people she loved.

At twenty Chris wanted to be the woman behind the man, as her mother had been. She would raise a beautiful family for this sharp young lawyer who had not even given his real name. But all she wanted was to be *his*.

She touched Carrie's curls.

"Mommy, you'll get me wet." Carrie looked up and smiled. "Should I get in?"

"You can have your own bath in a few minutes."

At twenty-five she had to start thinking differently. A divorced mother, short of cash and deep in debt, she couldn't remember who she was or what she wanted. More than to simply survive, though. She began writing, not masterpieces but simple stories for young adults. She wanted to give back some of the fantasies she had used through the years to sustain her impossible, illusive fancies. She knew she was fanciful. Hopeful and idealistic. She had almost lost that because of Steve, and it was what she liked best about herself. Hopeful idealists changed the world. They could also be perfect victims.

Chris was unlike Flo, who had been born to control, and unlike Mike, who addressed life expediently as a series of "informed risks." Chris made up stories for kids who, like her at six and twelve and sixteen, were dreamy, desirous and always wondering the same two things she wondered. One, what was going to happen next? And two, would it all work out?

It didn't take long for her to realize that she loved the way she felt when she was writing, and soon she knew she was fulfilling some kind of inner need and being alone was so much less lonely. Suddenly she found herself working harder than ever to learn how to do it, to make it right, to make it more than right. She took night classes whenever possible, she read how-to-write-and-market-your-book books and articles every Sunday in the library while the kids paged through picture books beside her. She read, studied, typed, tore her work apart, typed some more, scrapped it again. She *had* to get it right, because if she succeeded, she could be happy, she could make money to support her little family, and she could do it in a way important to *her* and the woman she was becoming.

Carrie scampered out of the bathroom, dripping water from her wet sleeves, and scooted back in with more bathtub toys. Chris watched and smiled as Carrie splashed and sang off-key. She decided then and there, looking at her older child, that she would never again call her marriage a mistake. Carrie and Kyle were healthy, smart and her greatest accomplishments. If she had it to do all over again, would she pay almost two million dollars for them? In a second.

"Mommy?"

"Hmm?"

"Mommy, where is my daddy?"

Chris felt her cheeks grow hot. "Well, Carrie, remember I told you that he went away when you were a baby? I don't know where he is. I haven't seen him or talked to him since he went away."

"Does he miss us, then?"

"I... I don't know, honey. But he should miss you, because you're wonderful."

"Mommy? Where is Mike?"

"He's working. We won't see him until tomorrow morning."

"Do I remember my daddy?"

"Well, I don't think so. Do you think you do?"

She shook her head. "Is my daddy the same as Kyle's daddy?"

"Yes," Chris said, appalled. "Of course."

"Is Mike supposed to be our daddy now?"

"Mike... Mike is our very special friend, Carrie, but I'm not married to him."

"He likes us to use his house," she said, smiling at her mother.

"Yes. He does."

"Will he go away from us, then?"

"No, Carrie. No, we will always know where Mike is, and he will always know where we are. Always. Even if we don't use his house forever. Even if we get a house of our own. Do you understand?"

"No."

"Well..." She'd better get used to answering difficult questions, because the older the kids became, the more serious the questions would be. "Well, even if we get our own house again, we will be good friends with Mike. We'll visit him, talk to him on the phone, see him sometimes. I'm sure of that. Do you understand?"

"No. I like Mike's house, and he likes us to use his house."

"Yes, but—"

"Can I watch cartoons until I have my own bath?"

"Yes. If you want to."

Of course she doesn't understand, Chris thought. Neither do I. She worked the drain release with her toe. So, twenty-seven years old, soaking out a headache, what did Chris want? Not a lot, actually. She wanted to keep the rain off her kids' heads, first. She wanted to reconcile with Flo so she could be rooted once more with the people, events and emotions that had shaped her. She wanted a man like Mike—the Mike who loved so deeply and with such involvement that loss made veldt-sores in him—to love *her*. To love them all. And she wanted a few hours a day to become the person she was destined to be—a creative, caring, independent woman. There should be room for all of that without any crowding. It wasn't much to ask. It was not a tiny bit more than those people she loved could afford.

Flo, though sometimes brassy, flashy and bossy, was not really a snob. Chris had been surprised at Flo's treatment of Mike, intimidating him, making it appear that he wasn't good enough. None of the Palmers, though well-to-do, had ever behaved uncharitably toward another human being; they had never taken their privilege for granted or placed themselves above others. Mike, too, had surprised her with his reverse snobbery—jabbing at Flo for having so much, insinuating that bounty made life too easy, accomplishments too effortless.

Grabbing at her was what they'd both done, and it made her very nervous, claustrophobic. Well, in another half hour she'd have it out with Flo.

"I don't know what to say," Flo said at breakfast. "I regret making you unhappy by pressuring Mike that way, but I honestly don't think I'm wrong. He doesn't have much to offer you, and I think you should be more practical."

Chris swallowed coffee as if swallowing fury. "Because he doesn't have a college education? You ought to be ashamed of doing that to him."

"I wasn't doing anything to him. Good Lord, Chris, if anything should happen to him..."

"No, that isn't it. If anything should happen to Mike, I'd have *you*. You're more afraid nothing will happen to him, that I'll stay with him forever. Just as he was afraid you were going to win and take me away. Well, I've got news for the two of you. This is a no-win situation."

"Chris, I'm not in a contest with this man. I feel responsible for you; I simply want you to reappraise the situation."

"Responsible? I'm not twelve, though you treat me as though I am. You keep forgetting that I've managed to keep my children and myself without state aid and without calling you. I did it myself. I didn't do it in designer labels, but I did do it. And reappraise what?"

"Your future plans. There are a lot of things I'd like you to consider. Your education, for instance. If you want to complete college, I think you should. Or if you'd like to consider business, I would be delighted. Whatever."

"Whatever? Or one of those two things?" she responded dryly. Chris reached for Kyle's plate, automatically cutting his room service pancakes for him. "Flo, I have future plans of my own that don't include either of those two things. Besides I don't want to decide my whole future in the next week, so I wish you'd stop listing my options for me."

Carrie tipped her milk and it sloshed onto the table, flowing toward Flo. Flo jerked into action, mopping, her movements almost as natural as Chris's. Flo didn't seem to worry about her expensive slacks; she merely acted, as if she had been mopping up Carrie's spills since birth. Flo had only known her children for three days, Chris reflected, yet they seemed bonded. Connected by blood. Chris shook her head absently. Flo didn't scold Carrie; she simply took care of her. The way she wanted to take care of Chris. The scolding hadn't started until Chris began trying to take care of herself.

"I'm only trying to help," Flo said. "I have no ulterior motives."

"Not consciously. You just want to do for me, show me your generosity and love. So does Mike. He wants to give and have me receive. Here I am being offered so much, from two people I care deeply about, and last night was a nightmare. When I saw the two of you together, I felt as though I didn't know either one of you."

"Well. Are we *both* sorry?"

"Yes," she said, swiveling in her chair to begin cutting Carrie's pancakes. "I haven't spoken to Mike yet, but he wrote an apologetic note before he left for work. I won't see him till tomorrow morning."

"Do you have any idea what you want, Chris?"

"Oh, yes," she said, laughing humorlessly. "I want to see if I can recapture the little bit of sanity I felt between the fire and *The Missing Heiress*. I felt . . . I felt alive, full of feelings that for once didn't conflict or frighten me. I had a sense of family—there was Mike and his people drawing me in. And even though I was too proud or stubborn to call you yet, I was getting closer. I had safety, pleasure, hope and desire. I felt protected but independent. And then it all changed."

"Come now, let's not get melodramatic, Chris. Did I make our reconciliation difficult? I may not have cozied up to the fireman too well, but—"

"Difficult? Heavens, no, it was just the opposite. Our reunion was so ideal I was spinning from it. You forgave me for all the trouble I've caused you when I'd half expected you to refuse to speak to me. I felt like a baby you'd waited seven years to give birth to."

Flo sighed and pulled out a cigarette. "I suppose I've failed again somehow," she said.

"When have you ever failed at anything? The fact is, you offer me so much that it's impossible for me to live up to it."

"Christine, let's not—"

"But it's true! You want so much for me that I find it hard to want anything for myself! You can dress me, style my hair, discuss my future, spoil my kids. We've barely talked in seven years. Do you even know me, Flo? Or are you trying to create me?" She felt her eyes well with tears. "I'm sorry. I didn't mean to cry about it."

"You're overwrought. You need—" She stopped herself.

Chris wiped her eyes. "You see? If you keep doing that, I'll have to keep fighting you. I want to have our friendship back, Flo, but with give-*and*-take. As it stands, the only thing I can give you is obedience, and I'm too old to be happy with that."

Flo pursed her lips, and when she spoke, her voice was scratchy. It was the closest Chris had ever seen her come to crying. "I just don't want you to be hurt. I don't want to lose you. Again."

"I'm going to carve a little niche out of this world that's all mine. Not a big chunk—just a little niche. I don't want to buy the world a Coke or conquer outer space, I just want to take care of my kids and work on becoming the best of who I really am. There's more to me than being your child, Stever's latest con or Mike's charity case.

That's what I was working on, Flo, when the house burned down."

"This has something to do with this idea of writing?" she asked. "Because if all you want is to be independent, to be able to write—"

"No. Yes. I mean, I was writing, and I plan to keep writing—I'm even crazy enough to think I'm going to succeed at it. What I have to do is make sure the decisions I make belong to me. I want to pay for my own mistakes. I want to take credit for my accomplishments. I don't want to be taken care of anymore."

"What I'd like to know," Flo said slowly, "is why it is reasonable for you to live in the fireman's house and eat his food and take his presents, but it's wrong for you to—"

Chris shook her head. "You don't get it, do you? I'm not going to give my life to him the way I did with Steve, and I'm not going to keep taking from him, either. I'm willing to share my life, my space, all that I am, but *share*, Flo. With you, with him and, hopefully, with others, because I've been alone way too long."

"And you can't come with me and share your life with him, only the other way around, is that it? He sounded as determined about what you need as I did, you know."

"If that turns out to be true, then it won't work."

"Why would you take that chance? Why not—"

"Because I love him." There. She'd said it. Shouldn't lightning strike or fireworks go off?

"That's ridiculous," said Flo.

"But it's true, just the same," she replied, exasperated.

"You're setting yourself up for some real trouble, Chris," Flo solemnly predicted. "You're going to get yourself hurt all over again. You hardly know this—"

"No, I'm not. I'm not setting myself up for anything at all. When I give up and let other people take over, then I'm in for it. I may be a lot of things—impetuous, idealistic, maybe even foolish, but dammit, I'm going to see if this is what I think it is. And if it isn't, I'll cry and be done with it. I won't lose two million dollars, I won't get pregnant, and I won't forget what I want from life. I'll cry. There are worse things."

"What about the kids? What about what they'll—"

"The kids," she said, "already love both of you." Carrie looked up. Her eyes were round and large; she knew there was something serious going on, but she didn't know what. "They shouldn't have to give up Mike to have you, or vice versa."

"He's awfully possessive."

"Said the pot," Chris quipped.

"We've never had any kind of family life together, Chris. Within a year of Randy's and Arlene's death you were gone. With that—"

"I got married. Maybe you didn't approve, but the reality is that I grew up and got married. And get this: I'm *glad* I did, because I have Carrie and Kyle. I'm a grown-up now, Flo. I can't go back to being the child you can spoil and discipline. We have to get together a new set of rules for our family life. I don't want to be all you have. I don't want you to be all I have. Go home, Flo," she softly advised. "It's the only way I can come home to you, which is all you really want, anyway."

"When is that going to happen, Chris? I don't want us to be estranged forever."

"It's never going to happen the way you think it should. When I go back to Chicago, I'll be a visitor or finding my own place. Flo, let go of me. Love me for myself, not for what you can do for me. Please."

They reached a tense compromise. Flo set up a checking account for Chris with a tidy sum deposited; she simply couldn't leave any other way. Flo took Chris's word that if the worst happened and the fireman turned out to be a big lout, Chris and the kids would rent something *decent*—with smoke alarms and everything. And they decided that if Chris remained in California through Christmas, Flo would have her tongue removed or her lips sutured shut and would return in time to celebrate with them all. She would be nice to Mike or else. Chris promised to call Flo frequently to reassure her they really were reunited.

And she still cried at the airport.

Mr. Blakely's address was in the phone book. Chris took the kids out for a hamburger and then pulled up to the landlord's house at just about the dinner hour. She was not in the least surprised to find he and his family occupied a substantial piece of real estate while they rented out hovels in poor repair. Still, she felt tension grating like sandpaper against her backbone—the backbone she was only just remembering she had. She wanted to do this exactly once.

"Hello, Mrs. Blakely. I'm Christine Palmer. Is your husband at home, please?"

"I don't believe we have any business with you. You can have your lawyer—"

Chris unfolded the tabloid so that her picture flashed in the woman's chubby, ruddy face. Mrs. Blakely looked like a mean, unhappy person; she had frown lines and downcast eyes that could flare wide in surprise, like now. She was about four weeks behind on her strawberry-blond dye job; her gray roots moored her frazzled mop. The house they lived in had been custom-built and appeared both well cared for and expensive. Mrs. Blakely, a fiftyish woman, looked out of place in the doorway. She was heavy, sloppily attired in a floral cotton housedress, and held a smoldering cigarette between her yellowed fingers.

"I'm the 'missing heiress,' Mrs. Blakely, and if you let me see your husband, we can complete this transaction in a few minutes. Then I will leave you alone. If you force me to call my attorney about this, it will cost you, because I am angry."

The woman stood still for a second, stunned. Then she slowly turned like a rotating statue. "Henry," she called.

He, too, looked out of place in such a decorous environment. He wore a white undershirt, slippers, baggy pants with his belly hanging obtrusively over his belt, and he had a nasty cigar in his mouth. The slumlord.

Mrs. Blakely passed the tabloid to her husband, who looked at the picture and then Chris, taking the cigar from his mouth. She gave him a minute to get the headline, but no more. "We can settle this in five minutes, Mr. Blakely. Your faulty furnace not only destroyed my every worldly possession, it nearly killed us all. In fact, I was rescued from the burning house. Now, I am not a difficult person, only fair. I would like some refunds and some restitution. There is the matter of the deposit—the first and last months' rent—the rent I paid for the month of November, and lost valuables." She reached into her purse. She unfolded an itemized list and held it out to him. Her children stood stoically on each side of her. "I take responsibility for fifty percent of the possessions lost in the fire because I did not have renter's insurance, which I should have had. I will take twenty-five hundred dollars now, or I will take you to court and sue for pain and suffering, as well. And I can get the best lawyer in the country."

"Um . . . maybe you'd better come in."

"No, that won't be necessary. I'll wait right here. It won't take you that long to write a check."

A teenager shrieked from inside the big house. "Mother! Where is my—"

"Shut up, Ellen! Just a minute!" Mrs. Blakely barked.

"I oughta check with my lawyer before I—" the landlord began.

"That won't take long, either. Here's what he'll tell you: if you have been approached with an itemized list of damages and you have made restitution in that exact amount, she really won't have a leg to stand on in court if she comes after you for more. Unless, of course, there are injuries, which there were not. Now, let's get this over with, shall we?"

Mrs. Blakely glared at Chris from behind her husband. She crossed her arms over her ample chest while Henry Blakely shuffled away with the list in his hand. The worst of it, Chris believed, was the fact that they had no remorse for the danger they had allowed in renting poorly maintained property. That the rent had been low did not absolve them. The malfunctioning furnace was Henry Blakely's fault, and he had never even called to see if Chris and her children were all right. Mrs. Blakely, who should be flushing in shame at her husband's callous evasion of responsibility, stood like a sentry in the doorway while the unrepentant man went in pursuit of a phone call or a check or a better idea.

These people were poor and didn't know it, Chris decided.

"Here," he said, handing her a check in less than ten minutes. "I don't want to hear from you again."

"Oh, you won't, believe me." And she walked away from them, pity for their selfishness leaving a sour taste in her mouth.

* * *

She was up, dressed and had the coffee brewed when Mike came home from the station early in the morning, beginning his four days off.

"We're on our own for a while?" Mike asked when Chris told him Flo had gone. "What does that mean?"

"I've convinced Flo to back off and give me some room. She acted like an ass. I'm really sorry."

"Not that I was any Prince Charming. I don't usually act that way around anyone."

"Neither does she."

"She, uh, spoke with some experience," he said.

"Oh, she's a born fighter, don't get me wrong. But she's not the snob she appeared to be. She wants me back, wants me home. It's been a long separation."

"But you didn't go."

Chris sighed. "Not because I don't love her. I need Flo in my life. She can be a real pain, but we have a lot of good history, too. The Flo you met was not my generous and strong friend, but a terrified mother lion afraid of losing her cub. I apologize for her."

Mike nodded, then changed the subject. "I had this idea about Christmas," he said. "The kids like the cabin so much, I thought we might go there, have a real Christmas, chop our own tree—"

"What about your family?" she asked.

"They could spare my presence for one year. What about yours?"

"She'll come back, Mike, if this is where I am through the holidays. You don't have to accept Flo, but I can't reject my family any more than you can reject yours. Flo has never been with the kids for the holidays."

"Maybe I should call up to Pembroke Pines and see if the caterer is busy. Or will she bring her own staff?"

She flinched.

"Sorry. It's just that she made me feel so damned inadequate. Middle class. I've never felt that way before. I guess I wanted to be the one to give you a chance to rebuild your life."

Chris bit her lip. "Maybe we should talk about this. Maybe you found me easy to care about when you thought I was helpless, destitute. Is it harder for you because I'm not? Just how far do you want to go to see if this crazy thing is real?"

He didn't hesitate to think it over. "I want to go all the way to the end. Wherever that is."

Chapter Eleven

Mrs. Cavanaugh is cooking an Irish stew,'' Hal said, placing the plates around the table.

Mike turned from the pot he was stirring and grinned at Hal. ''It's spaghetti,'' he said.

''Everything you cook tastes like Irish stew.''

''Hey, lay off,'' Stu said. ''I love Mrs. Cavanaugh's Irish spaghetti.''

''I'd put my cooking against yours any day of the week,'' Mike challenged Hal. ''My red beans and rice against your chili.''

''Against my potato soup, and you have a deal.''

''Name the day and put some green on it.''

''Hey, how are things with the heiress?''

Mike stirred the pot again. ''Don't call her that, okay?''

''Uh-oh. What's the matter, Little Mike? Chris go home to Auntie Flo?''

"I'd go for the aunt," Stu said. "In a minute, I'd go for the aunt. My wife would write me a note."

"My wife asked me to make a play for the aunt, and then send money."

"The auntie has gone away, for now, while Little Mike thinks about the furniture business."

Mike dumped the spaghetti into a colander. "You wanna eat, dog-breath?"

"No kidding, what's going on? You getting married?"

"Married?" he asked, as though amazed. Was he that transparent? "I've only known her a few weeks."

"What's taking you so long?" Hal asked.

"I'd have her in front of the priest," Stu said. "She's loaded, right? She's cute, too—I saw that much. Stupid me, I shoulda gotten into that house ahead of him."

"You're married already, Stuart. Although I know you tend to forget that from time to time."

"I have these blackouts. Spells."

"Yeah. You keep getting engaged."

"Naw. I go steady sometimes. A little."

There was laughter. Mike rinsed the spaghetti. He had a hard time with Stu sometimes—didn't like the way he handled personal business. Otherwise he liked him. Good fire fighter. A little green about life, but good in a fire. If Stu knew what it was like to lose a family, he wouldn't waste precious time away from his; he wouldn't fool around on his wife. Hal, young like Stu, still less than thirty, got a big kick out of Stu's antics, but Hal didn't fool around. He was serious about his young family. Mike liked that. Hal was a good cook, too. He had a little business on the side when he wasn't fighting fires, which was typical of firemen.

Jim Eble was Mike's closest friend besides family. They were nearly the same age and had worked the same rig for five years. They were alike in personal values as well as sharing many favorite pastimes. But Jim couldn't go fishing with Mike too often because he drove an ambulance part-time when he wasn't on duty; he'd be paying for college educations before long.

Mike was the only one, in fact, who didn't work at something else when he wasn't here. His income was plentiful for a single man, and with all the other kids in the family married and off doing their family things, he used his days off to make sure his mom and dad had everything they needed. And he liked to go to the cabin. Maybe he didn't have another business, but things like hunting, fishing, camping and riding took time. There was no work he liked more than this work. The furniture business? In a pig's eye.

"Don't let 'em get to you, Little Mike," Jim said while they did the dishes.

"They don't get to me. They're having fun. That's okay."

"Things are okay with Chris, then?"

"Yeah, I guess. I mean, she's the same person I pulled out of the house, right?"

"Well, is she?"

"Yeah, sure."

"Hey, Little Mike, don't let the bull from these guys get in your way, huh? You know what you want, right?"

No, he didn't know what he wanted. He thought he knew, but now he wasn't sure. Sure that he loved her a lot, yes. But all that other stuff, money, was getting to him. Getting him down.

How good he had felt when he carried bags and bags of groceries into the house to fill them up—to fill them up because they were empty. He had felt like a man, a dad, a provider. Maybe it wasn't his right, but he had. He liked to put himself to use that way.

That was what fire fighters did; they helped people who needed help. It didn't stop after the fire was out or the victim saved. They had their charities, individually and as a group. They were called upon to teach kids, help little old ladies, organize benefits. Brave men and women. Fire fighters helped people much more gracefully than they accepted help.

Then Chris didn't need so much anymore, and things changed. It wasn't his feelings for Chris and the kids and that stupid dog that had changed; it was this terrible discomfort he felt in his gut because he wasn't in charge anymore. Because without him they could survive just fine. He wanted to be the one they needed the most. He wouldn't have thought this would be so hard. This was a side of himself he didn't like.

Packages in Christmas wrap had arrived from Aunt Flo, in case Chris and the kids were still with him by then. Without opening them, he knew they were expensive presents. When he took his jacket out of the hall closet to go to work this morning, he had looked at Chris's jackets. More than one now. He had spent a lot on the jackets he bought for Chris and Carrie and Kyle so they could go up to the snowy hills. Now, in the front closet, was a new suede coat. Auntie Flo had probably paid ten times as much. He felt reduced.

Chris looked different now. Even though she looked better than ever, he wanted it all to have come from him. It was unfair, and he knew it, but it was still fighting inside him. He thought about his family and knew money shouldn't bother him so much. His brother Chris had a lot of money. Orthodontics was a good-paying profession, and Chris was a clever investor. Money could be loads of fun. He thought about his sister Mo who made way more money than her husband, and how stupid he thought it was that they should ever argue about it. What was the difference how much or whose or where it came from if it put food on the table and provided for the future? So why, he asked himself, was he feeling the opposite of his own beliefs?

On the first night he stayed with her in his own house he had opened up a secret part of himself and told her about his deepest pain. The shamelessness of it didn't humiliate him; he was ready to be as frank about his weakness as he had been obvious in his strength. But now, when he had this little injury inside over her money and her aunt, he didn't talk to her about it. He didn't say, "I'm in pain because you're buying new sheets when I want to buy them for you. I hurt because I feel not good enough. I'm afraid I can't give you anything." He said, "Looks nice." Then he sulked. And his pain popped out somewhere else. He yelled at the dog for chewing his socks, when he would have gladly fed Cheeks a thousand pairs for a feeling of security.

Jealous and stupid, he chided himself silently. He hoped he would get over it, because he was afraid to expose himself to Chris as the selfish jerk he really was. If she found out how tough this was for him, how much he hated that witch, Florence, how much he prayed Florence would somehow hit rock bottom, leaving Chris poor and needy again, she would leave him. She would have to. How could she stay with a man like that?

He tried to think of what he had instead of what he wanted, because he still had Chris in his bed at night, and through their intimacy an important part of his identity had returned to him. Sex with her was better than any sex he'd ever had because he loved her so deeply and wanted her so completely. Sometimes he felt surly and unaroused because of self-pity, but once it got rolling, it was fabulous. He tried not to imagine how good it would be if they had years to perfect it. They had already developed fun, lush games....

"Come on, smoky, put out this fire."

"In a minute, in a minute."

"Why do you wait so long?"

"I thought I was making *you* wait."

"I already didn't wait—twice."

And...

"Hug me for a while. Just hug me like you're not interested in sex."

"Hug you until you beg me to move, huh?"

And...

"I'm not even going to take off my shirt until you tell me what you want. No, until you *show* me..."

Well, actually, those things had happened before Flo and the money. Since then he had felt inadequate, insecure. But if Flo and the money disappeared, he would be all right again. Virile. Even with his troubles, bed was still one of their best places these days. Because of the way their bodies worked together like an efficient factory that ran on its own energy. Once it got going and he forgot his anger, she didn't ask him what was wrong and he didn't sulk or worry. He wanted it to go on forever.

He was terrified. He thought he caught a glimpse of the end.

"Flo is coming in on the twenty-third, Mike. She promises to be good. Shall we do Christmas here? Should we take her to your mom and dad's?" Chris had asked.

You can't turn family away at Christmas. You can't. Even if they're awful family. But Flo at his mom and dad's? "Let's do it here. My folks can spare me one year."

He didn't ask her if she was going away after the holiday. He didn't ask her if she was staying. She didn't mention her plans. She didn't ask him if his invitation remained open. Everything seemed to be moving out of reach. Except the money.

Chris had decided she had better not let her ex-husband get away with anything, for Carrie and Kyle's sake. It had been their grandfather's money. Flo could handle it. Chris didn't need it, didn't want it, but it could be put in trust for the kids, and some kind of dividend could be paid while they were growing up to help provide for them. They would never be poor again.

Mike had actually hoped he would be forced to take a second job to finance their college education. Like he had done for Tommy. Stupid thing to wish for, huh?

Chris didn't need that money because she was going to sell books. She loved writing, she was going to start selling, and she had big plans. A career. A good, satisfying one.

One way or the other, Chris was going to be well off. With or without him.

"Why don't you and Chris and the kids come over for dinner?" Jim asked as they washed and dried the last pot.

"Yeah, maybe. There's a lot to do with Christmas, though."

"Yeah, I suppose. Is her aunt coming out here?"

He was slow to answer. "Yeah. Not till the twenty-third, though."

"Little Mike, take it easy. You're not going to marry the aunt, you know."

"Who said I was going to marry anyone?"

"Uh, Mike? Joanie wasn't Catholic when you asked her to marry you, was she?"

"No. Why?"

"Did you tell her that was part of the deal, if you got married?"

"No. I wouldn't do that. I just told her it would make things a lot easier if she would think about it."

"Was it hard to ask her?"

He chuckled. "Yeah. Until I did. I guess I thought she'd get mad."

"What'd she say?"

"You know what she said. She did it, right? She said that wasn't too much to ask."

"Try and remember that, huh?"

Remember what? To ask for what I need? If Chris finds out how much I need, it'll scare her to death. Hell, it scares me to death. I cover up all my needs by filling the needs of others. I give a lot better than I receive.

Remember what? That people make changes in themselves in order to make a couple? I'm trying. I'm trying to change what I feel, but it hammers away inside me that I can't give her as much as Aunt Flo can—as much as she already has, for that matter.

Remember what? That when you lose the one you love, the one you counted on, you lose a part of yourself? Believe me, I remember. That was why I stayed alone.

I remember.

The bell came in. Truck and engine and chief. Mike's heart got a shot of adrenaline. He would only think about fire for a while now. Thank goodness.

* * *

Chris was scared to death of Christmas. Tomorrow Mike started his four days off over the holidays—quite a coup for a fire fighter, to have so much time. In a couple of days Flo would return. If they could get through this, amicably, maybe they could get through the rest. She hoped. But Mike was so distant and quiet that she feared Flo's presence combined with Mike's cautiously suppressed anger was going to drive the last nail into the coffin.

The tree was up in the living room. It was bulging with presents, more presents than she had ever seen in her life. Every time the UPS truck pulled up with another load from Aunt Flo, Mike went out and bought more. There was no telling who would win this contest. Meanwhile the kids were having a time like they had never had. Mike, fortunately, did not seem to discriminate against them because they had wealth and Aunt Flo. His lap received them as dearly as ever.

She had asked Mattie if she could drop by their house. She wasn't sure what she was looking for exactly, but maybe some Cavanaugh wisdom would teach her something about Mike that would make things work. She was willing to do anything—short of changing who she was. Since she felt she had only just discovered the real Chris Palmer, and since she had only just discovered she liked her, she would not abandon herself again. It wouldn't be worth it. Becoming who you thought people wanted you to be made a mockery of real love. Henceforth she would only settle for the real thing.

"Chrissie, you look so different. You're doing your hair different now, huh?" Mattie asked, after she greeted Chris and the children that evening.

"I just got it cut."

"You brought us presents. Oh, Chrissie, you shouldn't have done that. Really. We have so much. Bring everyone in. Come in, come in. I have a bundt cake."

"We brought the dog—I hope you don't mind. Carrie wanted Big Mike to see the dog."

"You brought that dog?" Big Mike asked, walking toward the front door with his newspaper in his hand, hiking up his low-riding pants. "You brought that Creeps to my house?"

Carrie and Kyle giggled happily, looking up at him. How did the children know he was funny, when he never smiled? How did they know he was making jokes? Cheeks stood just behind them, right inside the door, his tail wagging while he growled.

"I don't know why you bring him here. He hates me."

"He doesn't really hate anybody, but he's very crabby."

Big Mike hunched down and reached between the children to scratch under Cheeks's chin. Cheeks growled louder; his tail wagged. "This dog is a mess," Big Mike said. "Look at him. He wants to be petted, but he makes all this noise. What a terrible dog he is. I think somebody hit this dog in the head, huh?"

"We think somebody was mean to him when he was a puppy," Carrie said. "We think it was a *man*. He's always crabby to men, but not to girls."

"You're so tough, aren't you, Creeps. Come on then. Come on, Creeps," Big Mike said, straightening and walking into the living room, the wagging, growling dog following, the children giggling.

"Come in and have coffee, Chrissie. It's so cold. We might even get a little snow."

Chris took off her coat and tossed it over a chair. The kids were already sitting at Big Mike's feet, laughing as he said the dog's name wrong and made him look stupid, growling while he was being stroked.

Chrissie carried the presents into the kitchen. Mattie, who had waddled ahead of her, already had a coffee cup filled. "These are for the whole family, Mattie, but they're mostly for you. We picked them out together, and I want you to open them early."

"You shouldn't have, really. We have so much already."

"Go ahead. It isn't much."

It only took Mattie a minute to get inside the first box. Chris had tried to get exactly the right thing. A Christmas platter, a decorated lazy Susan, red napkins in green holly rings—enough for the whole clan, plus extras.

"I thought maybe you would like something like this. You have everyone here at Christmas, right?"

"Perfect, perfect. How nice you are to do this, Chrissie. How nice. Everyone will love it. Yes, they all come here, though I don't know why. Chris and Stacy have a big place with lots more room. They could have Christmas there, but they don't." Mattie lowered her voice to a whisper. "I think they don't like Big Mike to drive so much. At night, and all." She resumed in her normal voice. "Everyone comes here to this tiny house where we can't even move, but they come. I don't know why."

How they care for one another, Chris thought. As if they had secrets from one another, which they didn't. "I know why," she said, smiling. "This is where they belong. I love watching your family together. You're right, Mattie. You have so much."

"We've been blessed, me and Big Mike. Oh, we had our troubles like everyone else. Broken bones, for instance." She laughed. "You don't have four boys without broken bones. And the like. But we do okay, I think. Kids. They put you through it, huh?"

"You know, you've probably seen all that stuff in the paper about me, and Mike might have mentioned—"

"He told us a little bit about your aunt coming, but we don't ask him, Chrissie. It isn't our business, this with your aunt and all."

"Well, still, I'd like to explain some of that." Big Mike came into the kitchen to fill his coffee mug. "I want to tell you both," she amended, "that I haven't been taking advantage or—"

"You never mind about that, Chrissie," Big Mike said. "You don't need to tell us anything."

"It must seem so bizarre, all this 'missing heiress' nonsense. That's not really what I am at all. I was out of touch with my aunt because I was sure she would be too angry to even speak to me. I didn't know I was 'missing.' And I'm not an heiress. My aunt still runs the family business, which was half my dad's, but, well, it's not Exxon or anything. It's worth a lot, I guess, but that doesn't mean I'm really rich."

They looked at her, Big Mike by the coffeepot with his mug in his hand, Mattie at the kitchen table with her.

"I'm really not as different as I must seem."

"You don't seem different to us, Chrissie. We don't care about that story."

"But Mike..." Her voice drifted off for a moment. "I think Mike might have some trouble with it. I'm looking for a way to make him believe that I'm the same person who checked groceries at Iverson's. It's too bad it all came out so fast, and in such a bizarre way."

"Little Mike is a pretty smart boy," Mike said. "He doesn't do things he doesn't want to do. And he doesn't believe a lot of stories."

"Well, the stories are pretty much true," she said. "It just seems that Mike liked having us with him a lot more before he found out where I came from."

"You don't have to tell us about this," Mattie said, almost entreating Chris to shut up.

Chris was afraid she might cry. I love him, she wanted to say. I love him and I want him to love me the way I am, whether dead broke or monied.

"The boy likes to take care of everyone," Big Mike grumbled. "He does that with us, too. He's always taking care of us. He built that storage shed out back. He comes over, says he bought this storage shed. I say I don't need a storage shed, but he wants me to have it. So fine, I tell him. I have it. Thank you very much. But he can't let it go at that. He has to build it, too. Then he can go home, right? No. Then he has to put my lawn mower and things in it. Now he can be done with it, huh? No. He comes over to use the things he put in it. Sometimes he has to clean it out. And fix the roof. And trim the trees around the house. And paint this and that. Whew," he said, waving a hand. "He just likes to be useful."

Chris smiled in spite of herself. "How do you handle him when he gets like that. How do you act?"

"I act like I always act. 'What do I need some damned storage shed for?' I say. He builds it anyway."

"That's Little Mike," Mattie said, laughing. "We should slice up this cake."

"You just tell Little Mike you don't need it—he'll force it on you anyway."

"But," Chris said, "I can't do that."

"No, I guess not. Then you tell him to stick it in his ear if he doesn't like it."

"Don't tell her what to say, Mike," Mattie said. "Never mind him, Chrissie. He doesn't know what he's talking about. He's an old man who gets himself into all the kids' business. He gives them marriage counseling. If they listened to him, they'd all be getting divorces. Never mind him. We just want Little Mike to be happy, is all."

"Me too," she said.

"Then everything works itself out, huh?"

"You want to make him happy, huh?" Big Mike scoffed. "Tell him, 'Stick it in your ear, I don't want a damned storage shed,' or whatever. He'll be happy." Big Mike went out of the kitchen.

Mattie got out plates and started slicing pieces of cake. You couldn't come to this house and not eat, Chris decided. They fill you up in any way they can.

"What's hard for Mike," she told Mattie, "is that he wants very much to do for us, give to us. It makes him feel good."

"Yes, he's that way. He does for everyone."

"I think he's afraid there isn't anything I need anymore. With this business about my aunt, about money."

"Well, I didn't raise the boy that way, Chrissie. Little Mike knows the important things money can't buy. I made sure my kids knew that, growing up. We didn't have too much then, when they were little, but I was real careful that they knew what's important. And I was real careful they knew people learned that two ways. One way was if they didn't have a lot of money but they had a good life. The other way was if they had a lot of money and that wasn't all they needed."

Mattie put a plate and fork in front of Chris. "He's a bullheaded boy, Little Mike, but he's pretty sharp. Don't listen to the old man; just give Little Mike some time to remember about that. A little time. He had some trouble in the third grade. In the seventh grade, too, if I remember. Maybe remembering things takes him a little time."

It might serve just as well, Chris thought, to tell him to stick it in his ear. "A little time," she repeated.

"He'll catch on eventually." Mattie laughed. "Will the kids eat the cake?"

"They'd love it," she said. And then the sirens came. Time stood still. The shrill noise mounted. They lived near the firehouse. Mattie continued slicing cake and an odd staticlike sound came from the living room.

"What's that?" Chris asked.

"We turn on the scanner sometimes when we hear the sirens. We worry a little bit, but we don't tell him. He knows it, but we don't tell him. He likes to think he's on his own."

Mattie's hand went into her apron pocket, and something in there rattled softly. Chris knew without asking that they were rosary beads. "Bring your cake," Mattie said. "We'll listen."

Big Mike said it was a house fire. At first it didn't sound too serious. She heard Mike's voice on the radio. The engine, Big Mike explained. Then the truck with the hydraulics. Another engine—maybe it was getting a little hot. Then another alarm. Police and ambulances. Chris started getting nervous following the fire by radio calls like this. She would never have one of those things, never! Then she wondered if she could get to Radio Shack before they closed to get her own.

Next the hazardous materials squad was called in. There had been an explosion. Mike's company was initiating rescue, though it was not Mike's voice they heard. And then, with eerie screeching through the little living room, came the news that there were fire fighters down.

"God!" Chris said, straightening. "What do we do now?"

"Shh. We listen, that's all."

"Will they say the names?"

"No, they don't."

"Oh, God, why can't he be a house painter? This is horrible. Horrible!"

"No, they know what they're doing. They know."

"I don't know if I can take this."

"What would you change?" Big Mike asked. "What one thing would you change?"

"I would have sent him to law school," Chris said.

"Oh? He's been a fire fighter twelve years now," Big Mike said. "If I had had the money to send him to law school, maybe about twenty-seven people would be dead. He takes chances, yes. About twenty-seven people, alive right now because he didn't go to law school, should thank me because I didn't have the money."

Because, Chris thought, he goes into fires to pull people out whenever he has to, no matter how scary and dangerous. And he can't think in terms of luck or miracles, because how often can you expect your luck to hold or a miracle to happen? He can't think about being heroic; he's just doing the job he was trained to do. An informed risk. Like love. Please, God.

Mattie rattled her beads.

Chapter Twelve

Engine 56 was the first on the scene, followed by the truck with hydraulics in close pursuit and another engine on its way. Two engines and a truck were standard equipment response for a house fire. There were no cops yet. The fire fighters could count on an automatic response of two squad cars; they could also count on beating the cops to the fire. Mike's company's average response time was three minutes.

A civilian stood on the curb. He would have called in the alarm. The neighborhood was old but high-rent. The houses were all two-story, Victorian styles, around sixty to seventy years old but usually in excellent repair. The biggest problem with the houses here would be basement fires that could spread to the attic because of the absence of fire-stops. A maze of kindling.

This particular house had a nice big circular drive and an attached garage, from which smoke poured.

"I don't like 'em," Jim said, speaking of garage fires. Garages could be full of surprises; people stored paints, thinners, gas cans and such there. Not to mention cars.

As men sprang off the truck and engine, the neighbor jogged over. He was a little breathless, nervous. "There was a bunch of kids around here earlier—might've been a party. They have a lot of traffic around this place."

"Do you think there's anybody inside?" Mike asked the man.

He shrugged. "Could be. People coming and going all the time—parties and stuff. Could be a bunch of drunk teenagers in there."

Jim returned to the engine with a gas can in his gloved hand. He had gotten it from the driveway. He shook his head and set it down. This one might have been set; people didn't often leave empty gas cans in their driveways. Mike talked to the man briefly to determine when he had noticed the smoke, whether he'd seen anybody around—standard questions. He called for the peanut line to fog the site of the fire, while the ladder-company men approached the place with axes and pike poles. The truck men would cut the utilities and open it up; engine men would set up hoses and water. They pulled out tarps that would be used to protect the contents of the house from water, mud and other internal damage.

But the number-one priority was life. Structural consideration was always number-two. Jim was moving quickly, despite a hundred pounds of turnouts and equipment on his body, to the front door, next to the garage. He applied a firm shoulder to the door, pushed it open and went in.

Judging from a big bay window that faced the street and smaller windows above, the house might have a living room or dining room on the ground-level front, kitchen in the back. The front door and garage were to the right, bedrooms upstairs. Maybe as much as three thousand square feet, and a basement and attic. And this one just might have been torched.

The chief's car pulled up, and he relieved Mike with the civilian. Mike was moving to join Jim in the house when it blew. The garage door cracked down the middle, and debris flew down the drive. Two firemen en route to the site fell like dominoes. There was a medley of curses around the truck and engine while two fire fighters ran to the felled men to pull them away. But they were rolling over to stand up on their own steam.

Mike crouched away from the explosion for a second, but he couldn't take his eyes off the front door. It was no longer accessible, but blocked by debris and rolling gray smoke. Flames were licking out of the place where his best friend had gone in.

Then the chief was there beside him. "We have a man in the building," Mike told the chief. "Number 56 will initiate rescue; tell engine 60 to take over incident command. I'm going after Eble. Jim."

The chief called in a code 2 for the hazardous-materials squad. They didn't know yet what they had to deal with. They didn't know yet what had exploded or whether there was more. They'd use as little water on it as possible until they knew more about it.

Mike couldn't get in the front door, but the flames from the garage had not yet reached the living room window. A shovel lay in a flower bed at his feet, and he picked it up and smashed the big bay window. He hurriedly cleared the glass and climbed in, covering his mouth with the air pack mouthpiece. This meant, unfortunately, that he couldn't call out to Jim.

These old Victorian monsters were built like mazes with lots of rooms clustered amid stairwells and hallways. Jim would probably have gone through the downstairs quickly, looking for people, and then headed for the upstairs bedrooms.

The first thing that struck Mike as odd was the total absence of furniture. What kind of place was this? People coming and going, but no furniture? To have a lot of company, you had to have a couch to sit on. He got a sick feeling in the pit of his stomach. He was guessing what was wrong.

Typical of these old houses, there was a front staircase, now blocked by debris from the explosion and with flames climbing in through the damaged wall that separated house and garage. But there proved to be another set of stairs behind the kitchen. Mike took them quickly. At the top he looked down a hallway, with bedroom doors on each side, to the landing of the front stairwell. There he saw him, lying twisted, half on his side, half on his back, maybe dead, maybe unconscious.

Jim's blackened and bleeding forehead was either injured from flying debris or hurt by his fall but not burned. And he was alive, thank God. His red, watering eyes stared up into Mike's face. A wooden chest of some kind lay on top of his leg, a board across his ribs. His arm was stretched out toward his leg, as if he'd attempted to free himself. He was wearing his air pack, but his eyes were filled with agony.

Mike tossed off the trunk as though it weighed two pounds rather than fifty and threw off the board. He couldn't let Jim lie there or take the time to immobilize the leg. He grabbed Jim's collar and dragged him backward a little way before bending down to lift him. He heard the awful growl of his friend's pain. More than 260 pounds of

Jim Eble in his arms made Mike's heart pound, his muscles strain and bulge, but this was his best friend. There was no lighter load.

He started back the way he had come, toward the rear stairwell, but upon passing a bedroom door that was ajar, he looked in. There he saw what it was about. The room was filled with tables, glassware, sacks, tanks, tubing. A drug lab.

He grabbed the doorknob with the hand under Jim's knees and pulled it closed. And then he got the hell out of there.

He exited the building from the back door and carried Jim around the house to the front, where the equipment was parked. The chief met them. Mike couldn't talk until he laid Jim gently on the ground and pulled away his mask.

"Got a drug lab on the second floor, front bedroom. Maybe propane gas tanks in there. Do we have a code 2? They on their way?"

"Yep. I'll tell 'em when they get here. And a second alarm. How's Eble?"

"Jim?" Mike said to his friend.

"Goddamn trunk," he groaned. "Came flying at me, hit me in the back of the knees." He coughed. "Crunch," he said, tears pouring down his cheeks.

Mike heard the chief telling the police to empty out the neighborhood for a half-mile circumference, and the ambulances started arriving. There were three fire fighters down, but Jim had the worst injury. His leg was almost certainly broken, his head was cut and scraped and his jaw was already starting to swell. He had arm and shoulder pain as well, maybe a dislocation of the shoulder. The paramedics began cutting off his turnouts, trying to start an IV, applying bandages to his face.

Mike stayed nearby for a few minutes, looking on. He thought briefly about what Mattie and Big Mike were hearing on the scanner. On-site explosion. Code 2. Fire fighters down, ambulances dispatched. Injuries. Second alarm. Arson-investigation team called in. Additional police backup. Evacuation of neighborhood.

Mike guessed what had happened. A home drug lab, doing a big business in the area, especially for kids, and somebody got ticked off—maybe wanting a bigger piece of the action, or maybe unhappy they weren't being extended any credit. Someone had decided to set a little fire, burn them out. The do-it-yourself chemists were using propane gas and had extra tanks stored in the garage.

If the fire fighters couldn't contain the blaze in the garage, keep it on the lower level, it might reach the lab. It could turn this area into a gas chamber. Hydrogen cyanide, probably.

The Firebird—hazardous-materials men—came around the drive.

When the paramedics moved away from Jim for a few moments, Mike crouched beside him and asked, "You okay?"

"Damn. No. Got an aspirin?"

Mike smiled in spite of himself. "I gotta get back into the fire."

"Yeah," Jim panted. "Get the SOB. Please."

"You bet, bud."

Not a good fire. Oh, it would have been okay if there hadn't been chemicals that might blow, or injuries. Mike had tackled fires in old Victorians like this one, with hallways and rooms like mazes, twisting and turning and ending up blocked. Once inside you didn't know how you'd gotten in or where you might get out. It was a challenge.

But this one was no good and it had to be stabilized before the heat got to the lab. Otherwise...

They managed to get the hose in the front door, over the debris, and hit the garage from all sides, while above, the men opened up the roof with pike poles to let the smoke and steam escape.

Mike fought it like fighting time. With vengeance and anger. The HM squad in their rubber splash suits wandered through the upstairs, isolating the bad stuff, moving some of it out. Mike rallied to the race. It was a race to beat the fire before the fire beat them. And he wouldn't take a break, wouldn't call for relief.

He had not felt this good, or this bad, in a long time.

Dawn was dirty. The truck company would be left along with the Drug Enforcement Administration when engine 56 roared out. They smelled pretty bad. The structure was mostly intact; a lot of damage to the ground level, but the flames had never licked up against all those chemicals and gases. The DEA pulled orange tape across the site. A couple of lanky teenage boys were being cuffed and put in the back of a squad car. Arrests. For arson? Or for home chemistry? Mike hated to see anybody get away with either one. Especially since it had hurt a fire fighter.

Different kinds of fires led to different kinds of feelings, especially about injuries. When you had a man injured saving a life in a legitimate, accidental fire, that was one thing. You felt proud, somehow, that one of you could be there, doing that. But when a good fire fighter was downed in a torch job, or something like this, a vendetta among underworld slime that poisoned society with their drugs, it was like there was no justice. Putting out the fire just wasn't enough.

Mike noticed that Stu, dragging along in his filthy turnouts on his way to the engine, paused at the squad car. He took off his helmet and his gloves and stared into the back seat of the police car. He spit on the ground, then moved on.

It took a while for the talk to start after a bad fire. At first it seemed there was nothing to say. Then there was so much to say, you couldn't shut anybody up. But it was shift change. Not very many men would shower at the station; most of them wanted to get home, get out of there, before the next shift had time to think of a lot of questions.

There was one question, though, that no one would leave before having answered. And so Mike reported.

"Jim's got scrapes, a broken collarbone, broken femur—the big one, here," he said, tapping his thigh. "But he's all straightened out, no surgery, casted up, and higher than a kite on morphine. He'll be in a while, and it's too soon to know if there's any disability, but the doctor doesn't think so. Nice clean break."

Then he told everyone what a good job they had done. Then he thanked God for that little bit of luck that had Jim Eble all the way upstairs instead of on the steps when that propane blew. Five seconds, either way, would have cost them all dearly.

Chapter Thirteen

Mike went to the hospital when his shift was relieved. It could have been much worse than it was, but he was not surprised that Jim's wife, Alice, fell against him, releasing some of those pent-up tears. Hearing your husband was down in a fire was the dreaded news. Finding out he was alive was a huge relief, but temporary, because next you had to know how alive he was.

"It's only a couple of broken bones," Mike said. "How's he doing?"

"He's doing great," she said, sniffing, "but I thought I would have a breakdown. Thank God he's all right."

The newspapers sometimes ran stories about downed fire fighters—basically they covered the fire, part of which was a fire fighter hurt and hospitalized—but they didn't often follow up with stories about the ex–fire fighter locksmith or shoe salesman. The stuff they didn't print was the terrifying stuff. Like the early-retirement injuries. Fire fighters paralyzed by a fall. There were sprains, breaks and smoke inhalation—and then there were horrific injuries that made you wonder if life was the best deal for the poor guy. Like the fire fighter, some years back, who had been rendered brain damaged by carbon monoxide gas from a leaking air pack. Freak things.

Then there were the heart attacks. It wasn't only from breathing smoke or straining the muscles; it was from the alarms. The stress, not from the fire—but from the constant shots of adrenaline that presented the flight-or-fight conflict to the body. Like getting an electric shock on a regular basis. Young men, sometimes, fell because of this.

"You doing okay?" Mike asked Jim.

"No, I'm not doing okay," he said, trying to smile but giving a lopsided grimace through bandages that covered his right eye and chin. His arm cast was elevated, his casted leg hefted off the bed by weights and pulleys. "This had to happen right before my time off. Some luck, huh?"

"You're not going to be in here over Christmas, are you?"

"Hell, no. I refuse to be. Everybody else okay?"

"Yeah. You left early, so you don't know. They're still out there, but it's down to cleanup now. You were the big injury of the night."

"What some people won't do for attention."

"For once you didn't puke."

"Didn't have time. Never saw it coming, in fact. Boy, that sucker blew, huh?"

"Not a good fire. There were arrests before the sun came up, though. Nobody's getting away with anything."

"Yeah. Sure."

The response was cynical. They both knew that the little guys with the lab might get arrested, but the big guys who financed or set up or sold the stuff would probably never be discovered. Street drugs. Chemicals. Ether. Et cetera. Who would have believed they'd come up with something more volatile, more unpredictable, than a paint-store fire? Home drug labs.

"I owe you, bud," Jim said.

"You owe me nothing."

"I owe you big-time. In fact, you oughta get a medal."

"Don't you dare. I hate those damn things. Medals are for cops. They eat that stuff up."

"Go on," Jim said. "Get out of here. I want the nurse."

"What for?"

"Do I need a reason? She's gorgeous, that's what for."

"I think he's going to be fine," Alice said with a sniff.

"Yeah, he'll be all right. A minute, huh, Alice?" She nodded and stepped outside the room. Mike paused. He thought.

"Don't," Jim said.

Mike looked down. They were good at living dangerously, living on the edge of life and laying it all on the line. They were bad at being vulnerable, because in this they were unpracticed. You couldn't admit vulnerability and act completely in control at the same time. Those gears did not mesh. This was why Mike was in trouble with Chris, and he suddenly knew it. He didn't know what to do about it or why it had to be that way, but he knew what it was. It was one thing to tell her about weakness and pain that was ten years old; it was quite another to look her right in the eye and admit the fear and shame of the moment.

He looked at his best friend who had suffered severe bodily harm. He was about to try out emotion on him.

Scary thing. What if you admitted your fallibility when you were most apt to be fallible? Could you run into the burning building then? That's why they never talked about it. They were all afraid of the same thing—that if they thought about it too much, they'd come apart like a cheap watch.

"Don't start," Jim said.

"I have to. There are so many things I couldn't have faced without you. You know that."

"You face whatever you have to. You have before. You will again. Just don't start this."

"You're my best friend," he said, almost choking on the sentiment. He wanted to talk about the fear he had, a fear even worse than the fear that Jim had been killed. The fear of being all alone again. And the relief that he wasn't.

"You need more friends," Jim said.

"They can't take me. You can."

"Just take the thank-you and don't get sloppy. I'm in pain. I don't want to play with you now."

"Okay, then. But you're coming back."

"Sure. Of course. It's what I do. Anyway, lightning never strikes in the same place twice."

"Yeah." Mike laughed, remembering the old joke. "Because the place isn't there anymore after the first time."

"I'm here," Jim said, solemn.

Mike touched the fingers that stuck out of the cast. He wanted to do more, maybe hug him. But he had done all that he could reasonably do. *You're here, old buddy. Thank God.*

"See ya," he said.

"Don't bother me over Christmas. I'll be busy."

Mike knew what that meant. It meant that Jim didn't want him to feel obligated in any way; he should feel free to pursue his holiday plans without feeling obligated to visit the injured fire fighter, his best friend.

He stopped for coffee with Big Mike before going home. He felt grubby even though he had cleaned up. And tired, but too wired to want to sleep. And angry—about the fire, about near calamity, about the difficulty of life sometimes. And about Aunt Flo coming tomorrow...two days before Christmas. It had been building in him. He even wondered if his worry had been distracting him when they got to the fire. Otherwise, he might have been in the house and Jim might have visited *him* in the hospital. He was usually the first one in when there were people inside.

By the time Mike got to his house, it was nearly 11:00 a.m. Chris was pacing. She gave a gasp and ran to him, putting her arms around his neck and hugging him.

"Hey," he said, laughing. "Hey."

When she released him, there was fury in her eyes. "Why the hell didn't you call me?"

"Call you? What for?"

"I was worried sick! I told you I can't sleep through the sirens! You know I can't."

"Well, gee whiz, I was busy."

"You weren't too busy to call Mattie!"

"So? Did Mattie call you, tell you everything was okay?"

"Yes, but you could have called. Where have you been?"

"Look, Chris, don't get like this on me, huh? I'm wiped out, I'm mad, and I don't need this."

She ran a hand down her neck. "Okay. Sorry. I was worried. I was scared."

"Well, who knew you'd be worried? I figured you'd be polishing the goddamn silver."

He stared at her for a minute, then he turned to go through the kitchen and to the stairs. He wasn't going to his room to sleep; he thought he'd better get out of sight. He was already sorry, but he wasn't sure he could stop it. He should have known it would start oozing out of him sooner or later.

He passed a pair of chewed-up socks on the stairs and picked them up with a curse. He slammed his bedroom door. Oh, please, he thought, not now. Don't let me do this. Not like this.

But there was a new comforter on his bed. He gritted his teeth. Pillow shams. He wanted to shoot the place up. He went to his closet to change his shoes. Hanging on a hanger was a new shirt with a sweater hanging over it. He touched it. There were new pants. A new set of clothes. To wear while they entertained the aunt over Christmas?

He opened the bedroom door and called her. Loud. Angry. *"Chris!"* Then he closed the door, waited and seethed.

Chris opened the bedroom door and stepped in. "What?"

"She didn't really leave, did she. She just stepped behind her big ugly checkbook for a while, that's all. She might have seemed to leave, but she really just left you a big pot of money as a reminder of where it's at, huh?"

"She left me some money, but—"

"So you could decorate the place and make it good enough for royalty, is that it? You know, Chris, it's getting on my nerves to come home and find new towels, new sheets, new dishes—like my stuff isn't good enough for you. It's starting to really burn me up! If you want to buy a few things for my place, why don't you try asking me if I want any of this crap? Huh?"

"Look, I wasn't trying to—"

"And don't buy me clothes!" He was shouting now. He took the two hangers out of the closet and threw the things on the floor. "I'll dress myself! I'm sure it won't meet the standards of Her Majesty, Florence, but it meets *my* standards. If you want to buy me clothes, buy me some damn socks. I think the damn dog has eaten the last pair."

"I didn't buy you that because of Flo!" she shouted back. "I bought it because of *me*! I liked it. I wanted to do something nice. I'll buy socks, okay? Two thousand pair!"

"Like I don't have anything nice?"

"You have wonderful things! I don't have any problem with your house, or the way you dress, or— Jeez, I just wanted to give you something!"

"Well, I don't want anything from you, because anything you give me is coming out of Flo's pocketbook. And I've had it up to here with her!"

"What has she done to you that you didn't do right back to her?"

"Besides rub my nose in my middle-class existence? Besides outfitting you and the kids for your next appearance at court? Besides laying all these little traps for you, like your lost money? Not a damn thing, really!"

"I'm not spending Flo's money, you big dope. I'm—"

"Don't you *ever* call me a dope! Don't ever, ever—" He stopped. He knew without looking in a mirror that his face was red, his fists clenched. He took a deep breath.

"I didn't mean you were a dope in general, you dope. I meant you're acting stupid over this situation, which could be a good situation if you'd let it, but you're too stubborn and bossy to bend a little."

"Oh, man," he said, letting a mean laugh erupt. "I was a dope to think you could ever fit into a regular kind of life."

"Just because I came from a wealthy family doesn't make me *ir*regular. You didn't even know my family; you only met Flo when she was feeling threatened. You don't back a Palmer into a—"

"I didn't back her into anything. I sat there and took her abuse. *You* sure didn't stand up for me. I guess I know where *you* stand!"

"You, apparently, don't know anything about me! Did you hear me standing up for Flo when you went after her? You two were the ones determined to do battle."

"I don't want to feel this way," he said, his teeth clenched. "I don't want to feel shoddy. I don't want to care, but I do care that I'm a fire fighter and she has a damn empire waiting for you. I don't like the whole damn hoity-toity, highfalutin show we have to put on! Like I can't take her to Ma and Big Mike's because they're not good enough!"

"But they *are*. They're better than good enough!"

"I don't want you to be able to buy and sell me ten times over. Even if you wouldn't, I don't want you to be *able* to!"

"You're doing this to yourself! Nobody is doing this to you! You're being a snob. It's you. Not me. Not even Flo!"

"It was good before there were all these *things*. Before I came home every day and found new *things*."

"I can't do this. Stop it, Mike!"

"Is that how it would be?" he asked her. "There's something wrong and you can't deal with it? You can't fight it out? Chris, if there's a problem, *we* have a problem. What do you think? Think it'll go away? Huh?"

"You want to give it to me? Is that it? Yell at me for a while because you're mad? It was okay when I needed everything from you, huh? When I had nothing at all. Destitute, needy, sad little divorcée—you could tell me then, 'Go work on your book,' 'Be who you want to be,' 'Be where you want to be.' But you can't live with the real me, huh? Because my aunt's money makes you feel like less of a man? Maybe because you feel like a man only when someone's hanging on you, thinking of you as a hero, but you don't have any interest in someone who can stand on her own two feet."

The room was silent.

"Yeah," he said. "I don't want to feel that way, but I do."

"You feel different? Now?" she asked softly, tears coming to her eyes.

"I wanted—" He felt his throat closing up on him. "I wanted to hold on to a family that needed to be held. Not—" He stopped again to swallow before going on. "Not one that didn't need me."

"I don't have everything I need," she whispered.

"Then do something," he entreated. "Change it back."

"I can't. Don't you see? You loved the Chris who didn't have anything. I don't want to be that Chris. If you don't love me as I am, you were loving a fantasy, a hard-luck story."

"I did *not* love a hard-luck story! It was this feisty little babe making it through tough stuff that a lot of stronger people couldn't. But it wasn't true. You weren't gutsy—

you were *rich*. You always have been—you just didn't have it *on* you!"

"Oh, God," she said, shaking her head, "I should have known. I never should have stayed here. You think I've changed, but you're the one who's changed. I'm the same person, and you don't like me as much."

"No, you don't like it when it doesn't go your way. You gotta have it smooth as glass every second. That's it."

"Oh, yeah? I've been real spoiled, all right, the past few years of—"

"Oh, don't give me that bull! You never starved. You could always have called *her*!"

"Maybe I should call her now!"

"Well, maybe you should!"

They both looked stricken by what had been said. But it was too late to take it back.

Mike suddenly didn't know what to do. He yanked open the door. "I gotta have air. Gotta cool down." Reluctantly, helplessly, he left the bedroom and the house.

Mike drove around for a while but ended up at his mom and dad's. He'd pretty much known he would. It was years since he had sought his father's advice. Years since he had talked about his troubles. Years since he had admitted he had any.

"You oughta see what's under the Christmas tree," he told Big Mike. "I've never seen anything like it. And it's my fault as much as Aunt Flo's. But it'll never stop."

"It'll stop," Big Mike said. "You'll run out of money pretty quick."

"Do you know what she's got? I mean, like a million dollars!"

"Did you stop playing the Lotto? I thought you went for an idea like a million dollars."

"That's different. It would have been *mine*."

"'Mine,'" Mattie said quietly, half pretending not to get into this. "Kids says that when they're two. Usually they get over it."

"Ma, it isn't like you think. I thought a lot of money didn't mean that much to Chris, but she flaunts it now. I mean, she's buying things for my house all the time. Like when Flo was coming for dinner, she bought this whole new set of dishes, new tablecloth—the works. Flo can't sit down at a regular table? God forbid there should be a chipped dish. Can you imagine what it would be like if she came here? With the rest of us?"

Mattie shrugged. "She would sit down and eat or not. Makes no difference to me."

"Oh, you think that, but it isn't that way. It feels different to be surrounded by money. If I stay with Chrissie now, she'll build us a mansion."

"How terrible a thing, Mikie my boy. Just think of it—the pain of living with some money. Terrible break for you."

"Come on."

"So what would you change? What one thing?"

"The money. And the aunt."

"How would you do that?"

Okay, he thought. I can't make those changes. "Maybe I wouldn't have offered my house in the first place."

"Okay, if that makes it all better, okay. But for a minute there I thought you liked it. Maybe I was mistaken."

"I think you were." Big Mike *was* mistaken: it had been more than a minute, and he had more than liked it. He had felt restored, alive—before this whole issue of who had what and who was in charge got in his way. He'd already let it out, though, and if Chris couldn't face it any better than he could, then it couldn't be resolved. If you didn't know where the fire was, you couldn't put water on it.

He complained for a while longer, but he didn't tell them that the big problem was him. Probably they already knew. Stubborn and bossy. He liked to control things. On the other hand, *he* didn't want anything to do with a woman who would be controlled. The prospect for reconciliation didn't look good.

His parents said things like, "So what do you want? That she give the money away so you don't have to worry about it?"

"No, not that, but—"

"Maybe she should give it to you. Then it would be *yours*."

"No, but—"

I only want to feel good again, he thought. In control. Useful. Helpful. Needed.

At four o'clock he was ready, he thought, to go back to his house. His mother slapped his cheek affectionately. "Try not to be too stupid about this, Mikie."

"That will be hard for him, Mattie," Big Mike said.

"Don't do that. Don't say that. Chrissie called me a big dope."

Mattie kissed his cheek. "Did you see Jim? He's all right?"

"I saw him. He's doing fine, considering."

"Terrible thing," Mattie said. "Life is too short. Sometimes when you come that close to losing someone, sometimes it makes you want to shake everything up so you can fix it, huh?"

He thought for a minute. Was that why? He'd thought about losing Jim and then become afraid of losing Chris and the kids. Knowing that having them the way he did wasn't feeling too good, he'd wanted to shake it up. Maybe then they could put the pieces together right. But, no. He'd just made a big mess of things.

"Yeah, Ma," he said.

When he left the house Big Mike settled, shook the paper and hid behind it. "So?" Mattie asked her husband.

"That Chrissie. Good judge of character, that girl. He's a big dope, your son."

"He's always my son when he does something stupid."

"Was he the one who put Matthew in the clothes chute?"

"It was Chris in the clothes chute, and he put himself there after making Tommy go first."

"Was it? You're sure?"

"You think he's going to be all right?" she asked.

"I don't know. I'm betting on that terrible dog. I bet you anything that if she leaves, she doesn't take that terrible dog."

"I think you hope," she said.

The house was filled with the good smells of cooking. Chris was standing at the stove. This was not what he had expected. He had come in through the garage, and now he stood just inside the door and looked at her. "I don't know how to say I'm sorry about what I said."

"You said what you felt. You can't be sorry for that."

"I'm sorry I said anything. I don't want to feel that way. I wanted to work on feeling different before I said anything."

"But you were telling the truth?"

He nodded.

"Then I'm the one who's sorry," she said. "I cooked dinner, a special one. Do you think we can bury it for one night?"

"One night?"

"I think we should have an early Christmas. You, me, the kids. Flo is planning to get in at two tomorrow. If I can't reach her and get her to cancel—I've been trying—the three of us will meet her and go back with her. You two are incompatible. This isn't good for anybody anymore. I wanted it to work, Mike. And I'll never stop loving you."

"Is it because we're too different?"

"No. Because the differences are tearing us apart. And I don't think I can fix this."

"Try. Please. I'm willing to try."

"I don't think you can, Mike, and the past ten days—maybe the next ten years—you against Flo, against where I've come from, what I can provide..."

"But you don't have to provide. You—"

"I *do* have to. I have to give, too. And not just hot food and grateful sex. I have been working, working hard, so that I could make it on my own. That effort is as much a part of who I am as any other part of me. I don't have to live in a big fancy house or be like Flo or be able to afford the finest of everything, but I do have to be able to earn money, spend it, save it as I choose. I want this whole business about the amount to be irrelevant, like at Mattie and Big Mike's. Where whoever has gives, and whoever needs takes. Not just money, but all of it. I can't live with a man who will put restrictions on what I, too, could provide."

"You could give me a chance to try to—"

She shook her head, then walked toward him. Her arms went around his neck. "You mean struggle with this until it either works or crashes down around us? You wanted to be the one, you said, to give me what I need to build my life. Oh, Mike, you can't. Neither can Flo. I've got to do that for myself. Being loved because you're helpless is not very different from being loved because you're rich."

"You're comparing me to *him*? Chrissie, your husband didn't love you—he *used* you. He didn't say he'd try to change. You're just running away."

"Not exactly. I'm going to spend Christmas with Flo, but I'm not going to move in with her. I have some money from the landlord, and if I don't sell a book soon, I'll get a job. I've done it before. I want to do it on my own. I can share my life, Mike, but I don't want to be owned. I don't want to be kept down. This situation is hurting both of us too much."

"Chrissie, I have a bad temper. I'm bossy and stubborn, like you said. I got jealous. But maybe I can change some of that. Let's—"

"Look, I'm leaving, not dying. Maybe some of this can be worked out—a lot of it works already. But not while I'm in your house. I don't know which was harder, having you try so hard to be perfect and patient, or having you blow up like you did. Let's let the dust settle. We'll write, talk on the phone. Maybe after a while..."

"Don't leave. Don't."

"I have to. I think the kids and I have been through enough for now. For now, let's not put ourselves through any more fighting. Maybe later, when things have calmed down, when this business with the 'lost money' is settled, when my book is published, you know...maybe we can work it out. It's been wonderful, and I love you. Let's try to part friends. I'm not going to disappear. If it's meant to last longer, it'll survive a separation while we both decide what we need. Let's not put ourselves through a rough Christmas."

"Is it what you want?" he asked. "Would you love me better if I had some house plans drawn up...if I wanted to help you spend your money?"

"Mike, it isn't either love me for my money or love me because I'm broke. It isn't either-or. This is who I am. I am sometimes broke, and sometimes it looks like I have a lot of money. I want to be okay either way. I think it's the only way. We did what we set out to do, huh?"

"What if I beg?"

"Then that would mean you weren't telling the truth when you asked me to stay just long enough so I could get back on my feet and you could remember what you wanted again."

He shrugged. "I never asked you to promise anything, it's true. I said open invitation."

"But you made that offer to someone else. I'm not who you thought I was. That book. My stupid ex-husband. Will you be all right?"

"In a while."

"No veldt-sores?"

Open, bleeding wound. But he was one tough guy. "Those are taken care of now. But I think I drove you away when all I wanted was for you to stay."

"Maybe you couldn't help it, what with wanting one thing but being stuck with another. It's my fault, too. I should have told you that first night you asked me to stay. At least I should have told you before we..." She held back tears, looking away briefly. "It's been pretty rugged around here since Flo came and my past became my present and we forgot we only had one small, simple goal: I needed a roof, and you needed to get in touch with what you really wanted. We got a little carried away. I don't want them to hear that kind of fight again,'' she said, her head nodding in the direction of the living room.

''I suppose.''

''Kiss me, Mike. Kiss me so I'll never forget how wonderful it feels.''

Carrie's chin quivered. ''Mommy says that we're going to our Auntie Flo's for Christmas.''

Mike picked her up. ''Does that make you sad?''

''No. Cheeks makes me sad.''

''Why?''

''He's going in a kennel for Christmas. Because he can't go on the airplane. He doesn't have a box.''

''Oh, no, he's not. He'll stay with me. He can come to the cabin with me for Christmas. Okay?''

''You don't have to do that, Mike. Cheeks is pretty hard on your socks.''

''I like him. I'll buy him a bunch of socks for Christmas. How's that, Carrie? Can I keep him for you while you're away?''

''Yes.'' She smiled. ''And then you can bring him when you visit us. When are you going to visit us?''

''Oh, I don't know. Pretty soon, maybe. When are you going to visit me.''

''Pretty soon, too. Mommy says we will *always* know where you are. We bought you Christmas presents, and we're going to open them tonight. It is a 'practice Christmas.' ''

Let it be, he thought. Don't let me tempt fate by showing either too much joy in their presence or too much pain in their departure. Let them be happy, leave happy, as they were happy within my arms. All of them. And then, in my memories, I will be less lost.

Dinner was ham and things. Christmas ham. And a fire in the fireplace. And eggnog, cookies and an Irish whiskey, neat, for the grown-ups, which would either untense some tight nerves or loosen their tongues or start the tears flowing.

They only opened presents from one another; Flo's were put back in the boxes they had been shipped in to be carried back to Chicago. Chris had already made plane reservations. It was a miracle she was able to book them this time of year, but she called a travel agent and paid top dollar for first-class. It was all set.

And the opened presents would also be packed and carried away because, as Mike knew, they wouldn't be back soon. The kids were thrilled with their bounty. And Mike was surprised to be given things he had not thought they knew how to buy. A gun-cleaning set. Riding chaps. A rod and reel. And a big packet of socks. "We'll go fishing when you visit, huh, Kyle?"

"Fishing!"

"Our mother doesn't like guns very much," Carrie said. "But she said you are very careful with them."

"I am. When you're very careful and you know what you're doing with guns, as with fires, they're not so scary." Why then, he wondered, had they been so reckless with what they so briefly, so blissfully had? Had they never considered love volatile?

"Will I ride the horses some more?"

"Yes. Yes, you will. And I'll take pictures for you and mail them to you. And pictures of all the Cavanaugh kids.

And Big Mike and Gram. And I'll call you at your Auntie Flo's. Okay?"

"Okay!"

"Should we read a story? One of our favorites?"

"No, the new one. Read a new one."

"Okay, a new one, then." Which he did. A long, long one. But when they fell asleep, both of them, he did something he had never before done. He woke them. "Carrie. Kyle. Wake up a little bit. I'm going to take you to bed. It's my turn to tuck you in. There we go." And he hefted them up in his big arms and took them, together, to the beds upstairs.

There was an ache in his chest, but he would not give in. "I love you very much, Carrie," he told her. "And you can visit me whenever your mommy wants to." And then, "I love you very much, Kyle, and I promise to take you fishing if your mommy will let you go." And he held each one tight, kissed each one on forehead, cheeks, lips, chin. They were too tired to notice how desperately he behaved, and for this he was grateful.

He returned to Chris. She handed him another Irish. "I wish I had done better," he said. "Maybe you'll change your mind. Maybe when things are a little settled, you'll come back and work on this with me. I'm a big dope, but I'm not hopeless."

"Maybe. The timing has been all wrong. I'm not the coward I appear to be, Mike. And I'm not choosing between you and Flo—I'm only getting some distance from both of you while I think things through."

He lifted his glass to her. "That's probably good. Me and Flo, we've been lousy to you. You okay about the dog?"

"Carrie feels a lot better about it now. Do you think we'll have something to talk about on the phone, long distance? Do you think we'll keep whatever it was we had—"

"*Is*, Chris. Whatever it *is*. We haven't lost it. We just got sidetracked. Me. I got pigheaded. Our family's famous for it."

"But you're letting me go. Not arguing about it."

"I said I'd try. I don't know if I can change, I can only try. I became a different person when I started to compete with your big bucks. I didn't like the person I was becoming, but I couldn't get rid of the feelings. I want you to be where you ought to be. Here, there—it's all the same. I'll love you no matter what."

"I think if it's the real thing, we'll come back together."

"Yeah, well, you hit the nail on the head. I'm afraid if you go, you'll never be able to come back."

"Why?"

"I don't know. Because you'll find out what I've known all along: you're tougher than you think, and you have the moxie to make it on your own."

"You might find out something, too. You might find out you don't need all these complications."

"No, that's your line. I said I'll go all the way to the end. I just didn't know it would be such a short trip." He sighed deeply, fighting the feeling that the last shovelful of dirt was being tossed on the grave. "Like you said, we did what we set out to do. If you can stay, stay. If you can't . . . well, you're the one who thinks. I rush into things."

"Well, I could have gone earlier. I could have called Flo; then you wouldn't be feeling like you've lost something now."

"I feel fear, Chrissie, not loss. Afraid you'll decide leaving was the smartest thing you did. I want you to regret leaving, then decide it's worth it to come back. I just can't promise that I'll ever be easy to live with. And I might never like Flo. I can't make myself even *want* to like Flo. Just like Cheeks might never stop eating socks. Such is life. I'm sorry. My best isn't much sometimes."

"But I love you so," she whispered.

"Then show me. Here. In front of the fire. Show me where to touch you. Let me put out the fire one more time. . . ."

Much later he whispered to her, "I can't say goodbye, Chrissie. Not to the kids. Don't make me do that."

"Okay. Whatever you want."

"Then I want you to sleep in my arms. And when you wake up, be smiling. It wasn't long enough, but it was good."

Chapter Fourteen

When Chris awoke Mike and Cheeks were gone. She didn't have the time for the luxury of lying still and contemplating the past month and the decision she had made to end it; there was a great deal to be done before going to the airport. She hadn't made contact with Flo—where *was* her aunt these days?

As she hurried around the house gathering up their belongings, scraping their presence from his house, she could not still her mind. What was going to prove the most difficult to live without? The way he was with the kids? Like he should have a dozen. Natural and decisive, he never made hesitant or wrong choices for them. He spoke their language, found the right pastimes, the right jokes, and practiced affirmative discipline that showed them how good they were, how smart.

Or would it be even harder to live without the way he was with Chris's body? As though he had known it for twenty years and was, at the same time, just working up a sweat in the first round. How could you feel wild and nurtured at the same time? Frenzied yet companionable? Out of your mind with out-of-control passion but perfectly safe? You could feel this way with a man who trusted easily and gave everything he had.

Or would the hardest thing be giving up that fanciful, foolish, idealistic notion that one could have a unit of people bonded by love, fraught with ups and downs, fronts and backs, joy and pain, a circle that actually closed around them and was tied with the knot of trust? The belief that it could be settled, ironed out, renewed. Yes, that might be hardest. Had she really fantasized fighting and then making up? Sure. Before she had lived it. Before his temper had erupted and the first punch he threw hit her square in the only identity she had.

She had not, after all, asked him to become different from the man with whom she had fallen in love. Had she?

When she went into the kitchen she found his note.

"I did all the things I have to say. Love, M."

That was Mike. Mike was better with actions than with words. When he was forced to confront his feelings, they were pretty hectic. What he wanted, she guessed, would be for them to forsake Aunt Flo, the money, the past. She almost wished she could.

There was quite a lot to pack, plus Christmas presents, opened and unopened. Then there was the car, which she took to a used-car lot. She did not strike a bargain, but she did get a ride to the airport with all their things.

* * *

"You're doing *what*?" Flo nearly shrieked. The airport was a mess. Hundreds of frustrated travelers fighting for space on overcrowded planes, airlines offering money for people who would give up their tickets. Chris held four first-class seats. Nonstop, Chicago.

"We're going back to Chicago. Today. It'll be a long wait—we don't leave until five-thirty, but—"

"Christine, what in the world are you talking about?"

"Don't start on me, Flo. It didn't work out. I made a last-minute decision. I tried calling you, but—"

"You were so damned hell-bent to stay with this big, dumb fireman."

"Don't call him dumb. He isn't dumb. He's the smartest man I've ever known in my life."

"Well, then, why in the world are you doing this? Did something terrible happen? Did he hurt you?"

"Of course not. Of course he wouldn't hurt me. He's the gentlest man I've ever known."

Flo rubbed her forehead with her fingers, exasperated. "I'm sure I'll understand all this eventually." Chris shook her head, struggling with tears she had been alternately fighting and giving in to all day long. "Me," Flo said. "It's me. He can't take me. What a wimp. I knew he was a wimp all along."

"No, no, it isn't that. I mean, he is intimidated by you and your money, but it isn't anything personal. Not really."

"Well, then, so what? I'm not crazy about him, either. So what else is new? That's the way it goes, right? You don't like your aunt-in-law. Big deal."

"And the money."

"What about the money? Does the money matter? What matters is how people feel about each other, not how much they can spend. What happened? *When* did this happen?"

"Florence, *please*. Don't interrogate me. Please."

"All right. All right. Let's get my bags and go get a drink. We're going to be here for hours. Chris, when you go off the deep end, do you absolutely have to take everyone with you? Where is that stupid dog?"

"He kept the dog," she said.

"He *what*? He kept the kids' dog?"

"No, no, nothing like that. The dog was going to have to go to a kennel, and Carrie was upset, so Mike said he'd take care of Cheeks. He can ship him later or something—I don't know."

"He kept the dog so Carrie wouldn't be upset?" Flo asked.

"Yes, something like that. And I think he secretly liked the dog."

It took an hour to collect Flo's baggage and recheck it on the next flight. Then they found a corner table in an airport bar. The kids sipped soda. Flo had a Bloody Mary, but Chris couldn't drink; her stomach was still jumping. The kids, fortunately, were very resilient. They were excited about the plane ride, about Aunt Flo's house, and they were sure they would see Mike again soon. Chris was less sure, but she didn't tell them that.

"Now," Flo said, "let me see if I have this right. You are leaving because now that you have money of your own, he is intimidated by your ability to be completely independent of him? Is that it?"

"Yes," she said, blowing her nose. "It's just like with Steve—I mean Fred. Oh, damn, I'll never be able to think of him as Fred. It's just another way of using a person. I met Mike's needs by being needy."

"And you felt used?"

"No. Yes. I mean, I didn't feel *used*, but he was angry about the money. Angry—can you imagine? He came right out and said it, too. He resented my money. He didn't want me to buy things for him anymore. He said he'd like it better if I couldn't."

Flo lit a cigarette. "I know men who like having fat wives. It's testosterone poisoning. They're all defective."

Chris blew her nose again. Now that she was with Flo, the tears kept coming. "Well, everything was fine until he thought about going through life competing with my big bucks. It hurt his pride, I guess. It made him feel middle-class, less of a man. I wasn't prepared for that. Here was a man, I believed, who understood for better, for worse. I certainly can't change who and what I am. I *want* to contribute. I've worked hard at being able to contribute. If he can't take my inheritance, would he be any better at coping with a successful writer? It's all the same thing."

"Too bad he wasn't willing to work on that. I don't happen to think having money is the worst crime a person can commit."

"Well, he wanted to try, but I could tell he wouldn't be able to do it."

Flo's cigarette stopped in midair on the way to her lips. She was fairly slow to respond. "There were undoubtedly many other things."

"No. Everything else was wonderful."

"There is, obviously, some reason you *knew* he wouldn't be able to change?"

"It's part of his nature to want to do for people. When he doesn't feel needed, he doesn't feel loved. There would be a lot of trouble. I don't have the stamina for it."

Flo put out her cigarette. "I see." She leisurely sipped her drink. "Well, you did the right thing, Chris," she said coyly. "He wasn't good enough for you."

"Yes, he was! For a while he was the best thing that ever happened to me. You were right—I should have learned more from my mistake with my ex-husband."

"And I'm relieved you did. Just in time, too. You'll be much happier on your own. You don't need that crap."

Tears spilled over. "Oh, I don't know about that. I've been on my own for a long time. It's been pretty lonely. For a while, having you and Mike—my old family, my new love—it was so hopeful, so— Well, I just don't see that I have any choice. Regardless of what I think I want, I don't want to raise my children in a home where there's so much conflict, so much restriction on who can do what."

"Lord knows you don't need conflict and restriction after all you've been through. If anyone deserves a happily-ever-after life, it's you. You'll be much better off. Besides, I'm sure he wouldn't change."

"I won't know that, of course, because I— Well, I just couldn't risk it, Flo. I'm tired of fighting."

"He's probably relieved that you're gone. In fact, I wouldn't doubt that he's actually pleased. After all, his life was the way he liked it before you came along."

"He was lonely. I don't think he realized how lonely—"

"But these complications with money are too much for a man like Mike," Flo said. "He likes everything simple. He wants to be the big man, water down the big fire, bring home the bacon...."

"He doesn't like to think about things for too long," Chris said.

"No, and solving this problem would take a while. He wouldn't like that."

"He likes to face things straightforwardly—"

"Can't talk about his feelings," Flo said. "Come on, let's go down to the gate. This place is a madhouse. I don't want us to get bumped because of overbooking."

They began to gather up their things. They walked, a row of four, holding hands with the kids. "But he does talk about his feelings," Chris said. "He doesn't think he's very good at it, but really he is. I honestly don't know what was worse, when he was trying so hard not to say how he felt, or when he came right out and—"

"Oh, well, water over the dam," Flo said. "I'm so glad you've finally come to your senses. You'll never regret coming home. Not for one tiny second."

"I'm not going to move in with you, Flo. I'll stay until I can get my own place, and then—"

"You can stay as long as you like, of course, but I think you ought to know, I've made a few changes myself. Remember your little philosophy about betting you won't get cold? Ken and I have decided to get married."

Chris stopped dead in her tracks. "Really?"

"Uh-huh. Ken has always wanted to get married. I was the one who was too busy or too independent or, really, too scared. It's a big step. That's where I've been the past couple of days—with Ken...working this out." Flo nearly blushed.

"I'm happy for you, Flo. If you don't know him after all these years, you never will."

"I will never be accused of being impetuous, that's for sure. You're the one with that trait. I may be slow at deciding what I want, but you, darling, leap before you look. You couldn't possibly have known Mike very well."

"Oh-ho." Chris laughed. "Within a week I knew almost everything about him."

"He was holding back some vital information, though. Like not being able to accept you the way you are. It's a good thing you saw that in time."

"I had no idea he was holding back. In fact, he always seemed to give everything that was inside of him."

"You must have been pretty shocked, then, by the way he laid it on you about the money thing. After thinking he was so stable, so transparent, hiding that little tidbit..." Flo stopped at the gate. "Look at this place. An hour and a half until our flight, and it's mobbed."

"He didn't hold back for long. He put it on the line. He said what was the matter with him and wanted to fight it out."

"You don't need that, Chris. Life is tough enough."

"I wouldn't have lasted long. I hate to fight."

"No self-respecting Palmer wants to fight. Fighting lacks decorum."

"You're a born fighter," Chris disagreed.

"I'm a born *winner*. I don't like laying everything on the line. Never have. Probably why I never married. Look at that—they're *already* offering to buy back tickets. Good thing you booked us first-class. We are checked in, aren't we?"

"He wanted to face it. He wanted to try to work on it. He didn't want to feel the way he felt. What can I do about what he feels? I can't change his feelings. I can't—"

"I think maybe we'd better get our seat assignments," Flo said, "or we might have a problem. Oh, I'm so relieved, Chris. You would have been simply miserable through the holidays."

"I didn't want to argue through Christmas...."

"Last night must have been hell for you," Flo said. "The big jerk."

"Last night was..." Chris stopped. Tears spilled down her cheeks again.

"I could just kill him for hurting you this way. Here I thought he was a generous, strong man who wasn't afraid of anything, but when it came down to the wire, he just couldn't—"

"He *did* give me everything he had. Even the bad stuff."

"Well, honey, don't defend the big jerk. I think you got out just in time. And I'm certainly relieved that we don't have to deal with that dog."

"The kids are really going to miss the—"

"I wondered what I was going to do about that dog. That is not the most agreeable animal. Growly thing."

"Oh, he's noisy, but inside he's—"

"Where there's smoke there's fire. That dog had a hidden agenda, like the fireman. You *think* he's just growling, you *think* he's perfectly safe, then wham. He'll bite someone someday."

Chris's eyes widened, and she slowly turned toward Flo. She stared at her aunt's profile for a minute. Then Flo turned, and Chris met her eyes. "That dog will not bite if he's not abused."

"If you say so. But we're not going to find out at the expense of my carpet."

"I never had a fight with Steve," Chris said.

"Why would he risk fighting with you?" Flo asked. "If you didn't get along, you might have taken your money and gone home. I imagine he was very amiable. But don't think about that now, Chris. You're coming home. That's all that matters, right?"

Chris looked closely at Flo's eyes. "What are you doing to me?" she asked.

Flo put an arm around Chris's shoulders. "I'm agreeing with you, Christine. Don't you recognize it?"

"Flo..."

"If you're very careful, perhaps you can manage a life as tidy and enviable as mine. And maybe you'll be ready to take a few chances, again, when you're, say, about forty-one. What do you say, kiddo? Shall we get our seat assignments? Go home?"

It had been dawn when Mike arrived at his cabin with Cheeks. He had cried a little, then decided self-pity should be against the law. He wished he could have been stronger—strong enough to help them pack, take them to the airport, all of that. But he couldn't do it. His disappointment was overwhelming, and he would have broken down in front of them. There were certain things that children should be spared.

So he and Cheeks put on the coffee and built a fire to warm up the cabin. Later, they went for a hike. Then visited the horses. Cleaned up the cabin a little, shoveled some snow, cooked a steak on the grill, even though it was freezing out.

"Here," he said to the dog, giving him half the steak. "I'll give you a pair of socks later. For dessert."

What the hell, he thought. It had been a crazy, lunatic thing to do from the start—bringing her home like that, telling her to stay a while because it felt good. Who did stupid things like that?

Still, it might have worked. If she hadn't had money? No. It might have worked if he had not been bothered by her money. Or it might still have worked if she could stand that he was bothered. He might have gotten over that. If he had kept his mouth shut about it.

But he couldn't really live like that. It was about those changes, about that one thing that you would change to make things turn out differently. What if you got mad about the way someone squeezed the toothpaste but you could never say so? And if you said so, a whole major fight erupted and it tore you apart?

His whole family argued. At the Cavanaugh house you had better be able to hold your own during an argument, or keep your mouth shut. When something was wrong, you had better be able to either say what it was, fix it, or learn to live with it. You didn't grow up in a household crammed full of people and everyone politely tiptoed around saying, "Pardon me," "Oh, excuse me, did I do that?"

And in the firehouse, where the men were bonded by hard work, cooperation, danger, things were resolved quickly, too. You couldn't let bad feelings fester; it was critical to solve problems or learn to accept the fact that people had both virtues and flaws. Big ones and little annoying ones.

But Chris hadn't lived that way. Hadn't she told him that? There were only four of them—her parents and Flo. She was either struggling to be independent or giving in to let someone take care of her. Or she ran away. So it was just as well, then, that she left when she did. She would have gone eventually, at the first sign of trouble....

It wasn't just the money that made them different. It was the regard they had for risk. She could risk her life trying to save a dumb manuscript, but she couldn't risk the discomfort of an argument, a fight. What did she think? That husbands and wives didn't fight? He had thought she *was* a fighter. Turned out it was only sometimes.

"So, what one thing would you change?" he asked the dog. "What one thing that *you* could do would make everything different?" He nudged the dog with his toe. Cheeks growled. "That's what I thought you said. Nothing. Not a damn thing. Because it wouldn't have been better if I hadn't carried her out of the fire. I would have missed out on a lot of good things if I hadn't fallen in love with her, and if I *had* kept my mouth shut, I would have opened it eventually anyway. It all would have turned out the same. Like she said, you have to be accepted just the way you are. And that's the way I am. And that's the way she is."

And I hurt, he thought, because I feel loss. But I am better for what I had. I had my arms full again; I had love that was deep and rich. And because of that, maybe it will come back to me. Maybe I can have it again someday. Just maybe. My amnesia is over. *We did what we set out to do, huh?* When I'm stronger I'll write her a letter and tell her... thank you. Despite the problems, because of you I am better than I was. I had been in hiding too long, and I needed to learn what a mistake that was.

He heard the sound of a four-wheel-drive vehicle coming up the road. He suspected it might be someone from the Christiansons' house. Probably they saw the light and pitied him, alone. Or maybe they thought he was with Chris and the kids and were stopping by for a friendly chat. He wished they wouldn't. He couldn't refuse to answer the door. You don't do that in the mountains. He opened the door and watched the car come up the road. It wasn't the Christiansons' car. It was a big new Suburban. Oh, hell, he thought, recognizing his brother Chris's car. Why'd they do that? He had said he wanted to be alone.

Cheeks growled and wagged his tail. The Suburban stopped, but the headlights stayed on. The door on the driver's side opened, and she got out. He could barely make her out with the headlights shining in his eyes. She walked toward him slowly, until she stood in front of him.

He tried to keep from feeling that he'd won the Lotto. "Have you come back?" he asked her.

"I was wrong. So were you. I think that means we're not finished yet."

"Is that Chris's car?"

"Well—" she shrugged "—no matter how hard I try to be independent, I just keep asking for help, don't I?" Her smile faded, and she looked up at him, tears in her eyes.

He opened his arms to her, and she filled his embrace. "I love you," he said. "I don't care how hard it is, I love you."

She cried and laughed but would not let him go. He lifted her clear off the ground. "I'm going to keep you happy for a long time," she said, her voice breaking, "because there is so much I need from you."

They stood in their rocking embrace for such a long time that soon the children were beside them, greeting the dog, plowing past them into the house, but they didn't let go of each other. Mike's face was buried in her jacket collar. Until the door to the Suburban slammed and someone said, "Ugh. Oh, *Gawd*."

He looked over Chris's shoulder to see Aunt Flo ruining her fashionable pumps in snow up to her ankles. She couldn't move, of course, with her heels jammed into the packed snow. He laughed. It was tough for him to admit to himself, but he was even a little glad to see Flo. It meant they were going to face it, head-on, and work it all out together. That included family. And he felt strongly about family.

He let go of Chris—it figured that the first reason he would have for letting her go would be Flo. This time, though, he felt firm in his faith that he would hold her again and again, and he went to Flo. He looked her up and down with his hands on his hips. Then he scooped her up in his arms and carried her to the house. She complained the whole way, about her shoes, the snow, the cold, the long drive. He put her down inside. And once inside she looked around in silence, probably awed by the rustic sparseness of it.

Mike put his arm around Chris's shoulders. They watched the activity, the welcome fullness of it all. Cheeks was running in circles, barking. The kids were already looking in the cupboards for treats before even taking off their coats, and Flo was removing her wet shoes in front of the fire, grumbling.

"Did you bring the twenty-two midgets?" he asked Chris.

"Nope. She's going to do this without the caterer. Cold turkey."

"This ought to be good."

And it was.

* * * * *